Each knight aligned his lance, each took perfect position. They came together in the center of the lists with a resounding crash that reverberated throughout the valley like the ringing of a hammer on an anvil. Both horses sank to their knees. Both lances shattered. Neither knight was unhorsed.

Lucas stared at the stump of his lance and could not believe what had just happened. It was not supposed to break! First the sonic device malfunctioned, now the entire lance! Where in Christ's name would he get another?

1 TIMEWARS
THE IVANHOE GAMBIT

BY
SIMON HAWKE

ACE SCIENCE FICTION BOOKS
NEW YORK

THE IVANHOE GAMBIT

An Ace Science Fiction Book / published by arrangement with
the author

PRINTING HISTORY
Ace Original / January 1984

ISBN: 0-441-37762-9

Ace Science Fiction Books are published by
The Berkley Publishing Group,
200 Madison Avenue, New York, New York 10016.
PRINTED IN THE UNITED STATES OF AMERICA

For Richard McEnroe

No one can work in a vacuum. I would like to thank some people whose continuing help and support has kept me going. I am extremely grateful to Jeffrey Kraus and William Renn of Hofstra University, George Gordon of Fordham University, Tom Curley of CBS, Karl Hansen of the planet Mars, Don Kayne, the people at Finnegan's Tavern in Huntington, Long Island, Jack Dann, Gardner Dozois and Edward Bryant. I'd also like to thank my parents, the cast and crew, and all the little people . . .

THE
IVANHOE GAMBIT

PROLOGUE

Lucas Priest, Sergeant Major, United States Army Temporal Corps, was trying to figure out how to stop a charging bull elephant with nothing but a Roman short sword. Scipio had given the order to advance and Lucas wondered if the legion commander really believed that Rome's famed phalanx formations would intimidate a berserker like Hannibal. Sending foot soldiers against his pachyderms was not unlike attempting to stop a Panzer column with tricycles.

Lucas was a bundle of raw nerves. A short while ago, he would have given almost anything for a cigarette. He had managed to smuggle a few back with him, but he was almost caught smoking one by a tribune and it had given him such a bad turn that he had thrown the others away. Somehow, he couldn't see himself explaining to an ancient Roman what he was doing sticking a tubeful of burning leaves into his mouth. Now, as the elephants rapidly approached, he had forgotten all about his nervous urge for a cigarette and was instead wishing for a few pyrogel grenades or an auto-pulser. Unfortunately, all he had was his short sword, a shield and a spear.

He threw the spear and, of course, it didn't help his situation any. He decided that it was lunacy to go up against a herd of elephants with nothing but an oversized dagger, so he threw down his shield and ran. Not a few centurions came to the same decision and Priest had lots of company in his undignified, albeit prudent, retreat.

"Today's Army has Time for You!"

It was an effective recruiting slogan, but the army never stressed the manner in which that time was measured. A week's enlistment period didn't sound too difficult to take, but it was one *army* week, measured not by the time spent in the field on the Minus side, but by Plus Time. Present time.

On his first hitch, or assignment in the field, Lucas had clocked out on the fourteenth of September at 0700. He had spent close to a year pillaging and raping with Attila and his Huns. When he clocked back in, it was still the fourteenth of September, 0705. Nine months of sheer hell and only five minutes of Plus Time counted toward the completion of his tour of duty. He remembered thinking that if time flies when you're having fun, it positively *crawls* when you're in the Temporal Corps.

He had less cause to complain than most soldiers. He had enlisted voluntarily. There had been much better options available; no one had twisted his arm. He had scored fairly well on his Service Aptitude Tests, a mandatory battery of exams that everyone had to take when they turned seventeen. His score had enabled him to land a position in the labs at Westerly Antiagathics, doing research on how to add yet another hundred years to the human lifespan. The job had paid well, but it had bored him. When the army came around with their dog and pony show, he had fallen for it hook, line and sinker.

The recruiters really laid it on. The presentation took up most of the work day and since the company still paid for the time, the attendance was close to one hundred percent. The army spokesman had been a civilian from the Ministry of Defense. He had been dressed very casually in a mellow color combination, a clingsuit in peach and woodsy brown. He had a terrific tan and a marvelous voice. His official title was Director of Service Administration. That meant he was a salesman. His introductory remarks had been well laced with jokes and homilies and after he spoke, there came the testimonials. People "just like you" who had worked in "dull and undemanding" jobs came out and spoke about what a wonderful experience the army was for them. They always made sure, Lucas later discovered, that at least one of the speakers was "a former employee at your own place of business."

After the speeches, there was the Parade of Uniforms, a fashion show with something in it for everyone. The soldiers who modeled the garb of World War I doughboys, Apaches, Belt Commandos and Prussian cavalry were all good looking and they gave off a robust glow of health and vitality. The women were all beautiful, but somehow they never got around to explaining just what life was like for women back in "the good old days." Looking back on it, Lucas didn't believe that any of them had ever spent so much as one moment in the field. They had probably gone straight out of Official Social Courtesies directly into the recruiting program.

Following the fashion show, there came the part of the presentation they called Historical Orientation. It was a brilliant multi-media production complete with stirring music and holographic effects, all about how history had proved that nations always prospered when they were on a wartime economic standard, how war was an inevitable fact of human nature and how the advent of time travel had made it possible to avoid the "inconvenience" of the physical presence of a war in present time. There was a barrage of information about how international disputes were settled by evaluating the performance of soldiers of the present in conflicts of the past, a *tour de force* that looked and sounded very glamorous, even if the information did flash by so quickly that it was impossible to absorb it all. At the end, there had been a short speech about how it was possible to apply to the Referee Corps upon completion of your tour of duty. It was well known that the refs had the highest pay scale in existence and enjoyed a standard of living on a par with heads of state, to whom, as an extra-national arbitrating body, they did not have to answer.

However, the fact of the matter was, as Lucas was later to discover, only those scoring in the top five percent of the S.A.T.s could qualify for the Referee Corps School selection process. Even so, it was still necessary to achieve degrees in Temporal Physics, Trans-historical Adjustment and Maintenance, and Econo-political Management and Arbitration. Supposedly, according to scuttlebutt, there wasn't a single person in the refs under the age of one hundred. There were younger personnel in the Observer Corps, the lower echelon of that vaunted cadre, but few soldiers were able to succeed in rising through the ranks and surviving the selection process, to say nothing of making it through R.C.S., which was, by all accounts, a real horror. Lucas Priest had no illusions about ever being anything more than a simple dog soldier.

Jesse Fain's case was more run-of-the-mill. She had done poorly on her S.A.T.s, as most everybody who could not afford implant education did, and she had been presented with a truly enviable proposition. She had been given a choice between working in the radioactive waste disposal and reclamation system—mining in the asteroid belt—or service in the army. She had joked wryly that it had been a really tough decision.

They had just met and already they knew each other fairly well. Soldiers made friends quickly. They had no other choice. Jesse was a young corporal who had just clocked in from serving a hitch under Alexander Nevsky. It was not uncommon for Russian women of that time to join their men upon the field of battle and Jesse had been out there on the frozen surface of the Neva, swinging a broadsword with the best of them. It had been a welcome change of pace for her, since in ancient times a woman's place was either at home, out front as gun fodder or on the receiving end of a rape. Jesse, accustomed to modern equality between the sexes, hated the army with a passion.

"I can't tell you how *good* it felt," she said, "being in the thick of battle and splitting *men's* skulls! God, I never thought I could be so bloodthirsty, but after all that I'd been through . . ."

Lucas grinned. "I hope you got it all out of your system."

"Not quite," she said, smiling. "But don't worry, you're safe enough. I'll buy the next round. What do you say we get good and drunk?"

"No time like the present," Lucas said, and they both laughed at the old army in-joke.

For a soldier between hitches, getting drunk was almost a necessity. It was a way of coming down, of slowing down. Even if the drinking was pursued to the point where it was impossible to move, the army was very understanding. Each soldier wore dogtags color coded with the grid designation of their next departure point. Shuttles made periodic checks of all the bars. The M.P.s simply dumped insensible soldiers in the back along with all their gear, delivered them to the appropriate grid, threw them on the chronoplates and clocked them out.

Every soldier knew that there was nothing like a chronoplate to induce sobriety. Somewhere in the maelstrom of nonspecific time, what the enlisted personnel called the dead zone, there was an awful lot of vomit floating around. Clocking out made most people very sick. Eventually, most soldiers got used to it enough so that they could hang on to their food at least some of the time, but most people still barfed upon transition. It was yet another glamorous aspect of time travel in the army. Occasionally, people would get lost coming through and would become stranded in the limbo of the dead zone. No one ever talked about it.

There was at least one good thing that Lucas could say about the army. The booze was cheap and it was excellent. It was possible to order literally anything. He had once been a vodka drinker, but he had developed a preference for mulled ale, a taste he had picked up in the Middle Ages.

Jesse drank unblended scotch.

An army bar was never very noisy. There was an undertone of conversation, but there was never any music and rarely any shouting, no matter how drunk anyone became. Soldiers were never together for very long and chances were that when they separated, to go their different ways, they would never see each other again. Lucas and Jesse sat in their tiny booth, holding hands across the table. There wasn't anything romantic in it. Physical contact of some sort was important to soldiers. When, in the next few minutes, they could be called away to ancient Rome or to the Six Day War in the 20th century, it seemed important to reach out and touch someone, to be reassured of their reality.

"Do you ever wish that you could figure it all out?" said Jesse. She was already slightly drunk. "I mean, I'm getting tired of being just a button for the refs to push. Hell, I've never even seen a ref. Back there in Russia, in the middle of the goddam battle, would you believe it, I started thinking: if I live through this, just how does that affect the point spread? How does it really work? Why am I doing this? I would've thought that just trying to stay alive would have been enough to occupy all my attention."

Lucas had nodded, understanding completely. Jesse was still green and it was all new to her.

"Believe it or not," he told her, "you'll get used to it. There will come a time when you stop thinking about it altogether. It won't make any difference whether or not your part in the action has any effect on the resolution of some trade agreement or international incident a thousand years away. I like to think it makes a difference, that what I'm doing really counts for something, but I don't dwell on it. Sometimes it's best just to go on automatic pilot. Try to stay alive. Nothing else matters very much. It's strange, the sort of things that can go through your mind in the middle of a battle. You can't really control it. The best thing to do is try and put everything out of your mind. Just be empty. Don't think about the outcome. Otherwise . . ." He let it hang.

"Yeah," said Jesse, staring into her drink. "Ours is not to reason why, is that it?"

"Don't try to work it out, Jesse. It'll make you drop your guard."

"Thanks. I'll remember that." She sipped her scotch. "They tell you where you're clocking out to?"

"The Punic Wars."

"Oh. That could be pretty rough."

Lucas shrugged. "I'm about due for it, I guess. Knocking off Custer's 7th Cavalry was a piece of cake. The Sioux had a wild celebration afterward, in honor of Yellowhair's demise. It was an easy hitch. I figure I'm due for a tough one."

"I hate the waiting," Jesse said.

There wasn't much that he could say to that. It was something that all soldiers felt at one time or another. Not the waiting to clock out, but the waiting for that one unlucky moment that turns out to be your last.

There were soldiers all around them, some in the disposable transit fatigues, others already in uniform as Hessians, Huns, Centurions, Green Berets and Vikings. Nothing about the year 2613 seemed very real. They belonged to it, but it didn't feel like home, more like a part of some alcoholic dream. They spent another five minutes together before Lucas heard his code called over the P.A. They looked at each other, probably for the last time, and he left her sitting there, staring into her scotch and swirling the ice cubes around so that they tinkled against the glass.

Scipio sent his archers forward, regrouped his forces and

they struck again. As he had advised Jesse, Lucas went on automatic pilot, phasing out his brain and fighting like an automaton. He was drained of everything. Drained of energy, drained of spirit, drained even of fear. When he finally came out of it, he was astonished to discover that he was still alive. Scipio had won.

When the pickup squad made contact, he was still in a daze. He heard the tone inside his head—as they signaled him via his implant from somewhere close by—and he slipped away at the earliest opportunity. They tracked him and he was picked up by three men in Roman garb. He clocked back to the present, battered, weak and exhausted. He felt empty. He was back in the year 2613 and none of it felt right. The soldiers were sitting around in the departure station, waiting for their codes to be called. They were all in various modes of dress, a cross section of history on parade. Dollies shuttled around, carrying all manner of weapons and equipment. Men and women were loading up on cigarettes and coffee. Drugs were prohibited, but easily available. There was that same metronomical voice announcing codes and grid designations over the P.A. He had arrived, by chance, right back where he had started from, the Quantico Departure Station.

The snap-back hit. The old "it's-like-you-never-left" feeling. He felt vaguely disoriented with a heavy touch of *déjà vu*. He had some time left before he was due to pick up his new tags with a new code designation or to apply for a furlough. Some time. It seemed ironic. He was now eligible for a furlough, but most soldiers never took them. What was the point? The army gave credit only for time spent on active duty and time was precious. What he wanted, just that minute, was a drink.

He crossed the giant plaza and headed for a bar. It looked familiar and well it should have; it was where he had met Jesse Fain. Feeling a bit nostalgic for the present past, he headed for a certain table in a certain booth. The same booth he had shared with Jesse. It was unoccupied, but they hadn't had time to clean it off yet. On the table was an empty ale tankard and a single glass of scotch.

The ice was almost melted.

He checked the time. It couldn't have been more than a couple of minutes since she'd left. And he had been away six months. He sat down wearily and ordered an ale and a com-

puter terminal. Both were brought to his table almost immediately. He plugged into the line and voiced his request. There
were one or two people he wanted to check up on. At the same
time, he almost didn't want to know. He took a gulp of ale,
then gave their names and serial numbers.

The data was quick in coming. Johnson, Robert Benjamin,
serial number 777334-29-181-999-285-60 . . . . CS
(current status) active duty Napoleonic Wars—

That was all he wanted to know. At least Bobby was still
alive. So far. Some of the others weren't so lucky. Deacon
Bailey was MIA, Liz Carmody was KIA, Josh McKenzie was
KIA and Jesse Fain never even made it to wherever she was going. She was lost in transit, somewhere in the dead zone. Her
waiting was over. He didn't have the heart to continue. He
was about to turn off the terminal and have it taken away
when an update flashed across the screen.

Bobby Johnson had just clocked back in.

1

Master Sergeant Robert Benjamin Johnson sat on his duffel bag, a longbow resting across his lap. The plastic duffel, which had just been drawn from supply, made slight crackling noises as he shifted his weight upon it. Beside him was Finn Delaney, Pfc., dressed in the garb of a Saxon peasant and fast asleep on the plastic bench. Johnson heard someone call out his name and looked up to see a non-com dressed in transit fatigues threading his way through the crowd toward the bank of vending machines near which they waited. It took him a moment to recognize the man. Lucas Priest had aged.

"Lucas! Jesus Christ, you're still alive!"

"Only just barely," Priest said. They clapped their arms around each other in an awkward bear hug. "God, it's good to see you," Lucas said. "I wasn't sure I'd make it back from that last one. Nothing like a four week long forced march to prime you for facing Hannibal and his damn elephants. If it wasn't for the historical preservation regs, I'd have murdered that bastard, Scipio."

"That rough, huh?"

"Don't ask."

"I don't have to. You look all done in." He glanced at Priest's insignia. "I see you made sergeant major."

"And you've been bumped a grade or two as well. How long has it been?"

"It's been a while," said Bobby, grinning. "I haven't seen you since this morning."

They sat down to compare notes. The last time they saw each other, it had been at 0900 September 17, 2613. But that was Plus Time. Since then, Lucas had sailed with Lord Nelson, fought under General Pershing, picked up a saber scar in the Crimea and helped to kill Custer at the Little Big Horn. Now he had just clocked in from fighting in the Punic Wars and it was 1435 September 17, 2613. Lucas Priest had aged ten years. He and Johnson had been the same age five Plus Time hours ago, but now Lucas looked older. He had put in much more Minus Time. Lucas had about three days of Plus Time left to serve and Bobby had four days to go.

"It's great to see you again, Lucas," Bobby said. "I wish to hell we had time for a drink, but my code's on stand-by."

"I know," said Lucas, lifting his tags out and twirling them between two fingers. Bobby made a grab for them.

"Green 44! We've got the same departure code!"

Lucas smiled. "Well, fancy that."

"You knew!"

"Of course I knew," said Lucas. "I checked the data on you as soon as I clocked in. I told you I'd be doing it, didn't you believe me?"

"Yeah, well, everybody says that, you know? But it gets depressing, seeing all the KIAs and MIAs. . . ."

"I know," said Lucas softly. "My list of friends keeps getting shorter."

There was an awkward pause. Bobby finally broke the silence, anxiously trying to change the subject.

"How in hell did you come up with Green 44? You had a code choice? You look okay, but—"

"I never exercised my option after I got wounded in the Crimea," Lucas said. "I decided to hold off until the time was right."

"But why did you go for a code choice instead of bonus Plus Time?"

"If you had a choice between a lousy hour of bonus time and friendship time, what would you choose?" Lucas said.

"Well, since you put it that way, I guess I'd opt for spending a hitch together with a friend. But I'd still cry about the bonus."

"So you pick up another wound."

"Thanks, but if I can, I'll pass. I've been lucky so far, knock on wood." He glanced around. "You see any wood anywhere?"

Lucas grinned. "Tap on some plastic and cross your fingers."

He turned to see his squire pulling up on a dolly with his gear all packed. He had left word where he could be found so that he wouldn't have to wait around to meet whomever it would turn out to be. It was one of the few advantages of being a non-com. You could get an enlisted man to draw your supplies. In this case, the enlisted man was part of the supplies, since he would be going along as Priest's orderly.

Lucas Priest's squire was a whipcord thin young corporal named Hooker. It came as a surprise to him that he was not expected to call Lucas "sir" or "Mr. Priest." Where they were going, the term was probably going to be "milord," but Lucas tried to avoid military protocol as much as possible. He passed Hooker a cup of coffee. The corporal cracked the seal on it and the cup began to steam. They woke up Finn Delaney. It took some doing. Delaney was a surly lifer who was built like a gorilla. He immediately got into Priest's good graces by offering him a Diehard. Lucas pulled one out and rubbed it along the side of the pack, igniting it.

"*Code Green, Forty-Fowar, Code Green, Forty-Fowar, report to Seven Yellow, Grid Six Hundred, Seven Yellow, Grid Six Hundred.*"

"Well, that's us," said Lucas, taking several quick drags on the cigarette before stubbing it out with his boot. It would probably be a long time before he had another one, assuming he made it back alive.

The chronoplate left Lucas feeling slightly vertiginous, as it always did. He had never been able to get used to it, but his reaction was less severe than Hooker's.

"Didn't anyone tell you not to eat anything within two hours of clocking out?" he said.

Hooker looked puzzled for a moment, then got the joke. It was rare for the army to leave anyone waiting around at a departure station for much more than an hour. So long as a soldier was in Plus Time, the clock was ticking away. If a soldier was in Minus Time and had ample warning of a clock out, there might be two hours during which he could refrain from eating, but the pickup squads rarely gave anyone that much notice. They liked to cut it close.

"I think the last time I ate was a couple of thousand years ago," said Hooker, grinning weakly. "I could've saved myself the trouble. I didn't even get a chance to digest anything."

"Welcome to 12th century England, gentlemen," said the referee.

Lucas was surprised. Very surprised. It was not unusual to run across observers in the field, but what sort of hitch required the presence of a ref in Minus Time?

"Questions can wait a while, gentlemen," said the ref, a soft-spoken, professorial sort. "First things first. Mr. Hooker, you'll be pleased to know that we have third mess laid on for you and that you'll have the opportunity to digest your meal this time. If you'll follow me, please?"

Hooker and Delaney began to pick up the gear, but the ref told them to leave it. "It will be taken care of," he said. They glanced at each other, shrugged, then followed Priest and Johnson.

"We must be the last ones through," said Bobby. "Everybody else must already be at mess. With our luck, all we'll get is table scraps."

But such was not the case. They trudged a short distance to a prefabricated hut where they were served venison, kidney pie, roast pheasant, squab and potatoes cooked in an open fire so that their skin was black and crackly. They drank a truly potent ale. It was one of the best meals Lucas Priest had eaten since he had joined the service. That made him worry.

The referee sat with them, but did not eat and except for the orderlies who served them, no one else was present.

"Excuse me, sir," said Johnson, "where is everybody?"

"There is no one else, Mr. Johnson," said the ref.

"You mean that there are only *four* of us on this hitch?"

"Essentially."

"I don't get it, sir."

"All in good time," said the ref. "Meanwhile, don't feel that you have to stretch out your meal. There's plenty more where that came from and that goes for the ale, as well. You don't have any duties until tomorrow morning, so relax and enjoy yourselves."

He reached into his jacket pocket and brought out a silver cigarette case. "Would any of you gentlemen care to smoke?"

Now Lucas *knew* they were in trouble.

"With your permission, sir," he said, accepting the cigarettes. "I mean no disrespect, but I've been in the service long enough to know that this sort of treatment is hardly s.o.p. This is the first time I've seen a referee clocked out to the Minus side. Somehow I have the feeling that this hitch is hardly going to be a soft assignment."

The ref smiled. "Your point is well taken, Mr. Priest. You're quite correct in assuming that this is going to be an unusual hitch. There will be some risk involved, but you gentlemen should be accustomed to that. However, there are compensations. If you succeed in your objective, then the completion of this assignment will also constitute full completion of your tour of duty. That goes for all of you. The remainder of your service time, whatever it may be, will be waived and you will be given the option of retiring with the full pensions and benefits of first lieutenants or reenlisting as captains. And that goes for you as well, Mr. Delaney, even with your rather remarkable disciplinary record."

Delaney spoke the first words Lucas heard him utter. "Shit," he said. "We're dead."

Between the two of them, Lucas and Bobby had put in some pretty heavy service. Hooker was still fairly green, but Delaney was on his second tour of duty and had seen a lot of action. In spite of that, the training period that followed was the toughest any of them had ever gone through. Their drillmaster was a tough old bastard of indeterminate age. The antiagathic drugs made it difficult to accurately guess how old a person was, but the drillmaster looked like Methuselah himself. His name was Major Forrester. He was bald as an egg, wrinkled as a prune and as mean as a bear with hemorrhoids.

"You men might think you're old hands at this sort of thing," he told them. "Well, you're in for one great big fucking surprise. I'm going to work you till you drop and then I'll kick your asses right back up again and you'll work some more. And just for starters, I want a hundred push-ups, two hundred sit-ups and thirty chins."

"That's not so tough," Bobby whispered to Lucas.

"And if you're not done in six minutes, you'll do it all

again! Time starts right *now!*''

They were all used to strenuous demands placed on their bodies, but Forrester ran them ragged. Every night, they went to bed so sore that they could hardly move. The nature of their training left no doubt in their minds that they had been selected for a commando assignment. They were worked in the finer points of medieval combat, becoming accustomed to moving about in full armor and learning to control their horses by pressure of the knees. They were drilled in the use of weapons such as the broadsword, the axe, the mace, the crossbow and the long bow, as well. They trained with daggers and Hooker proved to be a surprise even to Major Forrester. He could throw almost any sort of knife with unerring accuracy. Lucas wondered where he had grown up and what sort of childhood he must have had. Hooker was barely nineteen.

Due to their varied past experiences, some things came easier to some of them than they did to others. Lucas had brought to the assignment extensive experience in fighting with all manner of swords, from foils and sabers to the Roman short sword. Bobby was an accomplished archer, surpassing all the others with his skill. As an expert in several of the Oriental martial arts, Delaney took to a quarterstaff like a duck took to water and he brought some innovative techniques to fighting with a broadsword.

A great deal of time and money had been invested in their training. They were subjected to everything from implant programming to conditioned reflex training, but it was not until they went in for cosmetic surgery that Lucas finally realized the true nature of their mission.

It was going to be a fix-it job. Somehow, someone had screwed up in this time period and a little Trans-historical Adjustment and Maintenance was called for. Lucas had often wondered how such things were accomplished. Now he was about to find out first hand.

By now, it was clear that they had been selected for their skills and general physical characteristics. With the sole exception of Finn Delaney, all of them were smaller than average. The physical size of a soldier had a great deal to do with his assignments. In the past, people were smaller and it wouldn't do to send a mess of six footers back into a time where they would stand out like sore thumbs. Most soldiers still wound up being somewhat larger than most people in the past, but within limits, this did not generally present a problem. Most soldiers were cannon fodder to begin with. History could not be changed, there was far too much risk involved. What modern soldiers could do on the Minus side was strictly defined within the parameters of what was known about their period.

Cosmetic surgery was not unusual in the army. Lucas had been a Sioux at the Little Big Horn. In order to allow him to properly play the part, they had changed his hair from blonde to black, enlarged his nose slightly and flattened out the planes of his face, as well as darkening the color of his normally fair skin with pigmentation treatments. When he rode out to do battle with Yellowhair, Lucas knew that history did not report that a particular Indian had killed him, so if he was presented with a clear shot at Custer, his course of action was entirely up to him. However, in battles that had been fairly well documented, a soldier's options were limited considerably. In such cases, they were always placed in relatively insignificant positions, historically speaking. They were, to all intents and purposes, expendable. History was never especially strict about such things as body counts. Therefore, soldiers from Plus Time fought side-by-side with their ancient counterparts and, if they were killed, their cybernetic implants relayed that information to the observers in that time period. MIAs, soldiers sustaining injuries, all went into the tally that became the basis for the complex point spread that governed the arbitration proceedings of the referees.

Being a veteran of many cosmetic surgical procedures, Lucas knew that in this event the changes made were subtle ones, rather than a general, superficial alteration. They were being made to resemble specific individuals, people who were either known to history or to certain key people who would be involved with them during their mission. This would not be a simple case of infiltrating a few soldiers—insignificant pawns from the point of view of history—into a Roman legion. This would be a covert operation. He wondered what the mission was going to be. If the training had been so intensive, what did the mission itself hold in store for them?

They had not been coached to play the part of certain individuals, at least not consciously. There was, however, the implant programming. Much of that information was already at their beck and call, but it made sense that a great deal of it was filed under "need to know," to be brought forth at the proper time, probably the mission briefing, by a key word or a key phrase. It made Lucas very apprehensive. Who were they supposed to be? When he found out, he almost wished that Hannibal had killed him back in Carthage.

It was the last day of their training. They were led into a small prefabricated building that had been, up to that moment, off limits to them. They were brought into a room which contained nothing save several chairs, a table, a couple of army cots and four cryotanks, with all the attendant read-out screens and servo-mechanisms. The two medical technicians paid them absolutely no attention as they entered and the referee, in turn, did not acknowledge the technicians' presence. The cryotanks were occupied by four men who looked exactly like them. Or, more to the point, *they* looked like the people in the cryotanks.

They sat down in the chairs and the ref perched on the edge of the table, leaning forward toward them, resting his hands upon his knees. He was the perfect picture of a kindly old professor. An old man with snow white hair, blue eyes, sunken cheeks and crow's feet. An old man who had total control over their lives.

"Gentlemen," he said, "in the year 1189, Richard the First, also known as Richard Plantagenet, *Coeur de Lion*, ascended to the throne of England. While he was off fighting in the Third Crusade, his brother, known as John Lackland, revolted against the justiciar, William Longchamp, and effectively took the place of the king. He thereupon embarked upon a series of intrigues to keep his brother from the throne. Richard had been captured and was held prisoner by the Duke of Austria. In time, the king was ransomed and he returned to England to pardon his brother, John, and to resume the throne. When Richard died at Chaluz in 1199, John finally realized his ambition and became the king of England.

"As king, John was, to put it mildly, something of a disaster. He warred on his nephew Arthur and eventually murdered him. He quarreled with Pope Innocent III, succeeded in getting England placed under an interdict in 1208, screwed up six ways from Sunday and generally bled the country dry to the extent that his own barons finally rebelled against him, forcing him to sign the Magna Carta at Runnymede on June 15, 1215. That, in a nutshell, is the story. Except, as you have doubtless deduced by now, we have a problem.

"The year is 1194. Duke Leopold has delivered Richard to Emperor Henry VI, who has released him for ransom and Richard is supposed to be on his journey back to England. Supposed to be. Here's where things get a little sticky.

"To my everlasting sorrow and deep, professional embarrassment, a member of the referee corps has gone rogue. To be quite blunt, he's gone off the deep end and has decided to live out some sort of Walter Mitty fantasy. His name is Irving Goldblum and he has succeeded in kidnapping Richard of England a *second* time. It's entirely possible that he has even killed him. In fact, it's highly probable, but I don't know for certain. Needless to say, in so doing, he has endangered history. His intention is to take the place of Richard Plantagenet and become the king of England. Nothing quite like this has ever happened before. It's a frightening situation. A highly complex situation, to say the least.

"What we have on our hands at this moment is a threat to the continuity of the timestream. There could be a massive split, the effects of which are completely unpredictable. Fortunately, we became aware of Irving's demented plan before he clocked out to Minus Time. He has studied this period extensively via computer tapes and he has had cosmetic surgery. The necessary preparations he had to make alerted us. Unfortunately, he was able to clock out before we could stop him. We acted immediately to organize an adjustment, hoping we could pull it off before any anomalies began to show up. We, meaning myself and my support team here with me on this desolate piece of rock, have already undertaken several attempts to rectify the situation."

The ref paused to take a deep breath.

"Our attempts, so far, have failed. We were able to estimate the time of his arrival in this period and we tried to intercept him. We did not succeed. We also tried to prevent his capture of Richard and we failed there, as well. He has the odds in his favor. He also has a chronoplate. This makes our job extremely difficult. He has used his chronoplate to outmaneuver us at every turn.

"We can travel through time, obviously, but that's how things can get completely out of hand. I am not about to become involved in a leapfrog race through time with him. That's sheer insanity, to say nothing of the dangers it presents. There is simply no way we could prevail under such circumstances. He knows it and I know it. Therefore, we must confine ourselves to doing battle, as it were, within this time period. Irving has gone to a great deal of trouble to set up this scenario and he won't move ahead in time unless I force his hand. At this stage of the game, we are fighting a limited war. It's our only chance to preserve the timeline, to prevent the potential split."

"Sir?"

"Yes, Mr. Johnson?"

"I realize that we're probably on a need-to-know basis here—"

"You are quite free to ask questions, Mr. Johnson. It's imperative for you men to thoroughly understand the situation within which you must function. What confuses you?"

"Well, we've all heard about adjustments before," said Bobby. "Nothing quite like this, but . . . What I'm trying to say here is that none of us really understands the process. You say this ref managed to stay ahead of you so far. What's to prevent you from using your plate to clock back and try to take him out again?"

"The mechanics of timeline preservation, Mr. Johnson. You see, I'm handicapped by the fact that I'm the one who's trying to preserve the timeline. Irving is the one who wants to change it. He wants to create that split. I'll attempt to explain it as simply as possible. The fact that we are here is the result of nothing less than an amazing piece of luck. We've been able to attempt this adjustment because Irving has not yet managed to take an action that would result in a timestream split. At this moment, the time from which we came is in a potential state of flux. You men are the third team to attempt this adjustment. The others have failed."

He paused a moment to let that sink in. It meant that they were dead.

"Now, remember that I have the not inconsiderable task of

preserving the timeline. Suppose, upon learning of the failure of the last team, I used my chronoplate to go back into the past and try again. That, in itself, would create a split, a parallel timeline. That must be avoided at all costs.''

"Sir?"

"Mr. Priest?"

"Hasn't this Irving character already changed the past, just by interfering with history?''

"Not yet. So far, there has been no paradox. The situation, as it stands, is as follows: Irving has clocked back into this period. So far, no paradox. He has not yet interfered with history. He has managed to intercept Richard on his way back to England. A potential paradox, but so far the timestream remains unaffected. My job is to keep it that way.''

"Good luck,'' said Delaney.

"Yes, quite,'' said the referee, dryly. "I see you understand the situation, Mr. Delaney. However, let's make certain that we *all* understand it. The fact is, our fake Richard can kill the real one and take his place, even regain the throne of England *as* Richard Plantagenet. With all that, the timestream still remains unaffected. There is a Richard on the throne of England. It's not the real one, but that creates no paradox in and of itself. What *would* create a paradox is if Irving were to take some action that would significantly alter the course of history. Let's set up a hypothetical situation. Suppose we're out of the picture. Suppose, also, that Irving takes the place of Richard and acts in exactly the same manner as the real one did, according to our history . . . up to a point. Let's pick Chaluz for the purpose of this discussion. The real Richard the Lionhearted died at Chaluz. Knowing this, the fake Richard will obviously avoid that fate, probably by the very simple expedient of staying out of France. It's still possible that the inertia inherent in the timestream could work against him, but that's all highly theoretical and I wouldn't want to bet on that. So now, we have a paradox. The real Richard was killed at Chaluz in 1199, but Irving, *as* Richard, lives on. Suppose he remains king for a long time after that. Suppose John never ascends to the throne. Suppose the Magna Carta is never even written, much less signed. Now we're talking about major paradoxes, gentlemen.

"The past is absolute. *Irving's* past is absolute. His timeline

—and ours—has Richard dying at Chaluz, John becoming king, etc. That cannot be changed, it already happened. The moment Irving takes an action that is significantly contrary to our history to create a paradox, he splits the timestream and creates a parallel timeline. And that means we've lost. If I clock back at a point beyond which he has done that, I'll only wind up splitting it again, creating yet another parallel timeline, which will only make things worse. I have only one course of action open to me and that is to proceed in a linear fashion through this mission. The first team failed. At the point I became aware of that, I sent ahead for another team. When that team failed, I put in a call for yet another team and you men arrived. Should you fail, I will try to get yet another team, *providing that Irving has not yet split the timeline*.

"You see, gentlemen, in a way it's very much like playing Russian roulette. All it takes is for that one possibility to arise in which I am not sent another team and Irving will have won. I have absolutely no idea what action he may take that would result in a change significant enough to create a parallel timeline. Nor do I know *when* he will take that action, when he will have the opportunity. It might even be happening right this very moment, in which case this is all a pointless exercise. In that event, I haven't the faintest idea what we would do. I don't even want to think about it."

He paused again, observing the men. They were grimly silent, all save Delaney, who groaned and put his head in his hands.

"There is, of course, another possibility," said the referee. "Once Irving splits the timeline, it is theoretically possible to clock back to a point *before* that split occurs and attempt to prevent it from occurring. However, that raises some very unpleasant possibilities. Split timelines must eventually rejoin. The moment Irving succeeds in creating the split, its effects show up in the future. It isn't possible to prevent the future from happening, but it is possible to warp our history and hurt a great many people. A great many. The moment the split occurs, from the standpoint of the future, an entire separate timeline already exists, incorporating God only knows how many lives. To go back and prevent it means to destroy everyone within that separate timeline. That would be nothing less than the most massive genocide in the history of the human race," said the referee, "and there's no telling how that would affect the future. Allow me to illustrate with yet another hypothetical situation. Suppose I send for another team, unaware that by that time, Irving has *already* created the split. Suppose I am sent a team. It could happen. The people who clock back could very well be coming from a future already affected by the split, for better or for worse. If I were then to attempt to eradicate the parallel timeline by preventing the split in the first place, a.—I would be risking causing a split myself and, b.—the people coming from a future affected by that split might never even have existed had not the split occurred. I would then be threatening *their* history, not to say their very existence. Under such circumstances, I expect that they would do their level best to kill me. Perhaps those would even be their orders, regardless of the problems created by the split. They would want to preserve *their* status quo, no matter how chaotic it might be."

"Christ," whispered Hooker.

"Scary, isn't it?" said the referee.

"How are we supposed to stop it?" Hooker said.

"I thought that was obvious," the ref said.

"We're a hit squad, son," Delaney told Hooker. "We're supposed to try and kill this Irving person."

"The rather archaic phrase is 'terminate with extreme prejudice,' " said the referee. "Should you succeed in doing that, *I* will then become Richard the First and act accordingly, as per our history." He grimaced. "I would prefer not to have to die in France in another five years, but I have no choice. So you see, gentlemen, I may be sending you out on an extremely difficult assignment, but I don't think you'd want to trade places with me."

"Sir?"

"Mr. Hooker?"

"Why only four of us, sir? Wouldn't we stand a better chance with more men?"

The ref smiled. "A good question. Yes, perhaps. Frankly, I wish I could have had an army at my disposal. However, I am somewhat handicapped—as are you—by organizational paranoia. It has been decided that the optimal number of men for this mission, in order to minimize the chances of temporal contamination, is four. Plus a support team, the other people whom you've seen here. Why not five, you ask, or six or seven or three, for that matter? Well, I argued that point, but . . . The situation calls for a small, highly effective unit that could be infiltrated into key positions in this time period. There is such a thing, the reasoning goes, as having too many spies. It was felt that a larger team would introduce a greater element of risk into this operation.''

"Chickenshit bastards," mumbled Delaney.

The ref smiled. "You're insubordinate, Mr. Delaney. However, I can't help but to concede the point. Nevertheless, that's how it stands." He indicated the cryotanks. "We have here four people who are of some significance in this scenario. These people are the ones whom you will be impersonating in this operation, so play your parts well, gentlemen. Your lives depend on it."

He got up and motioned to the technicians, acknowledging their presence for the first time. One by one, they swiveled the tanks into vertical positions.

"Mr. Delaney, you are now this man's twin," the ref said, pointing to the first tank. "His name is John Little, but he is better known as Little John. Mr. Johnson, if you have a touch of the romantic in you, you may be intrigued to learn that you will be assuming the role of the Baron of Locksley, otherwise known to history as Robin Hood."

"Holy shit," said Bobby.

The ref chuckled, in spite of himself. "Do try to maintain a sense of perspective, Mr. Johnson. Folklore notwithstanding, this man is only human, as are you. Mr. Hooker, you will notice that *your* counterpart has a fresh scar upon his face. I'm afraid we shall have to give you a matching one before we send you out. He gave us some difficulty. He proved highly resistant to drugs and we had to subdue him forcibly. You will take his place as squire to Sergeant Major Priest. Your name, the only one you're known by so far as we have been able to ascertain, is Poignard. Your not inconsiderable skill with knives will no doubt serve you well. And now, Mr. Priest . . ."

The final cryogen.

"I understand that your assignment to this operation came about as a result of your exercising a code choice option. You may be regretting that now. As it happened, rather ironically, you were ideally suited for this mission, better qualified than the man you have displaced. The moment you punched in, some soldier got off easy. He'll never know what he missed. Do you believe in fate, Mr. Priest?"

"Yes, sir, I think I do."

"Well, in that case, meet yours." He rested his hand on the edge of the cryogen. "Sir Wilfred of Ivanhoe."

2

Priest's suspicions about part of the implant programming having been subliminally inhibited were confirmed when they were dropped off on the mainland with their gear. He also saw that the ref was not without an ironic sense of humor when he faced them all and spoke the words, "Sir Walter Scott," and they instantly "remembered" things they never knew.

They stood upon the beach, watching the much-modified LCA making headway back toward the tiny, windswept island off the coast. Its engines were muffled to the point where they were barely audible and Lucas wondered what some passing Saxon would have made of the spectacle of their landing. But there were no passing Saxons, or Normans for that matter. The coastline was quiet and deserted. Nothing marred the stillness of the night save for the sound of wind, the crashing surf, and the cries of a few seagulls. They were on their own. Beached upon the shores of time.

None of them spoke as they started slowly moving inland, each experiencing unfamiliar memories. The four men in the cryogens had been drugged and questioned extensively so that the team might possess the information that would enable them to carry off their impersonations. Yet, there was no guarantee that the information that had been implanted in their minds would allow them to carry off their charade successfully. There were still a thousand things that could go wrong, such was the nature of covert operations. Risk was part of the game.

The men whose places they had taken had been snatched shortly before their arrival in Minus Time and they had been interrogated around the clock during the time in which the team completed their mission training. With the information extracted from Ivanhoe, Lucas was familiar with his background and with the status quo.

John Lackland was still controlling the reins of power in England. Richard had not yet returned from captivity. The main thing Lucas had in his favor was that Wilfred of Ivanhoe and Richard had been comrades in arms during the Holy Wars and Irving did not know that he was a bogus Ivanhoe. Perhaps the real Plantagenet would have been able to discern a change in his old friend, but Irving would be too busy playing his part to notice, unless Lucas made some dreadful error. Lucas guessed that Irving, despite the advantages that he possessed, would be as much concerned that his "friend and vassal" of Ivanhoe would not perceive a difference in his king as Lucas would be that he was taken at face value. It was to be a game of double bluff, with both parties striving to maintain a poker face to conceal the cards that they were holding.

Finn and Bobby, on the other hand, would be in a far more risky situation, since the people they would have to deceive would not be play actors, but the real thing. Robin Hood and Little John were both well known to all the "merry men," which meant that they would have to tread very lightly. As for Hooker, any concern he felt was being hidden beneath a stoic exterior.

The real Ivanhoe had been away, fighting in the Crusades. There were bound to be certain changes in him, but it was inevitable that sooner or later, Lucas would come across his "father." If anyone could penetrate his disguise, it would be Cedric. Since they were in medieval times, the likelihood of their being discovered for what they really were was virtually nil. Who, in this time period, would even entertain the notion of something like cosmetic surgery? Who would suspect that soldiers from a future time were masquerading as a knight, a squire, and two Saxon outlaws? Yet, these were very superstitious times. While no one would guess that Robin Hood was an imposter, they might well come to the conclusion that he had been somehow ensorcelled or that the person who identified himself as Ivanhoe or his squire, Poignard, was really some sort of wizard or warlock bent on evil. In his career as a fighting man, Lucas had many times contemplated the likelihood of death in all the ways that it could come to him, from a sword thrust or a bullet, from an arrow or the decapitating stroke of a headsman's axe. But he had never considered the possibility of being burned at the stake. He considered it now.

They made camp in the woods, electing to shiver in the night air rather than risking a fire. Lucas felt that they would have enough on their hands once they neared Ashby; there was no point to inviting trouble until they had some time to scout around. They had brought some provisions with them, so they did not go hungry, but they all ate in silence and then retired to sleep among the trees, taking turns at standing watch. It was like the quiet before a battle. The night passed uneventfully, giving Lucas a chance to contemplate his "memories."

Things had not gone well for Richard during this last Crusade. There had been yet another truce with Saladin, but it had been negotiated mainly in the interests of saving face. Saladin was a skilled and crafty warrior and his cause had only been advanced by dissension in Richard's ranks. A good sized faction of Richard's Norman knights had given their allegiance to Philip of France. Most of these knights belonged to the orders of the Knights of St. John and the Knights Templars. These same knights, the Templars and the Hospitalers, had taken the side of John of Anjou against his brother. While Richard was away, playing knight errant, John consolidated his power, egged on by that portion of the Norman nobility who stood to gain the most by his sitting on the throne. Most of the barons who had remained faithful to Richard and who had departed with him on his war had their lands and estates reassigned behind their backs by John, who neatly turned those properties over to his toadies in order to secure their backing. Among those unfortunate, now landless knights, Ivanhoe, a favorite of Richard's, had been among the first to lose his fief. He had returned to his native England, war-weary and penniless, without even a suit of armor to his name. That, at least, had been taken care of, courtesy of the U.S. Army. Lucas had a suit of nysteel that, while heavy in order not to arouse too much suspicion, was still lighter by far than the conventional armor of the day. It was far more flexible and impervious to swords and lances.

Ivanhoe had other problems on his hands, as well. It seemed that Cedric, his father, had been anxious to start a Saxon revolution to overthrow the Norman conquerors. To this end, he had hoped to arrange a marriage between his ward, Rowena, who was descended from the line of Alfred, and his friend Athelstane, a porker of a Saxon knight who was also of noble blood. This union, Cedric had hoped, would prevent the formation of factions among the Saxons, uniting them behind one house. The only hitch in his plan had been Rowena, who preferred Cedric's son to Athelstane. Wilfred had taken quite a fancy to her. When ordered to cease and desist, the son had rebelled against the father. Cedric was already displeased with his son. The old man did not approve of Wilfred spending time at court, learning the Norman art of fighting and picking up various Norman ways. When Wilfred began to court the woman Cedric intended to marry off to Athelstane and under his own roof, yet, it had been the straw that broke the Saxon's back. In a fit of temper, Cedric had disinherited his son, banishing him from his house and vowing never to speak his name again. Thanks to Ivanhoe's incontinence, Lucas now had an angry father and a pining sweetheart to contend with. As far as he was concerned, he didn't care if he never met up with Cedric and Rowena could pine away to her heart's content. He had enough to worry about. Still, if he ran into them, it could present a weighty problem.

Lucas attempted to consult his programmed memory on the subject of Poignard, but it was of little help. They must have questioned Ivanhoe concerning his squire and how he came by his services, but Wilfred evidently thought so little of the man who served him that all Lucas knew was that Hooker was supposed to be a fallen Norman of some sort whose services he had won in a passage at arms. Wilfred evidently thought as much about Poignard as he did about his saddle, which meant that he hardly thought of him at all. It wasn't really surprising. Property was only property, after all. Still, Lucas might have expected at least some sensitivity from the man toward his squire, but it seemed that Ivanhoe was not the most sensitive of men.

When he had been snatched by the Temporal Corps, Ivanhoe had been on his way to Yorkshire to purchase a horse and a suit of armor for the tournament at Ashby-de-la-Zouche. To this end, the gallant knight had waylaid a Norman monk, bashing his head in with a quarterstaff and relieving him of his purse. Having been issued his horse and armor, Lucas felt that the best thing for him to do would be to proceed on to the tournament as Ivanhoe had planned and to see what would develop. All the local nobility would be there, since the festivities were being hosted by Prince John himself in an effort to entertain the populace. Lucas recalled that the Romans had done much the same sort of thing. If you kept taxing the pants off the people, they were bound to get a bit annoyed, so it helped to take their minds off their troubles every now and then by putting on a show. The Romans had their circuses, the Normans had their jousts. *Plus ça change, plus c'est la même chose.*

They held a council in the morning to outline their plans. So far as either of them knew, Ivanhoe and the outlawed Baron of Locksley had never met, although they would know each other's names. Therefore, they had no need to get their stories straight. They decided to arrange a meeting later and the tournament seemed ideal for that purpose. They agreed to meet at Ashby and went their separate ways with no little reluctance. The journey could have been longer for his liking, but Lucas eventually found himself approaching Ashby, where the crowd was already gathering in anticipation of the tournament. Lucas put on his gear and donned his helmet, instructing Hooker to put on his hooded robe. He was not quite ready yet to meet anyone who knew Wilfred of Ivanhoe.

The galleries were all set up, as were the lists, which were nothing more than several fences running parallel to each other, forming tracks down which knights would hurtle toward each other from opposite ends, colliding as they passed. The battleground was in a small valley with the stands erected on a rise, a little hill that would afford the spectators an unobstructed view of the proceedings. On either side of the small valley, pavilions had been erected: tents with pennants flying from their peaks, the colors identifying the knights who occupied them. Some of these pavilions matched the colors of their pennants, revealing which of the knights were among the more well-to-do. As was the custom, one side of the field had been assigned to the hosts—or the home team as Lucas thought of them—the other to the challengers or visitors. Lucas had the purse which Wilfred had obtained by mugging some poor priest, so he gave it to Hooker and sent him off with instructions to secure a pavilion for themselves.

"Make sure it's one of the cheaper ones," he said. "It's still early in the game and it wouldn't hurt to economize."

When Hooker returned, he told him that they had a pavilion at the far end of the valley, out of the way of the center of activity, but close enough to enable them to observe the goings-on from within its shelter.

"Good enough, squire Poignard," said Lucas. "Let's go. Oh, and pick up a couple of those chickens that vendor's cooking over there. No point to jousting on an empty stomach."

Lucas stood just inside the tent flap, munching on a drumstick and watching the opening ceremonies. Hooker had collared one of the local lads and for a small price, they had a play-by-play announcer. Or blow-by-blow, as the case may be, thought Lucas. Under the circumstances, it was not an unusual thing for a knight to do. It was a large tournament and there were competitors present from all over the country. It was entirely within reason that a stranger to the land, especially one who had come from far away, would not be familiar with all the colors and heraldic devices. Lucas sat down on a crude wooden cot inside the tent, in a position so that he could see outside, yet at the same time appear to be resting for the time when his turn came. Hooker stood just outside with the boy, a youngster of about twelve who seemed to know everyone concerned, just as a modern kid would know all the players in his favorite sport.

"Describe everything to me in detail," Lucas told the lad. "I wish to close my eyes and rest awhile."

Then, while the boy stood outside and described what was happening in great detail, just as he was told, Lucas shifted his position so that he could see clearly everything the boy described. He could be forgiven for not recognizing all the colors, but it would look a little strange if he did not know any of them.

It was nearing midday and all things were in readiness to begin the tournament. It could have started hours ago, save for the fact that it was necessary to wait for the arrival of the nobility, who showed up in dribs and drabs, each delaying their arrival by a degree of lateness according to the positions they fancied themselves to hold in the social pecking order. Lord Bluenose couldn't possibly arrive at his seat before the Earl of High and Mighty. Finally, everyone was seated except for the prince and his retinue. They arrived with many fanfares from the trumpets, which sounded too much to Lucas like the braying of Hannibal's elephants. He was not in the least concerned about the passage at arms. Having been charged by a bull elephant, Lucas felt that an armored knight on horseback seemed rather tame by comparison.

John rode in on a handsome charger, surrounded by his knights. Priest's young announcer called them off to him, identifying each by their colors and the devices on the shields carried by their squires. There was Maurice De Bracy, riding at the head of a group of his Free Companions, which translated as mercenaries. De Bracy was all decked out in gold, which Lucas thought appropriate, and his shield bore the emblem of a flaming sword. Riding on John's left hand was the warrior priest, the Templar Brian de Bois-Guilbert. He was dressed in the black and white colors of his order, his shield emblazoned with a stylized raven, wings outstretched, holding a skull in its claws. Beside him rode Sir Reginald Front-de-Boeuf, a bullish looking knight whose appearance suited his name. He was in blue lacquered armor with a bull's head on his shield. Somewhat behind them, attired in brilliant blood red with a fleury cross upon his shield, was a knight the boy identified as Andre de la Croix. And in the vanguard was the prince himself.

John of Anjou was a dandy, dressed in the height of fashion, complete with a fur-trimmed short cloak and boots with turned up toes. His black beard was neatly trimmed and pointed and his hair hung down to his shoulders, curled at the end in a style that reminded Lucas of the way women wore their hair in the period following World War II. He flourished a small mace as he rode, a peculiar thing with a triangulated head that seemed more for show than for fighting. To top off the ensemble, John wore a velvet cap set at a rakish angle.

He took his small parade through the lists and around in front of the stands, preening before the crowd, which greeted him with some enthusiasm. Perhaps he was a tyrant, but he was the patron of the festival and the people seemed grateful for what small favors they could receive. Still, there were those in the gallery who were conspicuous by their refusal to applaud His Majesty. Richard still commanded some loyalty and, of course, the Saxons had little reason to love John. The prince seemed far less interested in them, however, than in their women. He took his time riding past the stands. He paused in front of the section where there had been the least applause and Lucas shifted his position slightly to see what had captured his attention. It turned out to be a pretty blonde.

"The prince gazes boldly on the fair Lady Rowena," said the boy, somewhat testily, betraying his strong Saxon pride. "This will ill please the noble Cedric."

Lucas got up and moved closer to get a better view. So this was his supposed sweetheart and his father. So much for my revealing myself at this tournament, he thought. He had no desire for a family reunion. As he watched, John moved closer to Rowena and Cedric, evidently displeased at this attention or at something John had said, interposed himself between the sovereign and his ward. John said something to De Bracy and Lucas saw the knight stretch forth his lance, as if to give Cedric a sharp poke in the ribs. The burly Saxon's response was to whip out his sword and, with a quick chopping stroke, knock the point off De Bracy's lance.

"Well," said Hooker, "things are getting interesting."

For a moment, De Bracy stared stupidly at his amputated lance, having been caught unprepared by the quickness of Cedric's blow. Then someone called out, "Well struck!" in a loud voice and the crowd burst into cheers and laughter. De Bracy turned beet red and grabbed for his sword, but found a gloved hand covering his own. He looked up and saw the smiling face of the red knight, who had ridden up beside him.

"You find this amusing, de la Croix?" De Bracy snapped.

"No, somewhat predictable, given Cedric's character," said Andre de la Croix, suppressing a chuckle. The two knights conversed in French, as did all Normans when they weren't addressing Saxons in the mixed tongue of *lingua franca*.

"Remove your hand," said De Bracy, very evenly.

"I will," said de la Croix, "only remember that this passage at arms has been arranged to curry favor with the motley masses, the better to enable them to forget, for a time at least, their empty purses. It would prove somewhat contrary to the purpose were you to skewer Cedric, who has their affection."

Sullenly, De Bracy loosened his grip on the pommel of his sword and de la Croix removed the restraining hand. John, meanwhile, had missed this interplay, having been preoccupied with his indignation at the man who had set off the outcry and the laughter by calling out, "Well struck!"

"*You!*" He pointed his truncheon at the offender. "What is your name?"

"I'm called Grant the Tinker," said the man.

"I don't like your face," said John. "Step forward!"

Bobby Johnson ducked beneath the railing and stepped up to the monarch's horse. He inclined his head in a small and totally inadequate bow.

"You are insolent, Tinker."

"I was merely carried away in my enthusiasm at seeing a blow that had been struck so well," said Bobby, casually omitting any use of honorifics in his address of the prince.

"What would a tinker know of such things?" said John, contemptuously.

"It's true that I'm no knight," said Bobby, "but I'm a fair hand with a bow and I can appreciate the skill one man displays in that which he does best."

"You fancy yourself an archer, then? Why would a common tinker concern himself with such a martial art?"

"These are hard times in which we live," said Bobby. "Bandits are abroad and a man must learn to protect himself."

"The man is insolent beyond belief, Sire," said Front-de-Boeuf. "Let me run him through and we'll have done with him."

"No," said John. "I am of a mind to have some sport with this rude peasant. We shall put him to the test. We'll see how well you shoot, Tinker, if your arrows fly as true as your mouth runs ready. Marshal, prepare the butts. We will begin with archery today. And if you do not prove to be as expert as you are rash, my loutish friend, I'll see you lashed for your impertinence."

As the heralds proclaimed the beginning of the tournament, John and his retinue took their places in the stands in a section separated from the others by being somewhat elevated above them and enclosed on all sides save the front, giving those sitting within the most commanding view of the field. The archery butts were brought out and Bobby stepped forward to take his place among the ranks of the competitors. There were not too many of them, since challengers would have to shoot against John's Norman archers, who were famous for their marksmanship.

"Now look what you've done," growled Finn Delaney, who had gone along with Bobby to hold his quiver and his cloak.

"Now look what you've done, *sir*," said Bobby, grinning. Finn was old enough to be his father.

"Shit, give me a break," said Finn. He ran a beefy hand through his thick red hair. "This isn't funny. He wasn't kidding about giving you a whipping. You think they'll stop with just tearing some skin off your back? These bastards will keep at it till you croak!"

"That's assuming I lose this contest," Bobby said.

"Who do you think you are, Robin Hood?"

Bobby stared at him in astonishment, then broke up.

"Okay, very funny," Finn said, frowning. "But what if any of these characters are better than you?"

"Then I guess we'll be in trouble."

"*We?*"

"Thanks, Finn. I knew you'd stand by me."

"Jesus, you could at least have called him Sire or Your Majesty or something. You had to go and piss him off. What was the point?"

Bobby handed him his cloak and hat. "You're supposed to be Little John," he said, "and I'm supposed to be the fastest gun in Sherwood Forest, remember? If I win this shoot-out, they'll be talking about it all over the place. Can you think of a better way of establishing our credentials?"

"Give me a minute, I'm sure I can come up with something."

"Well, think fast, because they're about to get this show on the road."

The trumpets blared again and the herald announced that each man would have three flights of arrows at a distance of seventy-five paces. The moment that had been announced, seven of the competitors dropped out. That left only nine, including Bobby. Each man shot at will, taking as much time as he wished to shoot three arrows in succession. Bobby hit the gold with every shot with no apparent difficulty and, to most of the people in the stands, it looked like he hardly even aimed. Only two archers did as well, which eliminated everybody else.

"That wasn't bad," said Finn.

"I had to make harder shots in training," Bobby said. "Besides, this isn't entirely new to me, you know. Remind me to tell you about the time I took archery lessons from Ulysses."

They moved the targets farther back, to a distance of about one hundred yards. They shot again and this time one man was eliminated. That left Bobby and Hubert, John's champion archer.

"If Hubert doesn't beat this insolent braggart," John said, "I'll have his guts for garters."

The targets were now moved back to a distance of some hundred and twenty yards.

"You sure about this?" whispered Finn.

"Piece of cake."

Hubert was to have the first shot. He drew his long bow back to his right ear, aimed carefully, waited for the breeze to die down and then let fly. The arrow described a graceful arc in the air and landed directly dead center in the gold. A cheer went up from the stands.

"Hah!" John exclaimed, jubilant at Hubert's shot. "Let's see the Saxon bastard beat that shot! It can't be done!"

Finn's heart sank.

"Hell of a shot," Bobby said. "I'd give my left nut for a laminated Browning recurve with stabilizers right about now."

"What are we going to do?"

"The only thing we *can* do."

"Resign and run for it?"

"No, cheat."

He turned his back to the stands, taking a position so that Hubert couldn't see what he was doing. He removed an arrow from the quiver that was colored differently from all the others. He fitted the black arrow to his bow.

"A little something the ordnance boys whipped up for me, just in case," he said to Finn.

"What's the gimmick?"

"Look inside the quiver and you'll find a little black box. When I nock my arrow, the bowstring depresses the arming trigger. The moment I let fly, you hit the button on that box. Inside the shaft, there's integrated microcircuitry coupling a ferrous metal detector inside the bronze arrowhead with a limited trim system on the fletching."

Finn grinned widely. "Now that's *style*," he said.

"I don't know about style," said Bobby, "but I've got a strong sense of self-preservation. The black arrows have shaped charges in the heads. Just stand between me and Hubert while I remove that, I don't want to blow up my target."

The whispered conversation with Finn was taken for hesitation on Bobby's part by Hubert, who began to grin broadly and act as though he had already won. Indeed, he had no reason to believe otherwise. When Bobby took his stance and drew his bow back, the crowd fell utterly silent. No one believed that there was any way the tinker could match the shot, much less beat it, but they respected his determination.

"He'll never best that shot of Hubert's," John said confidently. "I'll teach that Saxon cur a lesson in manners yet."

Bobby made a show of aiming, then let the arrow fly. The moment the shaft left the bowstring, Finn depressed the button activating the guidance system. The arrow was halfway to the target when the ferrous metal detector picked up the presence of Hubert's iron arrowhead just ahead of it. Fortunately, there were no other iron objects near enough to confuse the system and the arrow flew straight and true, the fletching adjusting itself imperceptibly until Bobby's arrow hit the end of Hubert's shaft precisely, splitting it right down the middle until it came up against Hubert's arrowhead with a shock that sent it halfway through the butt. There was a moment of complete, unbelieving silence and then the crowd roared.

Hubert's jaw dropped in astonishment. He could have sworn that the tinker's aim was off.

"By God, the man's a devil, not an archer!" John swore in

amazement, forgetting his annoyance with the tinker. "Any man who can shoot like that, I'll have in my service!"

He would have made the offer, only a mob charged out upon the field to congratulate one of their own, thrilling in a Saxon's victory over a Norman. When the tumult died down and the crowd dispersed, the black garbed tinker and his friend in lincoln green had disappeared. They did not show up to claim their prize. Vexed, John pronounced the man a craven coward and said that he hoped his Norman knights would make a better showing than his pathetic archers. Hubert left the field, looking miserable.

John flourished his truncheon and ordered the jousting to commence.

The Saxon boy was quite impressed with the tinker's performance. He could not contain his joy. Lucas thought that Bobby had showed off just a bit too much. It had been risky. Obviously, the last arrow had been a guided one. Lucas conceded that Bobby had no choice, since the Norman archer's shot would have been impossible to beat any other way, but still, he hadn't liked it very much. Fortunately, Bobby had been able to retrieve the arrow and melt away into the crowd. That, at least, had been prudent of him. The guided arrows were equipped with a fail-safe mechanism that would fry the circuitry inside the shaft if anyone was curious enough to examine them too closely, but he was still glad that Bobby had managed to get his arrow back and disappear. It had been an impossible shot. John might have decided to order him to duplicate it just to see if it was luck or skill. If it happened again, it would have been clear evidence of skill—superhuman skill. It was well to draw attention to themselves in order to curry sympathy with the locals and to flush out the renegade ref, but there was such a thing as carrying it a bit too far.

Now, his turn was coming up. Lucas decided to wait as long as possible to see how the competition shaped up. His nysteel armor would keep him fairly safe, but he could still be unhorsed and the whole idea was not to let that happen. He had no intention of risking a broken neck.

As the heralds announced the rules for the passage at arms, he sized up the other knights, watching as they were lifted up onto their horses. The rules were fairly simple. A challenger would ride through the lists to the opposing side and use his lance to touch the shield of the knight he wished to joust with. If he touched the shield with the butt end of the lance, then it was polite competition, lance points tipped with wood. It was still possible to be hurt, but at least the chances of getting skewered were somewhat diminished. However, if someone touched the shield of the knight he was challenging with the *tip* of his lance, then it was serious business. That meant either that he was bloodthirsty or that he had some personal grievance against the knight whom he was challenging, since then the joust would be carried out with untipped lances, like fencing with the buttons off the foils. For obvious reasons, most knights were polite to each other at tournaments. And for equally obvious reasons, the crowd simply loved it when shields were touched with tips of lances.

The first challenger rode out, heading toward the Norman side. The boy identified him for Lucas, engrossed in his role of play-by-play announcer and hamming it up to the hilt. Lucas wasn't paying very close attention. He wasn't interested in the challengers. They were not the ones he would have to fight. It was the home team he was watching.

The knight had crossed over to the Norman side and was slowly walking his horse past the pavillions, outside which the shields hung on upright poles. He hesitated at Front-de-Boeuf's shield, then smacked it with the butt end of his lance. He then returned to his side and waited until Front-de-Boeuf took his position. The fanfare sounded and both knights set spurs to their horses and thundered toward each other from opposite sides of the field. They entered the lists and dropped their lances into position.

Lucas noticed that Front-de-Boeuf dropped his lance fairly early, telegraphing his aim. They came together with a clash and clatter and Front-de-Boeuf nailed his challenger so hard upon his shield, directly in its center, that the knight was unhorsed immediately. Front-de-Boeuf took a hit himself, but he was built like the figure on his shield and although he swayed in his saddle slightly, he kept his seat. Home team 1, Visitors 0.

Two men at arms ran out carrying a wooden litter, but the challenger waved them off. He made an attempt to get up on his own, couldn't manage the weight of his armor and had to

be assisted to his feet. He stumbled about like a drunk for a
moment or two, then allowed the men at arms to lead him off
the field, supporting him. He was given some appreciative applause.

The next challenger out touched the shield belonging to De
Bracy. Lucas decided that this one, the mercenary, would bear
close scrutiny. Men did not hire themselves out as mercenaries
unless they damn well knew what they were doing. De Bracy
rode out briskly to meet his challenger. There was a tension in
his bearing, not a nervousness, but a tension of anticipation.
A man who liked to brawl.

He stared across at his challenger, nodded to him, the other
man returned the gesture and then they both dropped their
visors and took a running start. Lucas saw that De Bracy
waited until the last possible moment to position his lance
properly and he held his shield just a bit high, for which he
soon saw the reason. As the two knights came together, De
Bracy gave his upper body a slight twist in toward his opponent, using his shield to mask the movement. He really needn't
have bothered with the subtle ploy. His challenger had decided
to try for a head shot, the most difficult target. He missed
completely and De Bracy tumbled him to the ground easily.
The crowd gave him a cheer and Lucas noticed that once
again Cedric's section refrained from applauding.

Next came the Templar, Bois-Guilbert. The fighting priest.
It always fascinated Lucas how many men of religion were
able to preach Christ's doctrine and then go out and bathe in
blood on His account, such as the warrior pope, Julian.
Believe in peace and love or else I'll kill you, Lucas thought. It
was an old refrain. To get a closer look at Bois-Guilbert,
Lucas pretended to put on his helmet in order to check the fit-
tings. He lowered the visor over his eyes and dialed in some
magnification.

The Templar was good looking in a dark and swarthy sort
of way and he had the meanest eyes Lucas had ever seen. He
would have given Attila a run for his money in the "if looks
could kill" department. Then Priest noticed something funny
about his lance.

The wood that covered the tip had a faint, hairline crack in
it. And a tiny portion of the lance's tip showed through. The
moment that contact was made the wood would neatly splinter

and the point of the lance would be driven home. It would all look like an accident.

The trumpets sounded, both knights spurred and galloped at each other. Bois-Guilbert's horse was a heavy, muscular charger that had a definite advantage of height over most of the other mounts. He would be forcing his opponents to strike up, thereby placing them at a bit of a disadvantage. Also, his shield with the skull-toting raven on it was oversized and heavy. Nothing wrong with that, but it showed that this was a man who gave himself every possible advantage. Not that Lucas could fault him for that, with Bobby's trick arrows and his own nysteel armor.

Bois-Guilbert came in like a juggernaut, holding his shield low and his head down. Lucas couldn't find any fault in his technique. It seemed letter perfect. He caught his challenger behind the shield, squarely in the chest. The knight was lifted straight out of his saddle. Predictably, the wood broke and when the men at arms rushed out to give aid to the fallen knight, they found him to be quite dead.

And that seemed to be that. There were still other challengers, but having seen the strength of the home team, none of them were particularly anxious to try their luck. The remaining Norman knight, de la Croix, sat unhelmeted astride a chestnut stallion. The red knight looked vaguely bored. Lucas waited until they called for challengers two more times and then decided that it was time. No one else was going to take a crack at it. He told Hooker to pay the kid and send him on his way, then he went behind his tent and mounted up. He didn't need any help getting on his horse. The nysteel armor was considerably more sophisticated than that worn by the other knights. He took his lance and shield from Hooker, had him give his horn a martial toot and then he was off.

There was some muttering in the stands as he appeared, which was predictable. No one had the faintest idea who he was. Lucas was all in white, upon a white stallion, which amused him since he was supposed to be one of the good guys. On his shield, there was a somewhat druidic looking device, a leafy green oak with its roots exposed, as though it had been torn up out of the ground. He guided his Arabian through the lists by pressure of his knees and rode past all the Norman pavilions, pretending to give each shield a brief, cursory glance. He had already made up his mind, however. It wasn't what he would have liked to do, but it was the strategically advantageous move. Any one of the Norman knights he had seen could give him trouble on this assignment and he wasn't looking for trouble. Besides, Bobby had set him a good example and a hard act to follow. He raised his lance, set spurs to his stallion and galloped down the line, knocking each shield off its pole with the tip of his lance.

3

The crowd cheered wildly and many yelled encouragement to the white knight as he rode back to his side of the field. Up until that time, with the sole exception of the exhibition put on by the tinker, it had been a pretty dull show. No blood, except for the hapless knight unhorsed by Bois-Guilbert. Now the tournament would get truly interesting. It was a shame that this white knight would be killed, but they would applaud and cheer his bravery.

"This white knight is unfamiliar to me," John said to Fitzurse. "Do you know him, Waldemar?"

John's dignified looking minister, senior to the prince by twenty years, leaned forward so that he could speak into the prince's ear.

"The device upon his shield is one unknown to me, Sire. Possibly he may not be from these parts."

"An oak, uprooted," John mused. "What would that mean?"

"Perhaps it is meant to suggest that the knight has, himself, been uprooted from his homeland," said Fitzurse. "That appears to be a stout English oak. Perhaps he is a Saxon, one of those who went off to war on Saladin with your noble brother."

"If he is one of Richard's brood, then it is just as well that he has chosen untipped lances. It seems he has no great desire to live. If that be so, then we'll accommodate him. Front-de-

Boeuf will uproot him from his saddle soon enough.''

Both knights took their places and Front-de-Boeuf lifted his visor to the other knight. The white knight sat immobile at the far end of the field, his snowy stallion pawing at the ground. He refused to show his face. With a curse, Front-de-Boeuf slapped down his visor.

"Rude fellow, this new knight," said de la Croix to Bois-Guilbert.

"Some ill bred Saxon pig, no doubt, more fit to be a swineherd than a knight. Front-de-Boeuf will teach him courtly manners."

The trumpets sounded and both knights charged the lists. Front-de-Boeuf's lance splintered on the white knight's shield and both knight and horse went down, Front-de-Boeuf struck keenly on the head. The horse got up, Front-de-Boeuf did not. The men at arms carried the dead Norman off the field.

Cedric's section cheered themselves hoarse.

"Somewhat aggressive, these Saxon swineherds," said de la Croix, laconically.

The Templar spat upon the ground. "God smiles on fools and idiots," he said. "It was pure chance and ill luck for Front-de-Boeuf. Well, let the Saxons cheer their champion for a time. Maurice will lay him low."

The white knight returned to his side of the field and waited for De Bracy to take his position. De Bracy rode forward on his gray, helmetless. He sat and waited to see if the white knight would show him the courtesy of revealing his features, but the man made no move to lift his visor. De Bracy sat still, waiting. Finally, his patience broke and he called for his helmet.

"I'll knock the bastard's head off for him," he mumbled as his squire stood upon a wooden platform, putting on his helmet.

The trumpets blew and De Bracy was off like a shot, once again waiting until the last possible moment to couch his lance. Once again, the white knight took the blow on his shield, splintering De Bracy's lance while his own struck the gold knight in the shoulder, tumbling him from his horse and ending the tournament for him. The crowd went wild. De Bracy was on his feet in a moment, but there was blood on his armor where the lance had penetrated.

"It seems the leeches will be busy this day," said de la Croix in the same disinterested tone.

"Then I'll see to it that the gravediggers have more work, as well," said Bois-Guilbert, as he allowed his squire to put on his helmet. He rode out to take his place and did not do the white knight the courtesy of showing his face, matching rudeness for rudeness. The white knight touched his gauntleted hand to his visor in a casual salute, which only served to infuriate the Templar even more.

"Salute away, you Saxon pig," he mumbled. "You'll be saluting angels in a moment."

The trumpets blared and they were off, hurtling at each other at full tilt.

Lucas felt annoyed, to say the least. There was a tricky little gadget hidden in the tip of his lance that allowed it to fire a sonic burst, quick and very lethal. The only problem was that, when he dispatched Front-de-Boeuf with it, it did the job quite admirably and then ceased to function on the spot. Lousy army gear, thought Lucas. Trust it to break when you need it most. He thanked God he still had his armor and his shield. The nysteel was impregnable. Still, he had lost a good deal of his edge.

De Bracy was good, but he had spotted his weakness thanks to the magnification power of his helmet. When he gave his upper body that deceptive little twist just before impact, he left his right shoulder exposed for just a fraction of a second. That fraction of a second was all that Lucas needed. He took De Bracy right where he was vulnerable and tumbled him. De Bracy wasn't seriously hurt, but it would be a while before he could hold a lance or sword again. It would hardly endear him to De Bracy, but that was tough. If Lucas had his way, he would have killed him. He presented a threat and, as things had gone, he had gotten off easy. Lucas cursed his lance. Ordnance would hear about this. Now he had to square off against Bois-Guilbert and, priest or no priest, the Templar was no slouch with a lance.

He saw the Templar take position and he noticed that he didn't raise his visor as all the others had. His reason for not raising his own was simple. His "father" and his "sweetheart" were in the stands and it was best for them to think that

Ivanhoe was still off fighting the Saracens. He had work to do and he didn't want to complicate matters by inviting family problems. But the fact that the Templar didn't raise his visor showed that he had a temper. A temperamental Templar. Lucas grinned inside his helmet. That suited him just fine. When a man became angry, he was prone to making mistakes. And he hadn't seen Bois-Guilbert make *any* mistakes before.

The trumpets signaled the advance and Lucas kicked his horse, knowing that he would need every ounce of speed against the Templar. He chinned the switch inside his helmet that controlled the degree of magnification in the lens just inside his visor. This was something of a calculated risk. Using magnification power in action and at speed could affect perspective if he couldn't adjust from the magnified image back to the standard one quickly enough. If he was unhorsed and killed in the fall, the nysteel armor would not go to waste and someone would discover that it could do all sorts of interesting things. From a historical viewpoint, it could cause problems, but then if he failed in his mission, that meant far greater problems than just leaving a futuristic suit of armor lying around would cause.

Bois-Guilbert had very good form, indeed. But Bois-Guilbert was angry and that gave Lucas an advantage. The Templar's shield was large and he hid behind it well, offering precious little target. His horse was larger than the Arabian, and he would be striking slightly downward. He had seen Lucas going for a head shot with Front-de-Boeuf and succeeding admirably, so he was holding his shield slightly high, in order to enable him to deflect the lance in the event Lucas tried the same thing once again. There Lucas had him, dead to rights. Thanks to the magnification power of his helmet, he had caught it just as the Templar was entering the lists. There was an exposed thigh that would serve quite well. If he hit it just right, his upward strike would unhorse Bois-Guilbert. Not a killing shot, unless he was lucky enough to strike him solid and pierce the armor, hitting the femoral artery, but he would settle for whatever he could get. Given the Templar's excellent technique, it was no time to be picky.

Lucas chinned his helmet back to normal scan and let his breath out. Bois-Guilbert was going for a head shot and he didn't have the slightest clue that Lucas had already figured out his game plan. Lucas slipped his lance just below his shield at the last moment, leaning out to his right slightly as they came together, which was dangerous for balance, but it resulted in Bois-Guilbert's lance passing over his head by just a fraction of an inch. The impact of hitting him almost made Lucas lose his stirrups, but he managed to hold on. When he reached the opposite end of the lists and wheeled his horse, not having seen the results of his strike, he was satisfied to see the Templar draped over the fence, trying to wriggle himself to fall to either side. He had dropped both his shield and lance and his horse had continued on without him. As Lucas passed him on the return trip, he was disappointed to see that he had caused no visible damage. It was what he had been afraid of. He had felt his lance skip slightly upon impact and guessed that he had scraped Bois-Guilbert's tuille and caught him a glancing blow along his skirt of tasses, but it had been sufficient to unhorse him. He could not complain. With his sonic device out of commission, he hadn't done too badly. As he passed the hung up Templar, he gave him a shot with the butt end of his lance, an ignoble assist to his efforts to dislodge himself. The Templar clattered to the ground like so much scrap metal.

Prince John was furious.

"In the name of Heaven, this is too much to bear! First a Saxon tinker shames my archers and now this nameless knight deprives me of Front-de-Boeuf, pricks De Bracy and leaves the Templar draped over the lists like a dressed and hung up stag! Is there no one who can put an end to this effrontery?"

"There still remains the sanguine de la Croix," Fitzurse said.

John scowled. "It irks me to have to depend upon that smirking Basque with his invented name. He costs me more dearly than half De Bracy's Free Companions. Were he not well worth the cost, I'd pay just as dearly to be rid of his soft speech and laughing eyes."

"The impertinence of de la Croix is characteristic of his people," said Fitzurse. "And if his soft and mannered ways seem to be a mockery of ours, they are more than offset by his prowess on the field of battle, a quality that, with all due respect, Sire, you can ill afford to overlook."

"True, too true," grumbled John. "Let us hope he proves worthy of the fees he charges. This white knight has embarrassed my best men."

The object of their conversation sat quietly astride a chestnut stallion, staring thoughtfully out at the field as the white knight returned to the far end of the lists. The red knight's squire fastened de la Croix's headgear, then handed up the lance and shield.

"Do you think you can best him, Andre?" said the squire.

"I don't know, little brother," de la Croix replied. "There is something very strange about him. He comes in fast and low, and did you mark how easily he moves inside his armor? His shield has borne the brunt of strong assaults without a mark of damage. He found De Bracy's weakness in his shoulder in an instant, perceived a flaw in Bois-Guilbert's defense where the Templar rarely leaves one and I will not soon forget the blow he dealt to Front-de-Boeuf. There is more to this uprooted oak than meets the eye, Marcel. Still, we shall make a gallant effort, eh?"

The red knight clapped the squire lightly on the shoulder with a gauntleted hand before accepting the shield with its fleury cross in white on red. The fanfare called the start and de la Croix set spurs to the chestnut war horse.

The red knight's horse was fresher than the white knight's stallion, but still they sped toward one another like shafts shot from a crossbow. Each knight aligned his lance, each took perfect position. They came together in the center of the lists with a resounding crash that reverberated throughout the valley like the ringing of a hammer on an anvil. Both knights were nearly thrown from their horses by the force of the impact, each shield taking a lance strike. The meeting brought them to a grinding, shuddering halt as both horses sank to their knees. Both lances shattered. Neither was unhorsed.

Lucas stared at the stump of his lance and could not believe what had just happened. It felt as though someone had stuck his head inside a giant gong and then let loose with a pounding that threatened to burst his skull like a melon. His lance broke! It was not supposed to break! First the sonic device malfunctioned, now the entire lance! And one was all he had! Where in Christ's name would he get another?

He rode slowly back to his end of the lists, tasting blood, his vision blurred. His nose was bleeding from both nostrils. It felt as though he had been hit by a locomotive. He could see the crowd going totally insane, but he could not hear them. The only sound he heard was an *ung-ung-ung* inside his head, a never ceasing echo of the crash. His armor and his shield had saved him, but it was all that he could do to stay on his horse. And the animal didn't seem too happy about it, either.

Holy shit, he thought. He had been concerned about the Templar. Here he was, a 27th-century man, feeling superior as hell to these Neanderthals and along came de la Croix to throw cold water in his face.

He rode back to his position and saw Hooker looking at him with concern. He flashed him a helpless look, lifting his visor briefly and taking in a gasping gulp of air. *Now* what was he going to do? They didn't bring spare lances.

"The expression on your squire's face reveals your problem, nameless knight," said a voice at his side. Lucas barely heard it. He quickly slapped down his visor and turned to see a young man at arms standing by his side, holding a lance. "My lord and master, on seeing how you disposed of Front-de-Boeuf, charged me to seek out your pavilion and to bring you ale in celebration of your victory. I could not help but notice that you lacked for some spare arms, no doubt through some inconvenience which you could not control. I reported this to my lord and he bid me offer you the use of this, his lance, should you not be too proud. The noble Athelstane would be honored if you would grace his lance by testing it in combat on this day."

The young soldier held out the lance to Lucas. So, Lucas thought, chivalry is not dead. He realized how silly that thought was the moment it occurred to him and it was all that he could do to keep from laughing out loud. It was a trait he had that, whenever he was scared out of his wits, he had the disconcerting tendency to guffaw. A nervous reaction that, under present circumstances, could be misinterpreted. He held back, swallowing his hysteria.

"Tell your master that I am indebted to his hospitality of arms and that I regret that I cannot tell him who owes him a debt of gratitude. I am under vow never to show my face until certain conditions prevail. I will try to do honor to his lance."

He accepted the lance and nodded to the man at arms, who returned him a small bow. Then, belatedly, he realized just who his benefactor was. The Saxon noble on whose account Wilfred had been tossed out of his father's house upon his keester. As far as Lucas was concerned, Athelstane could have Rowena. He'd just earned her.

The red knight returned to the other side of the field to pick up another lance. There was blood coming from de la Croix's mouth.

"Andre!" said the squire, Marcel, visibly frightened at the sight of the blood when de la Croix raised the visor. The knight's eyes were unfocused.

"Water, Marcel."

The squire understood the request and knew that it was not for a drink. He ran into the pavilion and returned with a bucket of water, which he dashed in de la Croix's face. The red knight coughed and took several deep breaths.

"I may have met my match, Marcel. I do not know why this oak chose to challenge with his naked lance, unless he despises Normans. If he is a Saxon, it is something I can understand."

"But we are not Normans," said Marcel.

"We serve the Normans and it amounts to the same thing. If Saxons can breed men such as this, then John of Anjou has good reason to fear them." Andre de la Croix paused, taking several deep and ragged breaths. "But John doesn't fear them. More fool he. Well, let's have that fresh lance, Marcel. We shall see if the Lord means for me to die this day. Thus far, He has seen fit to bestow His grace upon the nameless knight. Should I fail to return, Marcel, you know what to do. And I charge you to pay the oak my compliments."

The visor was slapped down and the knights faced each other once again. Again the trumpets sounded and again they charged. Again both lances splintered on their shields and the white knight's horse stumbled and came near to falling, but was saved by the interference of the list fence, which gave beneath the animal's weight but provided the necessary purchase that allowed it to regain its footing. Both knights reeled in their saddles like willows in the wind. The red knight dropped the fleury shield and Marcel ran out to retrieve it. Lucas lost the magnification power of his helmet. The lens, being considerably weaker than the nysteel armor, cracked and was dislodged by the shock of impact. It fell to rest in pieces against his chin, cutting into the skin. Both knights obtained fresh lances. This time Lucas got one courtesy of Cedric, who said he knew him as a Saxon knight. He was wrong, but Lucas was not up to correcting him.

"This oak tree begins to irritate me," de la Croix said with a gasp. "Already he has cost me two lances."

Bois-Guilbert approached him.

"Have done with it, de la Croix! Unhorse this Saxon pig, unless you are determined to toy with him till nightfall!"

"I marked how well *you* toyed with him," said de la Croix. The red knight coughed and spat out some blood.

"Twice he ran at you and failed to find your weak point," Bois-Guilbert said. "Kill him and have done with it!"

"He failed to find my weak point because I do not have one," de la Croix remarked in an amused tone. "The trouble is, neither does he."

"You pick a fine time to jest!" the Templar said.

"I can think of no better time. Do you not find it amusing, Brian, two knights ramming at each other like rampant stags fighting over ground? They lower their heads, charge and smash together, horn to horn, then back off and ram once more. Perhaps in future years, someone will find a less strenuous way of making war."

"I hope I shall not live to see that day," said Bois-Guilbert, disdainfully.

"Judging by the account you gave of yourself this day, I think you have no need of concern," said de la Croix.

The trumpets blared their fanfare.

"Fuck," said de la Croix, slapping down the visor and spurring.

They did not ride at each other with quite the same speed the third time, but the shock of their impact seemed as great. Both knights were lifted from their saddles and, for a moment, seemed to hang suspended in the air before they both clattered to the ground like so much hardware. For a long period of time, both lay still as corpses. The men at arms ran out, but then both knights began to stir. Slowly, with great difficulty, the white knight regained his feet, having waved off the men at arms, refusing their assistance. The red knight flopped about weakly, like a fish out of water, but did not have the strength to stand without assistance. Raising the visor, de la Croix displayed a bloody, pale face and eyes that seemed to cross and announced that the white knight was the victor, since he had stood up on his own. The crowd went hoarse with cheering, especially the Saxons, who had claimed the white knight as one of their own.

Just a few moments longer, Lucas told himself. Stay conscious just a few moments longer so you can play the graceful winner and then you can slink back to your pavilion and throw up.

Someone brought his horse around and several men came to lift him into the saddle. Lucas had enough presence of mind to become dead weight in their hands, to prevent them from finding his nysteel armor unusually light. In the excitement of the occasion, no one seemed to notice. Then Lucas realized that they were spectators who had run out upon the field. They were yelling things at him, but he could not make anything out of it. He was led to stand before John and he had to hold onto his saddle with both hands for several moments to keep from falling off. It was a while before he could make out what John was saying, then he realized that he was being asked to show his face. He couldn't do that just yet, not with Cedric and Rowena watching him with glowing eyes, the unknown Saxon who had brought havoc to the Norman lists. He mumbled something about having taken a vow, similar to what he had told Athelstane's man. John did not seem too pleased with that, but chivalry demanded that he accept it.

He was babbling something about a banquet and a Queen of Love and Beauty and Lucas finally understood that he was expected to choose some lucky lady to officiate at the celebration and at the festivities the next day. Miss Blood and Guts of 1194. He was told to hold out his lance and John slipped a crown of thin, hammered gold onto its end.

Lucas had enough presence of mind to know that picking a Saxon woman to fill the office would only serve to irritate John even further and he felt that he had already done more than his share. He decided to play it safe and pick the daughter of some Norman baron. Ivanhoe, no doubt, would have picked Rowena and rubbed their noses in it, but that was the last thing he wanted to do. Besides, she was a vapid-looking blonde who looked as though her mind had never been sullied by the presence of a thought. To top it off, she simpered.

He managed to stay in the saddle somehow as he rode past the stands, looking for a likely candidate, someone who looked rich. The one he found not only wore expensive jewelry, but in point of fact, deserved the office of the Queen of Love and Beauty if it was to be handed out on the basis of looks alone. And in these times, women weren't judged on much more than that. This raven-haired young woman was enough to take anyone's breath away. Good, thought Lucas, you've got it, ma'am. You win. He dropped the crown at her feet.

Instant deathly silence.

She looked very embarrassed. Then Lucas realized his error. Even had he not seen the way she stood a bit apart from everyone around her, he should have noticed the man standing with her. He should have noted his dress, the beard and *pe-yot*, the Magen David he wore around his neck. He had supposed she was a Norman girl and having made his choice, he could not now take the crown back and say he'd changed his mind. He had hoped to avoid causing a scene by not picking out a Saxon girl, so he had chosen a Jewess.

Marcel was frightened.

According to the traditions of a passage at arms, Marcel was on his way to the white knight's pavilion with de la Croix's horse and armor, which were forfeit to the victor of the joust. Marcel was frightened of the strange knight and of what he had done to de la Croix. Marcel had never known Andre to lose.

Outside the white knight's pavilion, there was a small throng, including the squires of the other defeated knights who also waited with the gear of their respective masters. As was the custom, it was the decision of the victor to either keep the arms and horses or to ransom them back to their owners. Each squire had been charged by his master to offer a certain sum in exchange for horse and armor, but it was up to the white knight to accept or reject this sum. He would either keep the arms, or name a higher price, in which event he would keep the arms anyway, since each squire had been given a limit on the amount of ransom to be paid. The red knight had charged Marcel to allow the "nameless oak" to choose his own price for ransom. It had not escaped anyone's notice that the white knight had been forced to rely on Cedric's and Athelstane's generosity after he broke his lance, which meant that he was poor. Doubtless, if the ransom offers of the other knights were generous, as they were bound to be since none of them wished to appear unchivalrous, then he would accept the coin. If the other knights were as generous as de la Croix, it would allow the white knight to name a ransom which would exceed the value of the horse and armor. Marcel knew that Andre prized the armor highly.

The white knight's squire spoke to the others in the matter of the disposition of the arms. The offers were all generous and they were all accepted. When it came his turn, Marcel stood nervously before the fearsome and cruel-looking squire.

"My lord, the red knight, Andre de la Croix, charges me to tell your master, the white knight of the uprooted oak, to name his own price for the ransom," Marcel said nervously.

"Your master is a most generous and chivalrous knight," said the white knight's squire.

"My lord also charges me to pay his compliments to the white knight and to tender his respect, which, I add on my own, is not granted easily. My master says that he has never fought so fine a knight and that he hopes, despite the challenge to pass with naked lances, that your master is not greatly injured."

"I thank you for my master," said Hooker, "and charge you in my master's name to tell Andre de la Croix that he returns the compliment and, although fatigued, does not suffer any great injury. Further, my master charges me to say that the offers of the other knights were generous and have left him not so poor as he was before the joust. Therefore, out of respect for Andre de la Croix, he will accept neither horse nor armor, nor ransom for same, since the lessons he has learned at your master's hands today have enriched him in a manner that he prizes much more highly. Take this small sum for yourself, however, and if you are not too proud, use some small part of it to drink my master's health."

Hooker tossed a small purse to Marcel, then turned and entered the pavilion. Visibly relieved, Marcel returned to de la Croix and related what the white knight's squire had said.

The red knight sat on a wooden cot inside the pavilion, clad only in a loose-fitting doublet and boots. Andre de la Croix was tall and thin, with flaxen blond hair that fell shoulder-length. The red knight wore no beard or mustache and was strikingly good-looking in a youthful, boyish way.

"Thank you, Marcel," de la Croix said. "You've done well. I was afraid that I would lose my treasured armor, which I can ill afford to spare. These local artisans are not adept enough to craft so fine a suit as that which was given to me by our benefactor in return for secret services. In truth, I do not know what strange and wondrous craftsmen made this suit. I have never seen its like."

The red knight got up and ran a hand over the nysteel armor.

"I fear these secret services," Marcel said, "as I fear the stranger who demands them."

The red knight smiled. "We have shared many secrets since we left our mountain home, little brother. What is one secret more? Besides, no secret can weigh on us so heavily as that which we guard most closely."

The red knight turned and allowed Marcel to unfasten the doublet and remove it, revealing the cloth swathed around de la Croix's upper torso. Slowly, carefully, Marcel unwound the cloth and, when it was done, de la Croix sighed and breathed deeply. The men who had fallen to de la Croix's lance would have been surprised to see the red knight now. Tired, de la Croix sat down upon the cot and slowly massaged the skin to return circulation to her breasts.

4

If the wooden cot inside the pavilion was uncomfortable, Lucas didn't notice. He was simply grateful for the opportunity to get off his feet. He lay stretched out on his back, his eyes closed, listening to the din outside.

Hooker was keeping a throng of well wishers at bay. It seemed that almost every Saxon at the tournament wished to pay respects to the white knight and Lucas simply wasn't up to it. He was, however, somewhat more concerned about the so-called physicians, whom he could hear arguing outside with Hooker. Cedric, Athelstane, and several other of the more well-to-do Saxon lords had sent their physicians to see to his well-being. He had two reasons for not wanting to see them. The first was that they would know Ivanhoe and the second was that he had no desire to be bled.

As it began to grow dark, Lucas lay motionless inside his tent, feeling the growing evening chill and trying not to pay too much attention to the leeches, who had now turned to fighting amongst themselves for the privilege of bleeding him. Hooker stuck his head inside the tent.

"You all right?" he said.

"I will be if those bloodsuckers don't get their hands on me," said Lucas, wearily. "Can't you get rid of them?"

"I'm having a hard enough time just getting them to listen to me," Hooker said. "You've become very popular all of a sudden and a certain amount of professional pride seems to be at stake."

"Look, I don't care if you have to knock their damn heads together," Lucas said, "just get rid of them. I can't—"

There was a sudden commotion outside and Hooker quickly went to see what was developing. Moments later, a young woman entered the pavilion. She was dressed in a long, flowing gown of dark purple gabardine which clung to her shapely figure. She had long, wavy black hair and large dark eyes. Around her neck, she wore a diamond necklace hung with pendants and there were golden bracelets set with jewels upon her wrists. She was astonishingly lovely and she wore the thin gold crown which Lucas had earlier presented her with.

"This is Rebecca, daughter of Isaac of York, Milord," said Hooker. "She has come to pay her respects to the nameless knight and to see if you were injured." He cleared his throat. "She has, uh, sent away the leeches with some . . . enthusiasm."

"They have the temerity to speak of healing!" Rebecca said hotly. "They would bleed a man to death if given the chance!"

Hooker kneeled by the cot and whispered to him. "She sent those boys packing one-two-three," he said, so that she wouldn't hear him. "She has no idea who you are, so I figured it was safe enough to let her in. She only recently arrived here with her father, who's been loaning money to John, though I wouldn't lay any odds on his ever seeing it again. I figured we could use some well connected friends, if you know what I mean."

"How do you know this?" Lucas whispered.

"Are you kidding? The moment you gave her that crown, it was all anyone would talk about. You've rubbed their noses in it by honoring a Jew. Scuttlebutt has it that Isaac paid for your horse and armor in exchange for protection. He's not very well liked in these parts, being rich and Jewish, to boot."

While they conversed, Rebecca stood near the entrance of the tent, her hands clasped together, a look of grave concern upon her face. Lucas started to sit up.

"We should not whisper in the presence of a lady," he began. She rushed to his side instantly, gently urging him back down.

"No, do not get up, my lord. You're hurt," she said.

"I am somewhat the worse for wear," said Lucas, gently removing her hands from his chest and sitting up, "but I assure you, I'm not injured, only weary."

"I came to see if I could help," Rebecca said. "Waldemar Fitzurse, John's minister, suggested it. He said that since I was taught the art of healing by Miriam of Endor, I should see to your welfare, since you named me your queen." She lowered her eyes. "In truth, he meant you no great courtesy, my lord, since Miriam stands falsely accused of witchcraft by those ignorant of her skills and I fear the minister's request was meant less for your welfare than to spare these Normans the embarrassment of honoring a Jewess at their feast, which even now progresses. Pleased as I am at having been honored by you, my lord, I am distressed by it. It was not wise. You could not have known I was a Jew, else you would doubtless have chosen another to receive your favor."

"I didn't know," said Lucas, "and to be honest, I meant to choose a Norman girl to placate these nobles somewhat. In truth, honoring women for nothing save their beauty does not appeal to me. Such empty, vain displays are not to my liking. As to your faith and heritage, I have known many Jews in my travels and I know something of your beliefs. While I do not share them, they are far from abhorrent to me. I am not one of those who would persecute your people or take advantage of them."

"Then you are a rare knight, indeed," she said. "Is it true what the people say, that you are Saxon?"

"I fear that I cannot answer you," said Lucas. "There is much at stake and I am not yet ready to reveal myself. I must ask you to be patient."

She lowered her eyes. "Forgive me for asking, my lord," she said softly. "It was not my intention to presume."

"There is no need to ask forgiveness," Lucas said. "It is I who must ask your forgiveness. By choosing you, it seems that I have caused speculation that your father is my patron, having provided me with the means to enter the lists today. This will not make the Normans love him more."

She smiled. "It will not make them love his money less. I am well treated by the Normans, inasmuch as any Jew can be, only because it is well known that John borrows heavily from Isaac. So long as they can use the usurer, they will continue to treat us with some little kindness.''

"Your father treads deep water," Lucas said. "John is not likely to be fair in his dealings with a Jew. He may decide to force him to give up all his wealth and then where will you be?"

She shrugged slightly. "Where my people have always been. What is there to do? Our fate is in God's hands."

Lucas smiled. "He will decide the disputes of the nations, and settle many a people's case, till swords are beaten into plowshares, spears into pruning hooks; no nation draws the sword against another, no longer shall men learn to fight."

Rebecca looked at him with astonishment. "You quote the Prophet Isaiah? *And in Hebrew!*"

"Armorers are still making swords and spears," said Lucas. "They have not yet turned to making farming implements. I do not dispute your faith, but you would be wiser to take your fate into your own hands instead of trusting it to God."

"An easy thing for a man to say, my lord, but not so easy a thing to do for one who is both a woman and a Jew," she said. "I wish you well, good knight."

She inclined her head toward him and left.

"Interesting woman," Hooker said.

Bobby and Finn entered the pavilion. It was dark outside and all was quiet, most of the knights and nobles having gone to the banquet while the spectators dispersed until the next day's festivities. The sound of crickets filled the cool night air.

"Had to wait until your company left," said Bobby. "Striking looking woman. Who was she?"

"Rebecca, daughter of Isaac of York. A Jewish merchant whom John's been milking for money."

"How does she fit into all of this?"

"I don't know if she does, yet. I take it you didn't see the jousting?"

Bobby shook his head. "We made some contacts. What happened?"

Briefly, Lucas brought them up to date. "I don't know how our fake Richard intends to make his move," he said, "but he may not have an easy time of it. With people like De Bracy, Bois-Guilbert and de la Croix in his service, John's not going to be easy to displace."

"That's always assuming that our friend Irving's going to play by the rules," said Bobby. "Don't forget, he's a crackpot. He might just decide to come on strong with some technology and blow these boys away."

Lucas shook his head. "I don't even want to think about it. You said you made some contacts?"

Bobby sat down and sighed. "Finn and I met up with a few of Locksley's men."

"Any problems?"

Bobby snorted. "Problems? Try disaster."

"What happened? You don't mean to tell me that they didn't buy that you were—"

"Oh, I was accepted easily enough, that wasn't what I meant," said Bobby. "What did you expect these people to do, see through my cover? There's no chance of that."

"So what's the problem?"

"The problem is a bit of disillusionment," said Finn, chuckling.

"Hey, it's not so funny," Bobby said. He looked at Lucas. "The legend of Robin Hood was always one of my favorite stories, you know? The truth is somewhat less attractive. Seems Locksley wasn't quite the man I thought him to be. After the archery bout, we made ourselves scarce. Then we ran into a few of the merry men. You might say they were impressed. They never saw anyone shoot like that before. More to the point, they never saw *Locksley* shoot like that before."

"Turns out the famous Robin Hood wasn't all he was cracked up to be," said Finn. "The impression one gets is that he couldn't hit the broad side of a barn if he was standing in the hayloft."

"They were also surprised to see me sober," Bobby said. "See, Robin's been gone for a while, no one knows where to. Locksley's a fucking lush. Every now and then, he gets so blitzed he just takes off somewhere and doesn't come back for days. This time 'I' was gone for longer than usual. Marion's fit to be tied."

"You mean Maid Marion?" said Lucas.

Finn guffawed.

"Everything's a joke to this guy," Bobby said irritably. "Yeah, Maid Marion. Only nobody calls her that. That's because she's about as maidenly as Anne Bonney. Our referee friend who sent us out on this suicide mission didn't do his damn homework very well. The idea was that, as Robin Hood, I'd be able to use the merry men to help us out if need be. The only problem is, Robin Hood isn't in charge of the merry men. *Marion* is. Seems my main task is keeping her bed warm.''

"And he's in a bit of trouble because he's been delinquent in his duties," Finn said, grinning. "Fact, he's A.W.O.L. right now and if he doesn't get his ass back soon, the boys said, she'll put it in a sling!" He started laughing uncontrollably.

"God damn it, Delaney, put a lid on it! That's an order!" Bobby said.

"Fuck you, son. I've been busted from master sergeant, captain and lieutenant, just to name a few. Don't give me any shit about orders. I was getting my ass shot off with the Lost Battalion when you were still sucking at your mother's tit. I made it through some pretty bad scrapes and I intend to make it through this one, so if you're smart, you'll button it up and listen, both of you."

Hooker chuckled.

"And that goes for you, too, squire," Delaney said. "Plant it and listen up."

"Okay, Finn, no one's disputing your experience," said Lucas. "What do you suggest?"

"Well, for one thing, forget about the fucking rules," Finn said. "There's nothing in the manual about a hitch like this, so you can just throw out the regulations. If we play by the rules, we're going to die and that's all there is to it. All we have to worry about is nailing this Irving character and then we can leave it to the refs to clean the mess up, because they got us into it in the first place. Unfortunately, we don't have much in the way of ordnance to give us an edge, but we do have a few of those trick arrows Johnson here brought back with him. The first chance you get, you draw a bead on this whacked-out ref and blow him to hell and gone. The shaped charges might not penetrate nysteel if he's in armor, but the shock of the explosion will kill him very nicely."

"Suppose we don't get a chance to catch him alone?" said Bobby.

"So what?"

"It might look a little strange if an armored knight suddenly explodes in the middle of a crowd," said Bobby, wryly.

"Who cares?" said Finn. "Somehow I don't think it's going to change the course of history. At most, it will become one of those wild stories that no one will believe."

"I think you're right," said Lucas, "but we may not get that opportunity. If we do, then our troubles are over. But we've got to decide what to do meanwhile."

"I've been thinking about that, too," said Finn. "This character's no fool. He knows several attempts have been made against him already, so he will have taken precautions."

"But we do have the advantage of surprise," said Bobby. "He doesn't know who we are."

"Yes, and that's the only advantage we *do* have," Lucas said. "If we luck out and get a crack at him, one of those arrows should do the trick. But if we blow it, then we've given ourselves away."

"So we lay back unless we get that chance," said Finn. "And in the meantime, we forget about preserving the status quo. There's still a lot that can be done without revealing ourselves. The first order of business is to straighten out this mess with the merry men. If the rest of them are anything like the ones we met, they're the most dissolute bunch of comical buffoons I've ever met. Nothing but a bunch of low-lifes. We're going to have to whip them into shape, cause we may need them. Look at it this way," he said to Bobby, "the Robin Hood of history may be the result of what you're going to do."

"What about Marion?" said Bobby.

Finn chuckled. "Well, when those lads report back to her, she's going to expect a changed man, anyway. Surely, you can handle a simple 12th century peasant woman?"

"I'm not looking forward to it," Bobby said. "I doubt she's anything like the lady who just left."

"Well then close your eyes and hold your breath," said Finn. "Either that, or teach her how to bathe."

Bobby frowned. "Thanks."

"That doesn't leave me with much to do except wait around for the fake Richard to show up," said Lucas.

"That's where you're wrong," said Finn. "You've got a lot to do. You've already become a hero to the Saxons as the white knight. Now it's time to reveal yourself to Cedric and make it up with him."

"You mean throw Rowena over and convince him that I've changed my ways," said Lucas. "It might work. A lot can happen to a man while he's away at war. Cedric might believe that I've come to my senses. Then all I've got to do is convince him to throw his lot in with Richard when the time comes. That's not going to be easy.''

"Well, if you wanted easy, what the hell'd you join the army for?'' said Finn.

"It's a question I've asked myself frequently. I think I was looking for adventure,'' said Lucas with mock seriousness.

"Now's your big chance, son. Make the most of it.''

"What'd you join for, Finn?''

"The tests said I had no aptitude for anything else.''

"You think that's true?''

"I don't know. I've never done anything else.''

The banquet at the Castle of Ashby was a noisy affair. John sat in the place of honor at the tables in the great hall with Fitzurse sitting on his left hand and Bois-Guilbert upon his right. All around him, knights and barons were tearing into their food with both hands, ripping off drumsticks or lifting whole roast chickens up to their mouths. Wine ran down their chins and onto their doublets, gobbets of masticated venison were sprayed across the room as revelers erupted into laughter or shouted with their mouths full. Meat was tossed onto the floor for their dogs to fight over, tables were pounded upon, toasts proposed and drunk and curses shouted, oaths proclaimed and prowess boasted of.

It was all too much for de la Croix, who fled the banquet hall for a walk along the parapets. The scene was bad enough, but to her dismay, it seemed that she had gained an ardent admirer. In the absence of the Jewess, John had seen fit to grant Rowena the honor of presiding over the banquet. Cedric had reluctantly attended, along with Athelstane, and they sat there glowering while Normans made disparaging remarks about the Saxons. Clearly, Cedric had not wished to come, but his daughter had prevailed upon him, flattered by the attentions paid her by the men her father hated. Andre did not envy Cedric such a daughter.

What was worse, Rowena was blatant in her undisguised infatuation with the red knight, ignorant, as were all the others, of "his" true sex. She made cow eyes at de la Croix and made as if to swoon each time she glanced in her direction. She had contrived to procure for Andre the seat on her right hand, telling all other contenders for the same position that de la Croix deserved it, being the knight who had done the best against the white-garbed challenger. Once seated, Rowena took every excuse to create an opportunity for their hands to brush, for their thighs to come in contact. She had pressed with her knee and when that failed to provoke response, she had started rubbing Andre's leg with her foot. Failing in that, she sought to slip her hand between de la Croix's legs, at which point Andre fled, pleading dizziness as a result of the joust, for it certainly would not do for Rowena to grope about between her legs and not find what she sought.

Andre was not ashamed of being a woman, nor did she have any desire to be a man. Her decision to pose as a male had been one of simple pragmatism. In the society in which she moved, it was almost impossible for a woman to exist independently of a man. Certainly, it was impossible that she be treated as an equal and given the same opportunities as a man. Andre had lost her parents when she was only nine. They had been farmers. Her mother and her father had been hapless enough to slaughter a goat that had been contaminated. In the process of the butchery, they had breathed in the spores from the animal's hide. The same flesh, cooked, had not harmed the children, but for the parents, the die had been cast. Within a week, they had manifested the symptoms. Both had high fevers, their bodies racked with aches and pains as the infection spread. Their glands swelled, a fine red rash appeared, their blood pressure dropped and their lungs filled with water. They both became delirious, ranting for hours on end and hallucinating and finally, within another week, first the mother, then the father went into shock and died.

Thus, at the age of nine, Andre had become both mother and father to Marcel. She even tried to manage their tiny farm, but the children failed dismally. Leaving behind their simple home, and their parents, whom Andre had buried in the field, they started wandering, never knowing from one moment to the next what fate had in store for them or where their next meal would come from. Those meals were few and far between. They got by at first by stealing. Andre wasn't very good at it at the beginning and she often starved so that Marcel could eat, but she got better.

Their lives took a turn for the better when the orphans were taken in by an abbot who treated them kindly and taught them how to read, giving them what little education both possessed. The demands he made on her young body did not seem too much to give him in return. When he began to make the same demands upon Marcel, Andre decided it was time to leave.

It was very shortly after that that she took to passing as a boy. It made things easier, although not by very much. They traveled constantly, stealing what they could to see them through. They both learned how to fight and they survived, although the odds against them were incalculable. Then they met up with Sir Giles.

Andre never knew Sir Giles' full name. Giles, himself, was no longer certain what it was. A knight errant who had taken one blow to the head too many, Giles was addle-brained without any hope of recovery. He imagined himself to be upon a quest and, indeed, when he had set out upon his journey from wherever it was he came, he may have had some purpose in mind, but he could no longer remember what it was. Though he was a lost soul, Giles was a gentle man who had brief periods of relative lucidity interspersed with fugue states. He was a sad knight, barely able to take care of himself. Frequently, he forgot to eat and he was given to experiencing extremely painful headaches. In spite of this, however, he was supremely functional when it came to exercising his fighting prowess. It was as though his body could remember what his mind could not. Whenever it came to practicing his knightly art or speaking of it, something inside him clicked and, for a time, he was almost normal.

He had not seen through Andre's deception and he took her and Marcel at face value as two orphaned boys out on their own. They touched a chord of sympathy within him and he made them his squires and proceeded to instruct them. It was a touching, symbiotic relationship. They took care of him, and he gave them protection. When it came to instructing his two young squires in the art of combat, Giles was a relentless taskmaster. He transferred the feverish intensity with which he sought to grasp his past into his teaching and he rode them hard. Marcel, a delicate young boy, was ill suited to such work and he pleaded with his sister to run away from Giles; but even then, Andre understood that the knowledge being imparted to them had no price and that it was an opportunity that would never come again.

Although Marcel did not display much of an aptitude for knightly skills, Andre responded to the training well and quickly. She learned how to control a horse while in full armor, though Giles' armor was extremely large on her and she could barely move about inside it without his assistance. She learned how to use a crossbow, how to fight with a broadsword, which she had not even been able to lift at first. She was almost constantly in pain from the demands placed on her young and undeveloped muscles, but she was possessed of intense determination. As time passed and she grew, her muscles became stronger. She became concerned when she noticed that she was beginning to develop as a woman, but the fact that she was never meant to be voluptuous, coupled with the response of her muscles to the highly intense training, resulted in her developing a body that aided her in her deception. Her breasts, though firm, were small and easily, if uncomfortably, concealed. Her shoulders, though not as broad as those of many men, were nevertheless much broader than the standards of beauty dictated for women. Her arms were large for a woman and her legs did not have the coltish slimness indicative of indolence. Where women of the day were soft, Andre was hard. Where their skin was smooth, Andre's was rough. In short, as a woman, Andre de la Croix was too mannish to attract very many men and, indeed, she would have intimidated them. But in the aspect of a man, she gave the impression of possessing a studied, languid grace, a trim and compact body and a youthful prettiness that gave her a very boyish quality and frequently made others underestimate her.

When Giles succumbed to pneumonia, Andre and Marcel buried him in the forest and Andre took his horse and arms for her own. She applied the skills that Giles had taught her and improved upon them, selling her services to anyone who could afford to pay. In time, she was able to improve upon Giles' ill-fitting armor by commissioning an armorer to craft a suit especially for her. There were many knights involved in the Crusades and they proclaimed this by wearing the cross upon their chests and shields. Andre instructed her armorer to fashion a cross as a device for her, as well, only to make it different from those worn by the Crusaders. The armorer gave her a fleury cross and reversed the colors of the Crusaders from red on white to white on red and the red knight, Andre de la Croix, was born.

As she stood outside upon the parapet, feeling the cool evening breeze upon her face, Andre considered the unlikely part that fate had chosen her to play in the scheme of things.

She wished she understood more about the intrigue she was involved in.

"It is time for us to talk," a voice said at her side.

She jerked, startled. She had been all alone upon the castle
wall mere seconds ago and the hooded stranger had appeared
at her side as if out of thin air. It was not the first time he had
so surprised her.

"Would that I could learn to move so swiftly, or with such
silence," she told him. "Where did you come from?"

"That need not concern you."

"What do you want, then?"

"I want you to perform a service for me. You will listen
carefully and follow each of my commands to the letter. I will
not tolerate refusal or failure on your part. You—"

"I am not one of your serfs," said Andre.

"You are bought and paid for."

"You have purchased my services, my lord, you have not
purchased me. I care not if you are the rightful King of
England or Jesus Christ, Himself; it is all the same to me. So
long as I am paid, I will follow your instructions. It would
serve you well to consider that I could as easily inform your
brother of our dealings, should you become too inconvenient
a paymaster."

"I don't doubt that you could burn the candle at both ends
successfully," said the referee, "but I possess the means
whereby you might be singed."

"You threaten me?"

"With exposure as a woman, yes."

Andre stiffened and her fingers moved toward the dagger in
her belt.

"Yes, I know, but rest assured that your secret will be safe
with me so long as you follow my instructions."

Moving with lightning speed, Andre drew the dagger from
its sheath and stabbed at—but he was no longer there. Andre
looked quickly from side to side, holding the dagger out in
front of her. She was alone upon the parapet. Thinking that
her intended victim might have fallen over, she leaned out over
the edge of the wall to look down and—

—powerful hands pinned her down against the stone. If she
struggled, she could be thrown over the edge in a moment. She
froze, resigned to her fate.

"That was very foolish, de la Croix. Your life rests in the

palm of my hand, do you understand me? I could kill you at
any time. Any time at all. Now drop the knife.''

It spun away into the darkness.

"Better."

He let her up. She looked shaken. "Have I bound myself
over to a sorcerer?'' she said.

"You have bound yourself over to Richard of England.''

Andre shook her head. "You are not Plantagenet.''

Irving smiled. "Perhaps not. But I will be. Now listen
carefully, I have a task for you . . . .''

5 _____

The last day of the tournament was traditionally set aside for the melee, a mock battle staged for the benefit of the spectators. The melee held a great attraction for the masses, for it had all the elements of a real war. Once again, there was a great deal of milling about until Prince John showed up with his entourage, then the marshal began to organize things.

As the victor of the joust, Lucas was to captain one side while de la Croix, who took the second best honors, led the other. There were more entrants into this event than there had been in the jousting, not so much because it was less challenging as for the reason that with so many men upon the field, the fall of one was made less of a spectacle.

Predictably, Bois-Guilbert was among the first to enter on the side of de la Croix, as he was anxious to have another crack at the knight who had humiliated him the previous day. The bulk of De Bracy's Free Companions also took the side of de la Croix, while De Bracy himself was forced to watch the action from the stands, his shoulder bandaged and his pride a little hurt. There was no shortage of men to fight on the side of the white knight, however. Athelstane of Coningsburgh and several other Saxons entered the event on the side of the challengers, as did several Normans who wanted to try their hand against the mercenaries. When it was made certain that the numbers on both sides were even, the heralds announced the rules of the passage at arms.

Since the weapons to be used were real, whereas the battle was a mock one, there were certain prohibitions involved for the sake of preventing the melee from turning into a blood bath. Swords were to be used for striking only. Thrusting was forbidden. Maces and battle axes were allowed to be wielded with impunity, but daggers were forbidden. An unhorsed knight could, if capable, continue to fight on foot with someone in the same predicament, but then he could not attack or be attacked by a mounted knight. Any knight who was forced, by his opponent, to the opposite side so that some part of his arms or person touched the palisade was considered vanquished and his horse and armor were forfeit to the victor. If a knight was unhorsed or struck down and unable to get up, it was permissable for his squire to run out and drag him out of harm's way, but in such a case, he also lost his horse and arms. The melee would cease when Prince John threw down his truncheon. Any knight breaking the rules was to be stripped of his arms upon the spot.

All things considered, it was still possible to get hurt in such a donnybrook, which fact did not escape Brian de Bois-Guilbert, who was intent on embedding his battle axe well and truly in the white knight's cranium. The memory of their joust was still fresh in his mind and he still felt the burning shame of it. Everything about the white knight made him furious. The man would not reveal his face or state his name; he clearly showed himself to be a Saxon by declaring war upon the Norman knights and that a Saxon should prevail over a Norman . . . And on top of everything, he had chosen a Jewess as his queen, an open insult to every Norman lady and, yes, even to the Saxon wenches, as well.

Still, in spite of himself, Bois-Guilbert had to admit that the Jewess had been breathtaking. The Templars were not a celibate order; they granted themselves liberal dispensations. Bois-Guilbert was possessed of a hearty sexual appetite and, Jew or no Jew, the woman was a tasty morsel. Her lack of social standing made her quite vulnerable, a fact of which she was no doubt aware. She had absented herself from the day's festivities, leaving the Saxon girl, Rowena, to reign in her place as she had done at the previous night's banquet. Either the Jewess had chosen not to come in order to avoid any discomfort or someone had spoken to her, telling her she was not welcome. It irked Bois-Guilbert. On one hand, he was angry with the white knight for honoring a Jew and, on the other, he was irritated at her absence, since if she was not around, the chances of his getting between her legs were somewhat diminished. He was determined to take out his frustrations upon the man who had caused them all.

When both sides had taken their positions, the head marshal cried *"Laissez aller!"* and the fanfare sounded. Lances lowered, both sides thundered toward each other, crashing together in the center of the meadow with a clangor loud enough to be heard a mile away. There followed a cacophonous din, a pandemonium of metal upon metal as the knights hacked and flailed at each other with a vengeance, raising a thick cloud of dust that blew over the stands, adding the cursing and the coughing of the spectators to the general uproar.

In their first rush together, not a few knights were unhorsed and some lay still upon the field of battle, whether dead, wounded or merely stunned no one would know until their squires rescued them. It would have taken a brave squire, indeed, to rush out into such a press. Most of them waited until the dust had settled somewhat and the numbers thinned. Other knights struggled to their feet and took to bashing at each other, able to tell for which side they fought by the battle cries they voiced. Those on the side of de la Croix shouted out *"Tiens à ta foy!"* or "Hold to your faith!", the motto on the red knight's shield, while the white knight's men, to Prince John's great consternation, were instructed by their captain to cry out *"De par le roy!"* or "In the king's name!"

Lucas had less difficulty in the melee than did all the other knights. His nysteel armor allowed him to move far more freely than the others could and his helmet, though damaged from his joust with de la Croix, was still capable of filtering out much of the dust. While all around him knights sweated in their suits of armor, breathing in dust while risking heat exhaustion, Lucas felt relatively cool and unencumbered. As he lay about him with his sword, he found himself thinking that the melee was a good metaphor for the U.S. Temporal Corps. Soldiers on both sides battling it out while observers or, as in this case, marshals kept score. And even scorekeeping was a chancy proposition in this instance, as one marshal discovered who saw Philip de Malvoisin pressed against the palisade by his antagonist. The marshal pronounced Malvoisin van-

quished and the attacker turned away to find another to
defeat, whereupon Malvoisin promptly took advantage of the
interposition of another mounted knight between himself and
the stands to smite both marshal and victor with his mace.

As the spectators strained to follow their favorites, the air
became choked with dust and bits of plumage shorn from
the helmets of the knights. The deafening sound of metal upon
metal was falling off somewhat as arms grew tired and the
number of antagonists grew smaller. Many knights had now
been pronounced "dead" by the marshals and they had with-
drawn. The field was liberally littered with dead, dying and
wounded men and even a horse or two and there were but a
few combatants left. Now the squires began to risk running
out upon the field to drag away their fallen masters.

Bois-Guilbert, de la Croix and Malvoisin were the last remaining knights on their side, while on the other there were
the white knight, Athelstane of Coningsburgh and an unknown knight dressed all in black upon a jet black stallion.
His shield was black as well, bearing no device. He was not
well liked by the spectators, who had observed him to hang
back from the fray, fighting only when pressed by another
knight and, even so, doing nothing more than making a
defense. He was booed by the spectators as he simply sat
astride his horse and watched while Malvoisin and de la Croix
pounded Athelstane into the ground and then turned to join
Bois-Guilbert in doing battle with the "nameless oak." Many
of those watching called to John, shouting at him to throw
down his truncheon and end the contest, since it was obvious
that the white knight would be overwhelmed and the crowd
was sympathetic toward him. They did not want to see their
favorite beaten to a bloody pulp by superior odds, but John
held off, watching and smiling.

"Mark Bois-Guilbert," he said to Fitzurse. "The Templar
has a score to settle and I'll wager our white knight will not
live out the day."

Indeed, the Templar was pressing his attack with a fury,
hammering away at the white knight for all he was worth with
his battle axe while both de la Croix, on horseback, and Malvoisin, on foot, stood by to finish him off.

Lucas was doing his best to parry as many of the blows with
his sword as possible. They could smash away at the nysteel
until doomsday and make only the most superficial dents in it,

but he was anxious to keep up appearances. He had seen de la Croix and Malvoisin team up on Athelstane, with the red knight attacking him on horseback and Malvoisin standing by to complete the job the moment Athelstane was unhorsed. The Saxon now lay senseless, possibly dead, some few yards way. Now Malvoisin stood ready, waiting until Bois-Guilbert and de la Croix managed to unhorse him so that he could take his shot. John showed no intention of stopping the contest until he was stretched out full length upon the field.

It was at that point that the black knight chose to make his move. He spurred his horse and rode up alongside de la Croix, smashing the red knight in the side with his mace. The red knight tumbled to the ground, stunned by both the fall and the blow. The black knight then dismounted and advanced on Malvoisin. They met mace to mace and it took but a moment for the black knight to bludgeon Malvoisin into oblivion, using his advantage of size and strength to slam away at his adversary until Malvoisin dropped like a stone. That done, the black knight turned to de la Croix, but seeing Marcel dragging the red knight away, he took his own horse by the reins and led it from the field of battle to the cheers of the Saxons, who seemed to have forgotten his failure to help Athelstane.

Lucas was left to battle Bois-Guilbert.

"Die, Saxon pig!" screamed the Templar, hacking away at Lucas with all his might. He was becoming increasingly frustrated. The white knight had parried most of his blows, but some had gotten through and Bois-Guilbert simply couldn't understand why he had failed to draw blood. Whereas all around them lay knights who had been smashed and dented, leaving the impression that they had been dropped from some great height, the white knight's armor showed not a single mark of serious damage. It was infuriating.

Lucas, meanwhile, was beginning to grow tired. As the previous day's champion, he had had his work cut out for him, becoming the mark for every knight on the opposing side. While others had been able to pace themselves to some extent, he was constantly beset and not given even one moment's pause. His superior armor enabled him to survive unscathed, but he was still susceptible to the effects of all the pounding and he was exhausted. The timely intervention of the black knight had given him an opportunity to end it and he had every intention of taking advantage of it. He had only one shot, but one shot was all he needed. The Templar was obviously in a fine sweat from his exertions and that would serve very nicely. He waited for an opening and when Bois-Guilbert left him one, he gave him a casual swat with his sword. At the same time, he triggered the capacitor that discharged 25,000 volts at half an ampere through the blade and into the Templar's body.

The Templar spasmed and his horse broke wind prodigiously. Lucas took advantage of the moment to bash him once again, although it was more for the sake of appearances than anything else. Bois-Guilbert never even felt it. He tumbled from his horse, unconscious. Prince John threw down his truncheon in disgust.

Lucas, like the fused capacitor he ejected from his sword hilt, was completely drained. He wished he could have given Bois-Guilbert a lethal dose of electricity, but he was glad to settle for a TKO. He still had a part to play. Frying Bois-Guilbert would never do. What had happened had to appear to be the result of a sword strike, not a lightning strike. Just the same, he was thankful for the equipment designed to increase the odds of his survival. It was easy for a soldier from 2613 to succumb to the temptation to feel superior to a fighting man of the Middle Ages, since even the smallest modern man would be on a par at least with the largest knights. However, that did not take into account the fact that these were men who were accustomed to a harsher way of life, to more primitive conditions and, needless to say, to moving about in heavy suits of armor. These men were far from being weaklings. Lucas had taken quite a beating during the melee and much of it had come from Bois-Guilbert.

He was brought before Prince John, who was ill disposed to name him champion. The fact that Lucas had laid out John's best knights, not to mention doing so in Richard's name, did not endear him to the prince. John insisted that the white knight would not have defeated Bois-Guilbert had not the black knight ridden to his rescue. The black knight, therefore, deserved the honors. However, when the call was put forth for him, the black knight could not be found. John had him summoned three times and when he did not appear, he grudgingly acknowledged Lucas as the champion, at which point a great cheer went up from the stands.

"Come, Fitzurse, let's away from here," John grumbled.

"This day has soured my stomach."

"How, Sire, have you not accomplished your purpose this day?" Fitzurse said. "The people seem well pleased. They have seen a good day's entertainment, the champion is one to their liking and if a Jewess was initially selected as the queen of this tournament, at least the mistake was rectified and the Saxon girl, Rowena, installed in the office. All in all, a good day for the Saxons, one which they'll remember. It will make the new tax perhaps a bit more palatable."

"True enough," said John, somewhat mollified. "Still, I dislike these tournaments. They are a waste of manpower. This one has cost me Front-de-Boeuf."

"True again, Sire," said Fitzurse, "but this, too, can be turned to your advantage. The fief of Ivanhoe, which you had reassigned to Front-de-Boeuf, is now once again available to be assigned to a deserving knight. Might I suggest Maurice De Bracy? He and his Free Companions would serve you better if his interests were aligned with yours."

John smiled. "You are worth your weight in gold to me, Fitzurse. An excellent suggestion. I feel much better now. Well, then, since this nameless knight has opened up the way for me to award a fiefdom to De Bracy, thereby strengthening our bond, it would be well to honor him at Ashby. See to it that he comes. I am curious to see his face. Oh, and see to it that those Saxon churls, Cedric and Athelstane, attend as well, since they seem to love him. Perhaps we'll have some sport with them, and at the same time enjoy the fair Rowena's company."

Lucas accepted Prince John's invitation. It would have been inadvisable to turn him down. He was tired and sore, but he had already missed one royal banquet; to miss this one would constitute an insult to the prince. Besides, it was a good time to establish himself in his new identity. The Castle of Ashby was the domain of Roger de Quincy, the Earl of Winchester. While de Quincy was crusading, John had taken Ashby over for his own purposes. When the absent crusaders returned to their possessions, they would find them confiscated by the king's brother, who had strengthened his own position considerably. It would be interesting to see what effect his arrival at the banquet would have.

He had known that Ivanhoe's lands had been granted to

Front-de-Boeuf. Now John obviously intended to turn the fiefdom over to another of his toadies. What would he do when Ivanhoe showed up to claim his own? More to the point, what was Ivanhoe supposed to do? Lucas realized that his own position was becoming somewhat precarious. Ashby was the key. Whatever happened next, he was certain that it would occur at Ashby.

Hooker was not in sight as he approached his tent. With any luck, thought Lucas, he's gone to get something to eat. He was starved. Tired and hungry, Lucas entered the pavilion.

Hooker was lying face down on the ground. The black knight sat helmetless upon the wooden cot. He smiled.

"King takes pawn, Mr. Priest," he said. "It's your move."

As Lucas clawed for his sword, the black knight chuckled and disappeared into thin air.

Lucas was bending over to examine Hooker's body when he heard the sound of someone entering the pavilion, followed by a sharp intake of breath. Cursing himself for being caught off guard, he spun around, expecting to be attacked. Instead, he saw Finn Delaney and Bobby Johnson. And Corporal Hooker.

"*Hooker!*"

It was Hooker who had gasped. He stood looking down at his own dead body with a glassy-eyed stare. He had been garroted with a monofilament wire that had cut very deeply into his throat.

"*Christ,*" whispered Delaney.

After the initial shock had worn off, Lucas understood. Somehow, something had gone wrong up ahead. Irving had discovered who they were. Maybe he had known from the very beginning, wherever in time the beginning was. Now he was playing with them and it was a grisly game. Somewhere in the not too distant future, Irving had killed Hooker and he had brought his body back into the past—their present—to tease them with the knowledge that he knew and that they were doomed to certain failure.

Hooker doubled over and clutched his stomach. He vomited. Delaney grabbed him, holding him and steadying him until the shaking and the heaves abated.

"Well, I guess that tears it," Bobby said, as soon as Lucas

told him what had happened. "We've lost before we even had a chance to get started."

"Maybe," Delaney said. "And then again, maybe not."

"You mean maybe that's not me lying there?" said Hooker. He was trying not to look at the dead body, but his eyes kept straying back to it, as though the corpse exerted some sort of magnetism upon him. He was badly shaken and Lucas could hardly blame him. He could not imagine what his own reaction would be if he were confronted with his own corpse.

"Oh, that's you, all right," said Finn. "And I'll admit that you don't look too healthy, but that's not necessarily the way it's got to be."

"Are you telling me," said Hooker, "that *that's* not real?" He pointed to the body.

"It's real," said Finn. "It's a real possibility. Or, to put it another way, it's a potential reality."

"What the *fuck* are you *talking* about? I'm standing here and looking at the way I'm going to die!"

Hooker was on the edge of total hysteria. He was just barely keeping himself under control. Delaney took him by the shoulders and sat him down.

"All right. Take it easy. Take a couple of deep breaths. I mean *now*, boy, do it! Come on."

Hooker inhaled and exhaled heavily several times while Delaney stood over him.

"That's right, don't be afraid to look at it," Finn said. "Don't let it rattle you. He wants you to be rattled. That's why he did it."

"But I'm going to—"

"Don't talk, just keep taking those deep breaths. Again. Again."

After a few more breaths, Hooker relaxed a bit and nodded.

"You all right now?" Lucas said.

Hooker managed a very weak smile. "I'm not all right," he said, "but I think I can handle it."

"There's only one way we're ever going to make it through this thing," Delaney said, "and that's to act as though nothing is real as far as the future is concerned. *Nothing*. And that includes *that*." He jerked his head toward Hooker's corpse.

"Sure looks real enough to me," said Bobby.

"Yeah, and it *was* real," said Delaney. "It was real when it died. But the minute our friend Goldblum clocked back with it, it ceased to be real and it became only *potentially* real." He glanced at Hooker. "Maybe you're going to buy it this way, kid. And then again, maybe you won't. Because by bringing this corpse back here, Irving has created a time paradox. What's more, he knows it. Think about this, now. He can't possibly know everything. He can't possibly have this whole mission knocked, because if he did, then why are we standing here and talking about it right now? If he knew it all, he could take care of us at any time."

"Well, suppose he can," said Bobby. "He just might be playing with us. With that damn chronoplate in his possession, he can damn well do anything he wants to. He can take us out any *time* he wants to."

"So why doesn't he?" said Finn. "Why hasn't he?"

"Maybe he will," Bobby said. "Shit, maybe he already has. Maybe he's going back into the past even as we're standing here. Maybe he's going to arrive at some point prior to right now and do us in."

"Then what will happen to us?" Hooker said. "If he pops back in an hour ago and kills us, what will happen to us now? How could we even *be* here now if he killed us in the past?"

"Hold it right there," said Finn. "Don't start getting bent all out of shape. That's exactly what he wants. Let's talk theory for a moment. Here's how we stand right now: assuming Irving travels back into the past, *our* past relative to where we are right this very moment, then he might succeed in killing us. *If* he does that, then the timeline will have been disrupted and there will be a skip in it. There had to be a past for us not to be killed in, otherwise we wouldn't be standing here right now. In the same manner, there has to be a potential future in which Irving can come back to this time to mess things up. From the perspective of the future that we came from, history has not been changed. At least, it hadn't been changed up to the moment that we departed for this time period. We've got to preserve the status quo from which we came. As it stands right now, the timeline from here on is in potential flux. Irving has confronted us with a potential future in which Hooker has been killed. We know that there is no absolute future. There is only an infinite number of *possible* futures. There has to be a potential future in which Hooker did not know that he was going to die. We have been confronted with that very real possibility. By confronting us with it, Irving has managed to rattle us, which is precisely what he intended. He has also managed to *warn* us."

"You mean it might still happen," Hooker said.

"It might," said Finn. "What we don't know is this: when this Hooker died," he indicated the corpse, "he might not have known that he was going to die. Meaning, this Hooker might not ever have had the opportunity to see his own corpse."

"On the other hand, maybe he did," said Hooker. "Maybe *I* did."

"That's right," said Finn. "But we don't know for sure. So you've got a choice to make right now, son. You can either resign yourself to this fate," he pointed at the nearly severed head of the corpse, "or you can determine that you're going to do everything in your power to prevent this from ever happening. And that means you're going to have to watch your back."

Hooker took a deep breath and gritted his teeth. "Yeah," he said. "But *when?*"

"I don't have all the answers, Corporal."

"Thanks."

"Sarge," he said to Bobby, "why don't you take the boy outside and let him walk around a bit? He doesn't look too steady. Go on, get him out of here."

"Come on, Hooker," Bobby said. "Let's go out and get some air. It's getting a little close in here."

He led Hooker out of the pavilion. Finn stood at the entrance, watching them.

"They can't hear us now, can they?" Lucas said, softly.

Finn turned around and shook his head.

"You know what I'm about to say, don't you?" Lucas said.

"You mean about the paradox?" said Finn.

"What paradox?"

Finn nodded, glumly.

"That corpse doesn't represent a paradox," said Lucas. "At least, not yet. You smoked the kid, Finn."

"I had to. I had no choice. Surely you can see that."

Lucas took a deep breath and let it out slowly. "Jesus. What a mess. You know, something sounded wrong while you were talking to him, but I couldn't quite put my finger on it. I'm still not sure I can follow it through completely, but then

I'm just a simple dog soldier. So are you, for that matter. Or *are* you? You seem pretty well versed in temporal mechanics, even for a veteran with your experience.''

"I'm not a mission plant, if that's what you're getting at," said Finn. "What you see is what you get. I'm a lifer, son. I've served a lot of time. I've gone up and down in rank like a yo-yo, mainly because I don't always play it by the rules, but . . ."

"But?"

"Yes, well, there *is* a 'but,' Sergeant Major. I volunteered for the Corps. I didn't really have to. I finished in the top three percent of the Service Aptitude batteries. I chose the army anyway and I put in my time.''

"Which qualified you for Referee Corps School," said Lucas.

Finn nodded. "I got halfway through before I washed out," he said. "I couldn't handle Econo-political Management and Arbitration. Way over my head. Well, maybe not over my head, but beyond my inclination. I did get through Temporal Physics and Trans-historical Adjustment and Maintenance, though.''

"Which should have qualified you for the observers."

"It did," said Finn, nodding. "Only I didn't want it. You may think I'm crazy, but I missed this. Observing's not the same as participating, even though it pays better.''

Lucas nodded. "I understand. I can't say I would have done the same thing in your position, but that's beside the point. The point is, you bluffed him. You made him think that we can still do something to get through this thing alive. Only we can't, can we?''

"Not necessarily," said Finn. "We still have a chance. *We* do. Hooker, I'm afraid, has no chance at all.''

"I don't quite follow."

"Okay, I'll make it quick, they might come back at any minute. Time is fluid. The only thing that isn't is our subjective relationship to time. Time is like a river in that respect. Now you can take a boulder, let's say, and drop it in that river. It will create some eddies, but those eddies will have dissipated say, two hundred yards downstream. In order to significantly change the course of the river, or split the timeline, you're going to have to introduce a much more significant factor. Say, divert the river at one point and split it.

Now think of yourself as a molecule of water. Your relationship to that river is totally subjective, depending upon where you are in relation to its flow. If you move with the water to a point beyond which the river has been diverted, *before* it has been diverted, then that won't affect you. However, if I was to draw a cupful of water from that river, containing your little molecule, and pour you back in at a point upstream of the diversion, then that diversion could affect you."

"So we can't be attacked in our absolute past," said Lucas. "Irving can't kill me yesterday and expect that action to destroy me here today."

"That's right," said Finn. "You can't shoot five feet behind a clay pigeon and expect it to burst. What's happened to us has already happened. That's an absolute. Regardless of what Irving does in the past, it won't affect us right here right now. It will affect the past at a point at which the timeline will be split. From that point on, the future will be an entirely different scenario, depending upon when the timelines eventually rejoin. Irving can only kill us in a parallel timeline if he tries to attack us in our past. The point is, our job is to keep him from creating that parallel timeline. If he does succeed in causing the split, the future will be affected. And there's the danger. That game of Russian roulette the ref was talking about. His fate is sealed in that respect. If we succeed in stopping Irving, assuming that the real Richard Plantagenet is still alive and we can find him, then we have the possibility of our being able to clock back in to Plus Time with Irving, leaving the real Richard to sit on the throne. In that case, he'll have to be conditioned to forget all about Irving's intervention in his life. Not a problem. But then we'll have to clock back in at a point just *beyond* Irving's having gone back, so as not to create a paradox regarding our own experience. We will have restored the status quo of our own history. However, the possibility of that is almost nonexistent. I'll bet my life on the fact that Irving has killed the real Richard, in order to improve the odds of his success. In that case, we've got to kill Irving and let our ref become Richard, acting in a manner that will preserve our timeline. He will have to die, *as Richard*, in order to avoid a paradox."

"So where does that leave Hooker?" Lucas said.

"Hooker's finished," Delaney said. "We've still got a chance, because at this point, Irving has not confronted us with our own fates. Yet. He knows about Hooker. He knows about you. He may or may not know about me and Johnson. But the fact that we have been confronted with Hooker's corpse means that Hooker must die, because if he survives beyond the point at which Irving has killed him, assuming that it is Irving who's done it, then that will mean that he never died to be clocked back to right now. He will never have seen his own dead body. And that will change his experience. *That* will constitute a paradox and *we*, then, will have split the time-line. We have to make sure that Hooker is garroted."

"But we don't know when that's supposed to happen," Lucas said.

"That's right, we don't. With any luck, we won't be able to prevent it."

"*You call that luck?*"

"Compared to the alternative, yes."

"What alternative?"

"Well, there is the possibility that in order to avoid the paradox, we're going to have to kill him ourselves. And in that case, which one of us is going to volunteer?"

6

It was quiet and peaceful in Sherwood Forest. Finn and Bobby had walked all morning and now, at midday, they had stopped to rest by the side of the road, really little more than a narrow dirt path running through the forest, wide enough to permit two horses to travel closely side by side. They were not on horseback, however. They traveled on foot, at a leisurely pace. For a long time, both men had walked in silence, mulling over recent developments, especially what had happened in Lucas Priest's pavilion. The atmosphere in Sherwood Forest was conducive to quiet contemplation. All morning, they had not run into any other travelers. It was a bucolic scene, with the silence broken only by birdsong and the occasional hectic rustling of some small animal hurtling through the brush, frightened by their presence. The tree boughs made a canopy above them, through which shafts of sunlight streamed down to dapple the ground with light and shadow.

Finn had shot a rabbit and dressed it. They had cooked it on a spit and washed it down with cheap wine that tasted far better than it was supposed to. In another time and in another place, it would have seemed a very primitive and unsatisfactory repast, but in Sherwood Forest, it made for a veritable feast.

Finn leaned back against a large oak tree and lighted a cigarette. It was strictly against regulations, but neither of them cared. There was no one there to see them, so they passed the precious cigarette back and forth between them, hiding it with their hands just in case, staying very near the fire so that the smoke would not seem too noticeable to a prying eye. Finn had managed to smuggle several of the cigarettes from their island training base and he planned to ration them out carefully. They smoked in silence, neither man speaking until they were through. Then Finn field stripped the butt, shredding it and dropping what was left into the fire, which had almost burned out. That done, he leaned back against the tree trunk once again and shut his eyes.

"Finn?" said Bobby.

"Mmmm?"

"Suppose Hooker figures it out?"

Finn sighed. "It's possible, of course, but I don't think he will."

"Don't underestimate him just because he's still pretty green," said Bobby.

"No, that wasn't what I meant. This is going to sound pretty goddamn cold, but I don't think he'll knock it because, quite simply, he wants to live. When you're already predisposed toward one condition, your mind will tend to avoid considering any possible alternatives."

"I suppose you're probably right," said Bobby. "He seized on that bit of double-talk you fed him and hung onto it for all he was worth. He kept telling me how careful he was going to be, how he was going to refine paranoia to an art. He tried to make light of it, but he's pretty scared."

"Wouldn't you be?"

"I honestly don't know. I've been trying to put myself in his place and I just can't do it. I get sick just thinking about it."

"That's good," said Finn. "Keep thinking about it. It'll help you deal with Goldblum when the time comes."

"Yeah. I don't even know the man and I already hate him more than I've ever hated anyone in my entire life."

Finn nodded.

"But then I find myself thinking, perhaps he's really not to blame. What he's done is not the act of a rational man. He's sick, Finn. He's insane."

"Don't leave any room inside yourself for pity," Finn said. "Within the framework of their own insanity, people like that can be very rational, indeed. He's smarter than you are.

Otherwise he'd never have made it as a referee. Don't ever make the mistake of underestimating your enemy or feeling sorry for him. That's giving your enemy an advantage over you and Goldblum already has us pretty well outgunned.''

"Yeah, tell me about it."

"Wish to hell we could get our hands on a chronoplate," said Finn. "Let me know if you see any lying around."

"Lousy army," Bobby said.

"It's a living."

Bobby was silent for a moment. "It's more than that for you," he said after a moment. "It's a way of life, isn't it? I can't conceive of myself finishing up my tour of duty and then re-upping. To me, that's crazy."

"I guess maybe it is," said Finn.

"How old are you, Finn?"

"A hundred and six."

Bobby snorted. "I'm only sixty. And Hooker, Christ, nineteen years old! To have to go that young . . . I wish to God there was some other way."

"So do I," said Finn.

"Why do we do it?"

"I can't come up with any answer better than Lord Tennyson's," said Finn.

"I don't mean that," said Bobby. "I don't mean why do *we* do it, I mean why continue with these crazy time wars? Considering the risks involved, I just can't understand why they continue. Why can't we just stop it before something really nasty happens?"

"It may already have happened," said Finn. "That's why we're here. As far as stopping it goes, figure out when the arms race started, whenever in hell that was, and ask yourself why they didn't stop it then. Somebody would have had to stop it *first*. Your trouble is that you're thinking like a rational human being, not like a politician. Go back as far as you like, to the Belter Wars, the nuclear arms race, the first atomic bomb. . . . Okay, we've got the technology and we know how dangerous it is and how dangerous it is to escalate. To continue on the same course would be insane. But if *we* stop, there's no guarantee that *they* will stop and so the game of leapfrog continues. The trouble is that the people who make those damn decisions are never the ones most qualified to make them. Back when the time wars started, nobody fully understood the risks. You can't change history, right? You can't change the past, it's absolute. Anything you do back in the past will have to be canceled out one way or another by the inertia of time. And that's correct, but it's only partially correct. It's like I told Lucas before about diverting the river. Follow the analogy. You drop a big rock in the river, you're going to create a spash and make some eddies, which will dissipate in the flow eventually. That's why if you kill some poor redcoat at Breed's Hill, you're not taking much of a risk of changing the course of history."

"Unless you went back to the time of the Revolutionary War and snuffed George Washington," said Bobby.

"True," said Finn, "but nobody believed that was possible. They thought something would have happened to prevent it. But then there were anomalies, such as the Bathurst Incident, which Mensinger cited, the case of the British diplomat in Austria whose carriage dropped him off in an open courtyard. He walked around in front of the horses and simply disappeared, never to be heard from again. It didn't change the course of history, perhaps, but how do you ever really know for sure? Mensinger proved that parallel timelines could exist and that a split timeline will eventually rejoin. You take an even bigger boulder, some huge goddamn piece of rock, and drop it in the river and it will split the river, but the water will flow around the boulder and the twin streams will rejoin, forming a single stream once again. It's what happens during that split that scares the shit out of everybody. That's when they started getting really paranoid, but they were just as paranoid that the other side wouldn't stop if they did. So the Referee Corps got more power, they got really strict about soldiers killed in action. . . . You've got to bring back your dead because you never know just what might happen. You've got to send your Search and Retrieve units back to find your MIAs and you worry like hell when they can't. So you're sitting on a powder keg that could blow up beneath you. Does that worry anybody? Some, but not enough. You give 'em that argument and they'll say that that's what people said about nuclear waste and radioactive fallout, they said it about the hydrogen bomb, they said that sparks from the smokestacks of trains would burn down the countryside, they even predicted that the world would end in violence when the crossbow was invented. And we're all still here."

"So what's the answer?" Bobby said.

Finn laughed. "Well, we could always go back and kill the son of a bitch who invented the crossbow."

He yelped suddenly as an arrow embedded itself in the tree trunk against which he leaned. It pierced his left sleeve, grazing his arm and cutting it.

"Stand and deliver!"

Three men appeared, each holding a drawn longbow pointed in their direction. Both men jumped to their feet, Finn first yanking the arrow free and throwing it down upon the ground furiously.

"It's Little John and Robin," one of the men said, lowering his bow. The other two followed suit.

"Damn, Will, you could've killed him!" one of them said.

"Sorry, John," the one named Will said. "I couldn't see that it was you."

Finn glowered at him. "Come here, you . . ."

Will Scarlet approached hesitantly. "Now don't get mad, John. Could've happened to anyone, y'know."

Delaney struck him squarely on the jaw and Will Scarlet collapsed to the ground, unconscious. The other two began to back away.

"Stand fast!" said Delaney.

They froze.

"Now, you two eagle-eyed marksmen, I want you to cut me a staff, a nice-sized one, and then you truss up sleeping beauty here and hang him from it like a stag. Then you can carry him to camp that way."

Anxious not to provoke him any further, the two merry men hurried to comply with his orders.

"We're going to start whipping these cretins into shape right now," Delaney said. "Their cozy little forest retreat is about to become Finn Delaney's boot camp!"

Discretion seemed the better part of valor. Although he was tempted to reveal himself at Ashby, Lucas chose to postpone the return of Ivanhoe until a more opportune time. What he needed now was Cedric's protection. Ashby would provide a good opportunity to make it up with his "father," but not during the banquet. His arrival at the feast would have caused quite a stir, especially if he attempted to reclaim his fief and announced that Richard had returned to England, as had been his plan. Such an announcement, he had believed, would have thrown John for a loop. He guessed that the prince would have stalled for time. With many people at the banquet still loyal to Richard, the very people John was determined to win over to his side, Lucas thought that John would have made a show of loyalty himself by returning to Ivanhoe his fief and welcoming his brother's return. It would be so much lip service and nothing more. Returning Ivanhoe's possessions would have been a small sacrifice and a wise political decision. Meanwhile, John would doubtless send armed parties abroad in search of Richard, to find him and to do away with him posthaste. If Lucas could get John to do his job for him, so much the better. And certainly, anyone wishing Ivanhoe ill would not act during the banquet, where there would be so many witnesses. By giving up Rowena and begging Cedric's forgiveness, Lucas was certain that he would reestablish Ivanhoe in his father's good graces. It might not make Rowena very happy, but he would be safer leaving Ashby in the company of an armed party of Saxons. At least, that had been the plan. His growing sense of paranoia made him change it.

Finn was most likely correct in his guess that Goldblum had done away with Richard, rather than holding him prisoner somewhere. Holding the real Richard prisoner might have made for a bargaining point with the referees in case Irving failed, but Lucas was convinced that Irving was not even considering the prospect of failure. He was well ahead in the game and his possession of a chronoplate made the prospect of defeating him highly improbable. Unfortunately, that highly improbable prospect was all they had to look forward to. The alternatives were too frightening to consider.

Somehow, he had to discover where Irving was holed up. Either that, or wait until he made his move. So long as he was on his own, he was an open target. He had to change the course of events that had led to Irving's clocking back with Hooker's body. He did not know if that was possible, but he had to try. The danger was in second guessing himself.

He had fully intended to pursue his original plan. What he did not know was if he had already done so by the time that Hooker died. He thought back to Finn's analogy of dropping boulders in the river of time. His brain was in a muddle. Perhaps, by clocking back with Hooker's body, warning them that the boy would die, Irving had dropped a little boulder in the stream, had caused a tiny split in the timeline. Assuming that Goldblum had killed Hooker, at the time that happened —at some point in the not too distant future relative to where Lucas now was—perhaps Lucas had followed through on his original plan and revealed himself as Ivanhoe at John's banquet. Perhaps it was *that* event which had led to Hooker's death. What *was* the absolute past in Irving Goldblum's case?

Whatever had occurred up to the point at which Goldblum had killed Hooker was absolute relative to Irving's position in the timeline at that point. He killed Hooker, then clocked back with his body to confront them with it, to flaunt his superiority in the deadly game. Yet, there had to be a scenario in which Irving had not done that, there *had* to be. He had to kill Hooker before he could clock back with his body. Therefore, there had to exist an absolute past relative to Irving in which Hooker did not see his own corpse, because Irving had to kill him first before he could travel back into the past to confront them with his body. At the point in time at which Hooker had died, there had to exist a past scenario in which the timeline had been different. Irving had now changed that timeline or split it. The danger in second guessing the split, if there was one, lay in the fact that Lucas had no way of knowing what actions he was to take, which actions he had *already taken* at the point of Hooker's death. Had he, in fact, followed through on his original plan and announced himself at Prince John's banquet, which event subsequently led to Hooker's death—or had he altered his plan, as he was now doing? Which way would play into Irving Goldblum's hands? Or did it even make a difference?

Trying to solve the riddle gave Lucas a tremendous migraine. Maybe Finn was right. Maybe Hooker's fate was sealed, and with his fate, theirs as well. But if he was to accept that, then what hope could they possibly have of coming out of it alive?

Lucas decided and prayed that he had made the right decision. Without a chronoplate, he had no way of knowing. And if he had one, then things would have been even more confusing. Perhaps it was trying to solve such riddles that had led to Goldblum's insanity. For the first time in his life, Lucas was able to appreciate the difficulties involved in being a referee.

The first thing he had done had been to find a safe place to keep his armor while he was at the banquet. After some consideration, he had decided that the safest person to entrust his gear to was Isaac of York, Rebecca's father. He had already established a cursory sort of relationship with Rebecca and he knew that she did not think of him in the same way as she did the other knights. He had reason to believe that he could trust her. Secondly, he felt that he could trust to Isaac's business sense. What he had done was to send Hooker to Isaac and Rebecca, along with his armor, to use as collateral for a loan. He did not need the loan, but it made for an excellent pretext. They would keep his armor safe, obviously ignorant of its true nature and value, knowing that the interest Isaac demanded on the loan would exceed the price of Hooker and the armor if they sold them in the event of his default. After the banquet, he would simply repay the loan plus interest (which money would come from his winnings at the tournament) and reclaim Hooker and his armor. He felt that this would seem more natural than simply paying them outright to keep it safe for him. In that case, they might grow suspicious and wonder about his reasons for doing so and why he had selected them for the task. This way, as a poor knight errant, was a better way and it served to help keep up appearances.

He had purchased a simple suit of clothing that would enable him to pass for a palmer, a wandering monk who had made a pilgrimage to the Holy Land. Even though the banquet was being held by John for his knights and nobles, as well as for the wealthy Saxons, he would not be denied admission in this guise. They would allow him in and feed him, no doubt giving him an unobtrusive place in the banquet hall, which suited him just fine. It would enable him to observe the others without being too noticeable himself.

As he had expected, he was admitted to Ashby and brought into the banquet hall. The steward announced him briefly as a palmer just returned from the Holy Land. John made a curt bow of respect, inclining his head very slightly, and motioned for the steward to seat him. They made a small place for him in the corner of the damp hall and brought him food and drink. His arrival did not pass without comment, however. No sooner was he seated than Athelstane was on his feet, proposing a toast.

"My lords and ladies," the corpulent Saxon shouted, making himself heard above the noise, "the arrival of the holy pilgrim serves to remind us of those gallant hearts fighting to free the Holy Land. I propose a toast. To the strong in arms, be their race or language what it will, who now bear them best in Palestine among the champions of the Cross!''

Bois-Guilbert rose up then, goblet held high. "To the Knights Templars, then," he said, "who are the sworn champions of the Holy Sepulchre!''

"And to the Knights Hospitalers, as well," said the Norman abbot, Father Aymer. "I have a brother in their order fighting to defend the Cross.''

"I impeach not their fame," conceded Bois-Guilbert.

"What, then," said Rowena, noting her father's frowning countenance and smiling slyly, "were there none in the English army whose names are worthy to be mentioned with the Knights of the Temple and of St. John?''

"Forgive me, my lady," said Bois-Guilbert. "The English monarch did, indeed, bring to Palestine a host of gallant warriors, second only to those whose breasts have been the unceasing bulwark of that land.''

"Second to none!" roared Athelstane. He turned in Lucas' direction. "Tell us, holy palmer, were there not gallant knights of *English* blood second to none who ever drew a sword in defense of the Holy Land?''

All eyes were on Lucas and he rose slowly to his feet, thankful for his cowl and the fact that he was in the shadows. Ivanhoe had been away for quite some time, but surely his own father would know him if he had a clear look at his face. Lucas took a deferential pose as he replied, holding his head slightly lowered as if uncomfortable to be made the focus of attention, which he was, acutely.

"I am but a palmer," he said, "and as such, know little of the way of warfare. Yet I did see when King Richard and five of his knights held a tournament after the taking of St. John-de-Acre, as challengers against all comers. On that day, each knight ran three courses and cast to the ground three antagonists. Seven of these assailants were Knights of the Temple, as Sir Brian de Bois-Guilbert can vouchsafe.''

It was one of Wilfred's favorite memories. Under questioning, it had been difficult to get the doped up knight to speak of anything else. He had been quite well pleased with himself.

The Templar did not take that well. He scowled and his hands clenched into fists.

"Their names, good palmer!" shouted Athelstane. "Could

you tell us the names of these gallant knights?''

"The first in honor, as in arms, was Richard, King of England," Lucas said. "The Earl of Leicester was the second. Sir Thomas Multon of Gilsland was the third."

"A Saxon!" hollered Athelstane, joyfully.

"Sir Foulk Doilly was the fourth," said Lucas.

"A Saxon on his mother's side!" yelled Athelstane, to the growing displeasure of the Normans. "And the fifth? Who was the fifth?"

"Sir Edwin Turneham."

"Saxon, by the soul of Hengist!" Athelstane's voice grew even louder, echoing throughout the hall. "The sixth! Who was the sixth?"

"I fear the sixth knight was one of lesser renown," said Lucas, "whose name dwells not in my memory."

"Sir Palmer," Bois-Guilbert said, tensely, "this assumed forgetfulness after so much has been remembered, comes too late to serve your purpose. I will tell you myself who this knight was, whose good fortune and my horse's fault gave him the victory. It was Sir Wilfred of Ivanhoe and there was not one of the six who, for his years, had more renown in arms, as Sir Wilfred would himself be first to tell you. Yet I will tell you this, that were Ivanhoe in England, I would soon demonstrate which of us is second to none in arms and valor!"

"Well, then," said John, smirking, "we shall include Sir Wilfred in our toast, whose absence prevents his answering the challenge. Let all fill to the pledge, and especially Cedric of Rotherwood, the worthy father to so gallant a defender of the Cross."

"No, my lord," said Cedric, turning his goblet upside down upon the table and spilling out his wine. "I will not drink to a disobedient youth who despises my commands and relinquishes the manners and the customs of his fathers!"

"What," said John, "can such a gallant knight be an unworthy son?"

"His name shall not pass my lips," said Cedric. "He left my home to mingle with the nobles at your brother's court, where he learned your Norman ways and tricks of horsemanship. He acted contrary to my wishes and commands and in the days of Alfred, such disobedience as his would have been a crime severely punished! Nor is it my least quarrel with my son that he stooped to hold, as feudal vassal, the very lands which his fathers possessed in free and independent right!"

John smiled. "Then it would seem that we would have your sanction, Cedric, if we were to confer this fief upon a person whose dignity would not be diminished by the holding of it. Sir Maurice De Bracy, will you keep the Barony of Ivanhoe, so that Sir Wilfred shall not further incur Cedric's displeasure by being a feudal vassal of the Crown?"

"By God," said De Bracy, "I'll be called a Saxon before Cedric or Wilfred or the best of English blood shall take away from me this gift, Your Highness!"

"Anyone calling you a Saxon, Sir Maurice," said Cedric, "would be doing you an honor as great as it is undeserved."

"No doubt the noble Cedric speaks the truth," said John. "His race may, indeed, claim precedence over us in the length of their pedigrees. The pictish blue with which his fathers painted themselves doubtless imparted the nobility of color to their veins."

"They do go before us in the field," said Father Aymer, "much as deer go before the dogs."

"And we should not forget their singular abstemiousness and temperance," said De Bracy, chuckling at Athelstane, who stood literally quivering with rage.

"Together with the courage and the conduct by which they distinguished themselves at Hastings and elsewhere," said Bois-Guilbert.

"Whatever be the defects of their race, real or imagined," said the heretofore silent de la Croix, "as one who has had occasion to partake of Saxon hospitality, I can at least vouchsafe that I know no Saxon who, in his own hall and while his own wine cup has been passed, has ever treated an unoffending guest to such a display of discourtesy as I have seen here on this night."

There was a long moment of uncomfortable silence, broken finally by Cedric, who rose to his feet ponderously.

"My thanks, Sir Knight," he said, controlling his voice with difficulty. "At least there is one among you who does not stoop to use a guest in such a wanton fashion. As for the misfortune of our fathers upon the field of Hastings, those may at least be silent who have within the past few hours once again been tumbled from the saddle by a Saxon lance!"

"By my faith, a biting jest!" said John, laughing. "Our Saxon subjects rise in spirit and courage, become shrewd in wit and bold in bearing in these unsettled times! Alas, I fear it may be best if we were to board our galleys and flee for Normandy in the face of such an uprising!''

"What, for fear of Saxons?" said De Bracy. "We need only shake our hunting spears to set these unruly boars to flight."

"A truce with your raillery, my lords," Fitzurse said. "Perhaps Your Highness would do well to assure the noble Cedric that there has been no insult intended by these good-natured jests."

"Insult?" said Prince John. "No, surely the noble Cedric perceives our humor and knows that I would not permit such insults to be offered in my presence. My lords, I fill my cup and drink to Cedric, since he will not abide our pledging his son's health."

"And to Sir Athelstane of Coningsburgh," Fitzurse said.

The guests all echoed the sentiment and drank, though Cedric and Athelstane remained visibly unappeased.

"Now, good Cedric, noble Athelstane," said John, "since we have drunk your health, is there not some Norman whose mention may at least sully your mouth, so that you might wash down with wine all bitterness?"

Cedric sat silent for a long moment, then at last raised his goblet, having made a great show of filling it.

"I have been asked to name a Norman deserving of all our praise and honor," he said. "This is not an easy task, as it requires a slave to sing the praises of his master. The beaten dog is asked to lick the hand that wields the whip. Yet I *will* name a Norman. I will name the best and noblest of his race. And those who will refuse to pledge his health, I term false and dishonored. I give you Richard the Lionhearted!"

John, who had been smiling, expecting to be named himself in a show of courtesy, now had the smile freeze upon his face. No one touched their goblets until his hand reached for his and he stood, a bit unsteadily, holding his goblet out before him.

"Richard of England," he said tonelessly. Then, after a pause, "Long may he live."

"Richard of England," echoed the other guests, all save De Bracy and Bois-Guilbert, whose goblets remained untouched upon the table.

Cedric set his goblet down, looking long and hard at Bois-Guilbert and De Bracy.

"I thank you, my lords," he said. "And now, having partaken of your hospitality, I think the time has come for us to leave. Come Athelstane, Rowena. . . . Perhaps these Normans will share some of our Saxon hospitality another time. I warrant they'll find our manner not so courtly, but I doubt our courtesies will suffer by comparison, overwhelming though their own courtesy has been."

As they passed by Lucas on their way out, he lowered his head, bowing low to Cedric.

"If you are on the road to Rotherwood, my lord," he said, "perhaps you would not mind if a poor palmer traveled with you. The hour is getting late and I hear these woods are dangerous at night."

"Come and you are welcome, pilgrim," Cedric said. "As welcome as the news you brought us of your journeys and the sights that you have seen. I find myself sore in need of some diversion on this night."

"It came to pass, just as you said it would," said de la Croix. "Maurice De Bracy was granted the Barony of Ivanhoe by Prince John and the Templar swore to meet with Sir Wilfred when and if he should return to England. I sat in wonder, watching as all came to pass as you predicted."

"Did you doubt me?" Irving said.

As they spoke, Andre was removing her armor, changing one suit for another. Irving was dressed in a black cloak, barely visible in the night where they stood among the trees.

"If I did, I shall not doubt you again," said Andre. "Perhaps, when this is over, you will predict my future. Or, better yet, do not. I am not sure I wish to know."

"I can safely predict that your future will be dim if you fail me tonight," said Irving.

"I will not fail if these men know their work." She glanced at the group of men who stood off at a distance, talking quietly among themselves. They were all equipped with daggers and longbows and dressed in suits of lincoln green.

"They are the pick of Sir Guy's men at arms," said Goldblum. "They will not fail you. Now turn around. Let's have a look at you."

Andre complied, standing erect and turning for his inspection. She was dressed in gold and carrying a shield with a flaming sword upon it.

"Excellent," said Irving. "No one will know you from De Bracy. Tonight's escapade will prove more than the local Saxons can bear. When Normans, aided by the outlaws, start attacking them and carrying off their women, they will eagerly rally to my cause when I come to rescue them from such oppression. You know what is to be done. Now mount up and ride. The Saxons have a fair head start."

7

The miserable Will Scarlet arrived back at camp hung from a pole as though the victim of a hunt. Finn ordered his two companions, Oswald and Ian, to carry him around the camp three times, which they did to the delight of the other merry men, who greeted Scarlet with hoots of derision and pelted him with sticks.

The camp itself was primitive in the extreme. Built around an ancient oak, in which was built a tiny wooden platform for one man to keep watch, the camp was situated in a grassy clearing and surrounded on all sides by thick undergrowth. The merry men lived a carefree and slovenly existence in small, poorly constructed wooden huts covered with thatch. There was one large pit dug for a cooking fire and several smaller ones, these being uncomfortably close to the highly combustible dwellings. From one of these haphazardly built shelters came a short and heavy curtal friar, a man almost as wide as he was tall. His cassock was coarse and filthy and what little hair he had was matted to his head as though plastered down by water. The friar waddled up to them and both Finn and Bobby became uncomfortably aware of the fact that he was sweating profusely. His perspiration had an overpowering smell of garlic to it.

"John! Robin! What *were* you thinking of? Disappearing like that for days on end and then entering a Norman tournament! Marion was furious when she found out!"

"So?" said Finn.

"*So?* So she'll flay you two alive, that's what's so!" said Tuck. "You had best hope her hunt's successful. If she comes home without her meat, she'll be in an evil humor."

"Whether she comes home with venison or not," said Finn, "Marion will find that there have been some changes made."

"Changes? What changes?"

Bobby put his arm around Friar Tuck's shoulders, doing his best to ignore the odor. "The time has come for us to change, Tuck," he said. "I have given it much thought. This going off on drunken binges and stumbling through the forest and falling in the brambles ill serves our cause. We saw the exercises put on by the Normans and from my days at Locksley Hall, I still recall some of the teachings of the drillmaster to our men at arms. John and I have devised some methods whereby we might all become the more efficient at the plying of our trade. We must begin to work immediately."

"Work?" said the friar. "Did he say work? Have you gone mad?" He turned from one to the other. "Has he gone mad?"

"More to the point, good friar, we have both gone sane," said Bobby.

"And what of Marion?"

"Yes, and what of Marion?" said a new voice and Finn and Bobby turned to see a small party entering the camp, two of them carrying an eight-pointer on a pole. In the vanguard of this group was a young woman dressed in lincoln green. She was perhaps nineteen or twenty years old with her dark blonde hair worn uncharacteristically short for a woman of the time. She looked like a Saxon peasant youth and only her distinctly feminine figure gave the lie to that impression. She wore two long daggers at her waist and carried a longbow in her hand, even though she looked hardly strong enough to string it.

"Godfrey, Neville, see to that stag," she said. "And as for you two springals, where the devil have you been?"

"John and I had thought to go to Ashby to watch the Normans flail at each other," Bobby said. "It seemed good for some amusement. On our way, we both became quite paralyzed with drink and, to our misfortune, we ran across some of the sheriff's men. We both barely escaped with our lives. It was a sobering experience. So sobering, in fact, that we came to the conclusion that we must bring to an end our dissolute existence. We both lay in the forest, shaking and sweating as we struggled with our demons and, at long last, the crystal clarity of true sobriety returned to us. And, with my sobriety returned, so were my long lost skills at archery, as you have doubtless heard by now."

"Do you mean to tell me that it's true that you split Hubert's shaft and won the tournament?" said Marion.

"It is the very truth," said Bobby. "And if I, who have always been the most dissolute amongst us, have so benefitted by my new abstemiousness, think what the rest of the merry men could do if kept from drink and given some direction. Why, we would be the very terror of the forests!"

"We *are* the terror of the forests!" protested Tuck.

"The only terror that we cause, good Tuck," said Bobby, "is in the rabbits and the woodcocks whose poor ears are assailed by our noise of drunken revelry. As for the gentry hereabouts, the only terror which we cause them results from fear that they might die of laughing at our bumbling prowess."

"If you were as abstemious of words as you claim to have become of drink, then I would be impressed, indeed," said Marion. "But that would be asking for the moon, no doubt. Hold out your hands."

Bobby held his hands out before him.

"They appear steady enough," said Marion, dubiously. "But I have heard this claim of temperance many times before. How long will it last this time? One day? One hour?"

"Well, wait and see," said Bobby.

Marion made a wry face. "You'll never change. You'll ever work your mouth far better than you shoot a bow. You, John, and that other wastrel, Alan-a-dale. Forever drinking yourselves blind and making up those absurd songs about yourselves. *'Robin Hood, Robin Hood, riding through the glen,' my buttocks!* You've got half the shire singing that drivel and believing it, as well. You forget that *I* know better. Singing and carousing were all you were ever good at." She chuckled. "That, and perhaps another thing or two, besides."

"Marion!" said Bobby, with a great show of indignation. "I have had a most profound experience! How can you doubt me?"

"I am to believe you *split* a shaft of Hubert's? Prince John's *finest* archer?"

"But some of the men saw it! Did they not tell you?"

"Oh, they'll say anything to please you and you know it. Am I also to believe that you had a confrontation with my husband's men and came away to speak of it?"

Bobby glanced at Finn. "Your husband?"

"Are you now forgetting the very lies that crossed your lips mere moments ago?" she said. "Did you or did you not claim to have met the sheriff's men and lived to tell the tale?"

"Oh, well, yes, of course . . ." said Bobby, trying desperately to recover. *Marion was married to the Sheriff of Nottingham?*

"Oh, you're contemptible!" she said. "I ought to thrash you!" Then she smiled. "But just the same, I'm glad to have you back. I will forgive you if you come give me a kiss."

Bobby smiled as she held her arms out to him and he approached her, pleased to note as he did so that she took at least some pains to keep herself clean, for while there was a slight musky smell about her, she did not stink anywhere near so badly as did Tuck. She put her arms around him and kissed him energetically, but the moment they broke the kiss, she hauled off and smashed a right into his jaw.

Bobby staggered and almost fell.

"What was *that* for?"

"You never kissed that well before! Where have you been taking lessons?"

Finn burst out laughing.

"You find it funny, do you, John?" she said, advancing toward him, her right hand going to the hilt of one of her long daggers. When he wouldn't stop laughing, she drew the dagger and waved it at him threateningly. "Stop your laughing, or so help me, I'll—"

Finn quickly pivoted on the ball of his left foot, bringing his right foot around in a lightning fast spinning wheel kick. He caught her knife hand just at the wrist and the dagger went flying out of her grasp. For a moment, she stared at him, stunned, then she furiously drew the other dagger and lunged at him. Finn trapped her wrist, then using her arm as a lever against her, he casually flipped her. She fell flat on her back. The other merry men stared at him with their jaws hanging open. It was the first time in their lives they had ever seen a demonstration of the Oriental martial arts.

Marion got up slowly, rubbing her hip. "Where did you

learn *that* trick?'' she said, no longer angry.

Finn shrugged. "It's no great feat," he said. "It is a way of fighting they have in the East. It was taught to me and Robin by a knight returned from the Crusades."

"A knight! Why would a knight bother with a Saxon outlaw?"

"This was a Saxon knight," said Bobby. "We met him at the tournament. He was much impressed with the way I handle a longbow and offered to teach me and John some of the art of this foreign way of fighting in return for instructing him in archery."

"*You* taught a knight the longbow?" she said, astonished.

"Well, it was not completely foreign to him, being a Saxon," Bobby said. "And he already had some skill with a crossbow."

"*You* taught him? *You?*"

"John, I don't think she believes me," Bobby said.

Finn shrugged. "Show her."

Bobby strung his bow. He looked at Marion and grinned. "What shall we shoot at?"

"I think you're starting to believe your own fantastic boasts," she said. "You could never beat me."

"Ah, but that was before I gave up drinking," Bobby said.

Marion strung her own bow. "I see it's time to put you in your place again," she said. "Very well." She nocked an arrow and, choosing a stout oak tree on the far side of the camp, she drew her bow back and let fly. The arrow sailed across the camp, narrowly missing one of the men who had just exited his hut. He yelped and dove back inside. The arrow struck the tree trunk and stuck there.

"Right," said Marion. "Let's see how close you can place your shaft to mine. Perhaps you'll even split it as you did Hubert's." She laughed, mockingly.

Bobby removed his quiver from his shoulder, handing it to John.

"Hold that for me, will you, Little John?"

Finn winked at Bobby as Bobby drew out a black arrow. With Bobby standing between him and Marion, Finn reached into the quiver and drew out the little black box.

"A black arrow?" Marion said.

"A new idea of mine," said Bobby. "I thought to have all the merry men use black arrows."

"Why?"

"To strike fear into the hearts of our enemies, to mark that the arrow comes from one of Robin Hood's merry men."

"Ah, I see," said Marion, with mock gravity. "Perhaps we should all wear some sort of crest upon our chests, as well? Crossed black arrows upon a cask of ale?"

By way of an answer, Bobby nocked the arrow, first taking care to quickly disarm it, drew the bow back to his ear, and let it fly. The black box did the rest. Marion's arrow was neatly split.

The merry men cheered, throwing their caps into the air and pounding one another on the back. Marion stared at him with total disbelief.

"I could not believe that story about your winning the tournament," she said, "yet now I see it with my own two eyes! You really *can* shoot!"

"And you doubted me," said Bobby.

Marion unstrung her bow, then swung it with both hands. It whistled through the air and struck Bobby on the side of his head.

"*Jesus!*" He clapped his hand to his left ear, wincing with pain. "Are you crazy?"

"*All this time, you could shoot so well, and yet you deprived me of such marksmanship by being a drunkard!*" She grabbed him by the hair and shook his head furiously. "*If I ever see you touch a drop of drink again, God be my judge, you'll live out the remainder of your life a gelding!*"

She shoved him away from her, then turned to face the merry men, who all instantly grew silent.

"Tomorrow, we start to learn these new tricks of fighting," she said. "And from this moment on, any man who cannot hold his drink will be hung up by his thumbs! Neither are you excluded, Tuck, holy friar or not." She stalked off to her lean-to, but paused and turned around before entering. "One more thing," she said. "From now on, we use black arrows."

The merry men glared balefully at Finn and Bobby.

"Well, how about that?" said Bobby.

"She sure is some kind of lady," Finn said.

"What kind is that?"

Finn grinned. "I guess you'll find out tonight."

"I have a feeling we're not very popular around here right this minute," Bobby said.

Finn nodded. "We'll be even less popular tomorrow morning, when I start in on these rampant specimens of manhood."

"We may have some desertions," Bobby said.

Finn shook his head. "I don't think so."

"Why not?"

"Because the only alternative to us is honest work."

"Good point."

"*Robin!*"

"I think the lady's calling you."

"*Robin!*"

Bobby sighed. "Lousy army."

Finn chuckled. "It's a living."

Cedric didn't make it easy.

Lucas was waiting for the right moment to confront him, but the old man began ranting about the "Norman dogs" the moment they left the castle. There wasn't a pause in his tirade until they had reached the edge of the forest. By that time, he had commented extensively upon the ancestries of all the Normans present at the banquet, excluding Andre de la Croix, who, conceded Cedric, was at the very least a better mannered knight than the rest of "those swine from Normandy."

"That despicable Templar is the worst of their lot!" said Cedric, showing not the slightest sign of winding down. "If I were a younger man, I would have it out with him upon the field of battle! Athelstane, you should have split his skull! No, no, it was well that you didn't. Never let it be said that a Saxon drew sword upon his host, no matter what the provocation! We must see to it that his skull is split at the very next opportunity, however. Would that the white knight had split it for him! Oh, how my heart sang when I saw how well he humbled them! Would that I knew who he was so I could hold a great feast in his honor!"

Seeing his chance, Lucas quickly said, "I can tell you who this white knight is, my lord."

"*What, you know him?*" Cedric reined in his horse and slipped a small golden bracelet off his wrist. "Good palmer, I will give you this bracelet if you name him to me!"

"Keep your bracelet, my lord. I will proudly do you this service without payment. This white knight was a Saxon who had gone off to fight for the Holy Land with *Coeur-de-Lion*."

"Ha! I *knew* he was a Saxon! I cannot say that I hold with

any true Saxon going off to fight in foreign lands while his own nation is held hostage, but for the way he unhorsed those Norman bastards, I forgive him!''

"Then forgive your son, my lord," said Lucas, "for his name is Ivanhoe."

"No! It cannot be! I *have* no son!"

Lucas pulled back his cowl. "I plead your forgiveness, Father. Can you find it in your heart to take your son back?"

"*You!*"

Rowena gave a small shriek and almost fell from her saddle. At that moment, de la Croix attacked.

The first thing Lucas became aware of when he came to was that his head was throbbing. He put his hand to his forehead and was surprised to encounter a bandage. He was also surprised to find himself lying in a bed. He gradually became aware of his surroundings. He was in a small wooden cabin with a planked floor. There were shutters on the windows and these shutters were closed, but there was light inside the cabin. He moved his head slightly and saw a light bulb hanging from the ceiling. There was music in the cabin. A Bartok concerto for the recorder. He sat up quickly and immediately collapsed back on the bed with a groan.

"Take it easy there, pilgrim," said a man's voice. "You've had a nasty crack on the head and you've got a concussion."

Lucas looked up and saw the man bending over him. He looked like an old man at first, but then Lucas realized that what gave that impression was his extremely long hair, which was streaked with gray, and his long, full beard. The face behind the foliage was youthful and the blue eyes were clear and bright. The man wore a long, clean, beautifully embroidered velvet caftan. There were dragons on both sides of his chest, their tails curling down to his knees. When the man turned around to pick up something from the table, Lucas saw that the back of the caftan was embroidered with the words "Hong Kong."

"Here you go, pilgrim. Have some chicken soup. It's good for what ails you."

"Jesus, I'm hallucinating," Lucas said.

The man in the caftan pursed his lips. "Don't think so. I can fix that, though. I've got some dynamite acid here from 1969, that oughtta do the trick. But with you being in the shape you're in, I don't think a trip would be such a good idea.''

Lucas sat up, much more slowly this time. The man sat down on the bed with the bowl of soup in his hand. He spooned out some of it and fed it to Lucas.

Lucas swallowed the hot broth. "Who the hell are you?"

"Name's Hunter," said the man. "Lieutenant Reese Hunter, late of the U.S.T.C. Here, have some more soup."

"Where am I? What am I doing here? What happened?"

"Just relax and eat your soup, son. We'll take things one at a time, okay?"

Lucas nodded and opened his mouth as another spoonful approached.

"Answer to number one: You're in my cabin. We're smack dab in the middle of the woods here, you can barely get around without a machete. It's not that bad, actually, but we're off the beaten track and no one's likely to bother us. As for answer number two, what you're doing here is recovering from the answer to number three, which I can only take a wild stab at, but as near as I can tell, it appears that your head sideswiped a mace. I found you wandering around out there in shock and I brought you in and sewed you up."

"How'd you know I was a—"

"Whoever hit you not only busted you up pretty well," said Hunter, "they also smashed your implant. I'm a pretty decent surgeon, which is a lucky thing for you, and I removed it. I'll show it to you if you like, but the little suckers are tiny and your vision probably isn't going to be so hot for a while."

"You're an observer," Lucas said.

Hunter laughed. "Oh, no, not me. I'm through with that gig. I'm just a plain old citizen."

"I don't understand."

"I'm a deserter."

"I don't believe it."

"It's the truth. See, I just sort of . . . well, retired, you might say. I take it you're here on an adjustment."

Lucas nodded.

"I figured as much. There's some kind of circus going on back here, a real crazy merry-go-round. They've been sending people back and forth and back and forth, I mean, it's really frantic. At first, I figured maybe they were on my trail, but that just didn't add up, so the only other answer had to be a threatened timeline split. That's a bad deal, friend. Heavy business. Standard duty's bad enough, but an adjustment on a split, that could be a real killer. If you're smart, you'll just throw in with me and take a real long vacation. You're KIA now, with your implant out. They'll never trace you. I've got a pretty nice set-up here, all the comforts of home. I could do with some company. What do you say?"

Lucas looked slowly around the cabin and, at first glance, he took in the sound system, the microwave oven, the holovision and the cassette file, thousands of books, a reading lamp and chair, several Persian rugs, racks of pipes with tobacco humidors beside them . . .

"How on earth did you . . ." His voice trailed off as the answer became obvious.

"What, all this stuff?" said Hunter. "No sweat. I've got a chronoplate."

8

The sheriff sat at the table in his chambers at Nottingham Castle, scratching his head and frowning. He poured himself another goblet of wine to help him think. He was an extremely large man and very muscular, a giant by the standards of his time. He towered over the man who paced the floor in his chambers, but that did not change the fact that this man intimidated him. The sheriff scratched his square, clean-shaven jaw and his slate gray eyes never left the pacing man. Richard had changed since he had returned from the Crusades. The sheriff, who was senior to his king in age (or so he thought) by a good ten years, decided that fighting Saladin had matured Richard. Always fiery, fierce and impetuous, the Lion Heart was now tempered with maturity. He had developed cunning and a cold, methodical ruthlessness that impressed him greatly.

"Damn me for a dullard, Sire, I *still* don't understand," he said.

Irving, dressed as the black knight, although sans his armor, stopped his pacing for a moment. He looked at the sheriff much the way a patient schoolteacher might gaze upon an inordinately slow pupil.

"All right, Guy. I shall explain it once again, but listen carefully this time. John has obtained a great deal of power in my absence. He now holds both York and Ashby and he has

reassigned the lands of many of my faithful knights to his own
followers. He has his own men at arms, whose number he has
significantly increased, as well as the lances of De Bracy and
his Free Companions. He also has the formidable Templar,
Bois-Guilbert, in his good graces and Sir Brian has but to snap
his fingers and the knights at the Preceptory of Templestowe
will be at his beck and call. John has granted them complete
autonomy within their province and they will be anxious to
protect their interests against me. My differences with the
Knights Templars and the Knights of St. John in the Holy
Land will not aid my cause.

"I have my loyal followers," he continued. "I have Andre
de la Croix in John's camp; I have you, Sir Guy, and your well
trained men at arms, but we are still vastly outnumbered. I
cannot afford to take direct action against my brother at this
time. There are yet other forces about who seek to bring us
down. The time to strike is not yet ripe. You and I must make
it so."

"This much I understand," the sheriff said, "but I do not
see the purpose served by the abduction of this Saxon and his
party. Will it not serve to alienate the people from our cause?"

"Oh, *think*, Guy, for pity's sake!" said Irving. "To what
end does de la Croix impersonate De Bracy? How do you
think the people will respond when it becomes known that De
Bracy, John's paid vassal, attacked a Saxon lord, carrying off
not only Cedric, but Athelstane and Rowena, the last of the
royal Saxon lines? For what reason did your men at arms who
accompanied Sir Andre wear lincoln green?"

"It would make them appear as outlaws," Guy said. "But
then, if you want it thought that outlaws did the deed, why
dress Sir Andre as De Bracy?"

"*Think*, Guy! Must I explain everything to you?"

The sheriff put on a heavy expression of concentration.

"Stop that," Irving said. "You look as though you're suf-
fering from piles."

The sheriff stopped frowning and shrugged.

Irving sighed. "Very well. I will explain it to you. And you
will feel heartily ashamed for not seeing it yourself. Why is it
that you have had so little success in bringing the Saxon
outlaws to justice?"

"Because they are led by the cleverest shrew who ever—"

"Spare me. I have no desire to hear of your marital difficulties. They enjoy their liberty only because they know the forests better than your men at arms and because they are supported by the people, who see them as figures of romance.''

''Yes, I've heard those silly songs about their robbing from the rich and giving to the poor,'' said Guy. ''Alan-a-dale should be hung for his minstrelcy if for nothing else. Yet, those songs always fail to mention that these wolf's heads deduct a goodly percentage of their plunder for themselves.''

''Be that as it may,'' said Irving, ''the people love them because they rob the Normans. The Saxons are taxed into penury and they are grateful to see their oppressors suffer any disadvantage. Occasionally, these outlaws might beard some wealthy Saxon, but it is another thing entirely if it should become known that they have taken to working hand in hand with mercenary knights, abducting Saxon women and holding them for ransom. And rest assured, we will make it known. In such an event, the affection that the people bear these outlaws would begin to wane somewhat, would it not?''

''How does that help us?'' said Sir Guy.

''It prepares the people to greet us with open arms when we come to free them from such tyranny,'' said Irving. ''It also puts the forest outlaws at a disadvantage. They would have to prove themselves innocent. What better way to do this than to confront De Bracy?''

''But Sir Maurice will deny it all.''

''Do you expect the Saxons to believe him?''

''So while De Bracy and his Free Companions are beset by outlaws, we move against Prince John with the odds for our success being much improved.''

''There, you see? Was that so difficult to reason out?''

''But there still remains a problem,'' said Sir Guy. ''Cedric and his party will know the truth of the matter.''

''Will they?'' Irving said. ''Even as we speak, de la Croix delivers Cedric and his party to Nottingham Castle. The Saxons will be bound and blindfolded. They will have no idea where they are. Andre de la Croix, in the guise of Sir Maurice, will see to it that they are safely locked away within our dungeons. They will never know that it was not De Bracy who had taken them.''

''But surely De Bracy will have some response when he is accused?'' the sheriff said.

''What does that matter? By that time, it will be too late. Of course, there is always the possibility that the truth will eventually emerge. But then, the dead do not tell tales, do they? The prisoners will have to be dispatched when the time comes. It is regrettable, but their lives will have to be forfeit to affairs of state. We are fighting for a throne and the welfare of England is at stake. As for De Bracy, you leave him to de la Croix."

The sheriff shook his head in admiration. "You seem to have thought of everything, Sire."

"Not quite everything," said Irving. "At least, not yet. There are other matters I must see to presently, for which purpose I must now retire and contemplate. See to it that I am not disturbed."

"As you command, Sire."

Irving left the sheriff and made his way to his private chambers in the castle tower. His remark to Sir Guy had not been merely an excuse; he needed time to think. He was growing worried. He reached his chambers and closed the door behind him, then shot the bolt. Wearily, he threw himself down upon the bed.

He had to tread with extreme care. If possible, he needed to take at least one of the adjustment team alive. That opportunity had not yet presented itself. He needed enough time to make the snatch, and to convey one of them to Nottingham, where he could use the fine equipment in the dungeons to discover the location of the adjustment referee. Once he accomplished that, it would all be over. But he had to be extremely careful. He had failed each time before. The men had died before divulging the necessary information.

His past was absolute. He knew that clocking back once more would not create a paradox if history remained unchanged. Yet, that was the very game that he was playing. He had to be supremely cautious, staying within the limits he had set for himself.

He knew that small actions taken in the past were canceled out in the flow of time. Any small ripple in the timeline became evened out through the inertia of the flow. Traveling back into the past and taking an action that would significantly change history, or clocking back to confront oneself would cause a more significant ripple in the timestream. At that point, the timeline would be split, creating an alternate timeline running parallel with the absolute past. Each such instance created yet another parallel timeline and, theoretically, this could go on *ad infinitum*. However, a split timeline had to eventually rejoin. This action would occur at some point beyond the action taken to create the split.

This was what Mensinger had cited in his famous work on "The Fate Factor." He had used the "grandfather paradox" to illustrate his point. The grandfather paradox postulated a fascinating dilemma, a riddle that had not been solved until Mensinger had proved the potential for parallel timelines. The paradox stated that if you went back into the past and altered the history of your grandfather, killing him before he ever met your grandmother, then he would never have met and married your grandmother. Your father, then, would not have been born and, consequently, *you* would not have been born. And if you were never born, how could you go back into the past to kill your grandfather?

Conventional wisdom had held that it was impossible to create such a paradox, at least until Mensinger had proved that it was. It had been believed that since you *were* born and since your past was absolute, something in the past would have prevented your taking your grandfather's life. However, given the potential for parallel timelines, it was very possible, indeed.

Mensinger hypothesized that if you went back into the past to kill your grandfather and succeeded in so doing, the action would create a ripple in the timestream, a split in the timeline. Since there had to exist an absolute past in which your grandfather did *not* die, a past in which he met your grandmother, married her and procreated your father, which action led to your own birth; *that* past was absolute for you taking the action and could not be changed, since the past had to occur before you took action to change it. Once you took that action, a parallel timeline was created, one in which your grandfather had died. These two timelines, the one which represented your absolute past and the one which you had created by your action, ran parallel to one another in a linear fashion.

Yet, these two timelines had to rejoin at some point in the future. The danger therein lay in the fact that in the timeline in which your grandfather had died, there existed the distinct possibility that your grandmother would marry someone else. She could very possibly give birth to someone other than your father, which action progressively led to other events. Theoretically, wrote Mensinger, the timelines would become re-joined when the traveler to the past returned to the future (or the present) from which he came. However, he wrote, given some common degree of longevity on the part of the two grandmothers in the parallel timelines, when these timelines rejoined, there existed the possibility that grandmother would be duplicated, sharing with her twin an absolute past prior to the split. This raised all sorts of fascinating possibilities.

Mensinger's "Fate Factor" came into play at the point at which the split in the timeline was created. The moment that the action taken to create the split occurred, the future was in flux, creating an infinite number of potential scenarios. Any disruption in the timestream, like eddies caused by throwing a rock into the water, had to eventually respond to the inertia of the flow. The inertia of time, on the grand scale, worked to minimize the effects of such disruptions. This was the "Fate Factor." However, according to Mensinger, the grand scale in terms of time was not necessarily what would be defined as a grand scale in human terms. Disasters on the human scale were possible. Significant changes at the point of the rejoining could occur.

Irving had thought that he had spotted a flaw in Mensinger's theory. He had become obsessed with it. Mensinger had postulated that parallel timelines would rejoin when the traveler to the past returned to the time from which he came. In such an instance, the rejoining of the timelines would most likely have abrupt and jarring effects. However, what would happen if the traveler to the past *did not return at all* to the time from which he came? Suppose this traveler lived out the remainder of his life in the parallel timeline which he created. Would it not be possible, in that event, for the timelines to eventually rejoin at some point far beyond the point from which the time traveler departed? On the grand scale of time, there had to be a point at which past history was insignificant, unknown completely to the people living in that time, much as the history of man in his most primitive stages was totally unknown to modern scholars. Under such circumstances, could history not be changed to the benefit of all mankind? Irving had discussed his theory with other referees, which he now knew had been a great mistake. He had expected that they would agree with him wholeheartedly, but such had not been the case. They had argued that taking such an action could have disastrous consequences, that he had misinterpreted Mensinger's work. In order for his theory to prove valid, they had argued, it would be necessary for him to exert a continuous influence upon the timeline. Even though, as he hypothesized, he would travel into the past never to return, the parallel timelines would have to come together the moment his splitting influence ceased to become a factor. The moment that he died, they said, the rejoining would occur. There was no chance of the grand scale split which he proposed.

He could not accept that. He could not accept that his influence, the role that he had played, would end with his demise. They were wrong. He would *prove* them wrong.

The single mistake that he had made was in sharing his theory with the other referees. They were fools, bogged down in their bureaucratic roles, interpreting the moves of pawns upon time's chessboard. They shook as if with ague at the very possibility of an upset in the flow. They were totally incapable of making the intuitive leap that was so necessary to the great discovery. As had always happened in the past, they—with their feet firmly planted in the mud—decried the attempts that he, the visionary, made to transcend the boundaries of ignorance. Genius is never appreciated in its own time, thought Irving. He chuckled. He had put a new slant on that cliche.

Once he became the king, once the interference of the adjustment teams was ended, there would be no limit to what he could accomplish. He never should have told them, never. He had given them ammunition against himself, warned them of what might happen. They had been prepared to move against him and they *had* moved against him before he could affect the changes he had planned. If he was not careful, very careful, if he made even one mistake, they could still win.

But he would not make any mistakes.

Hooker was convinced that something had gone wrong.

The plan had been for Lucas to secure a place in Cedric's party and, at the very first opportunity, to reveal himself as Ivanhoe to Cedric. Whichever way things went from there, whether Cedric would forgive his "son" following his change of heart or whether he would remain intractable, Lucas was not to continue on to Rotherwood, but to return to Isaac's house and to reclaim his squire and armor. He was to repay Isaac the loan plus the interest—which was exceedingly high, doubtless owing less to Isaac's greed than to the fact that John was bleeding him dry—and from there they were to proceed to Sherwood for a rendezvous with Finn and Bobby. Ideally, if those two had managed to establish their position with the merry men, they would then use them to make inquiries concerning the whereabouts of the black knight.

But Lucas was overdue.

He should have been back by morning or, at the latest, by the afternoon. Now it was growing dark outside and Lucas still had not returned. Something must have happened.

He had to get his hands on the nysteel armor. The only problem was, Isaac was jealously protecting it. There was an additional problem in that he didn't have a horse. Finding a horse presented no great difficulty, but he still had to get away from Isaac. Technically, he was Isaac's property for the duration, until Lucas came to redeem him. As such, he was Isaac's guest, kept in a small room that was sparse and spartan, although clean. Bondsmen, as the collar on his neck identified him, were notorious for running away at first opportunity. His station was somewhat better than that of the average bondsman in that he served a knight, but he was still that knight's property. Isaac treated him well, seeing to it that he was fed and comfortable, which cost had been included in the interest, but Isaac felt that it was his responsibility to see to it that Hooker was still there when the white knight came to call for his belongings. He had two choices. He could escape and search for Lucas on his own, or he could attempt to persuade Isaac to assist him.

The latter prospect did not seem to present an insurmountable problem. Isaac had been planning on journeying back to York. He would have been en route already had not Lucas presented him with a business opportunity, one that promised not to delay him overlong. The story Lucas had given Isaac had not been too far from the truth, at least insofar as their cover story was concerned. He had told Isaac that he had family nearby, which would be Cedric, and that since he had enemies among the Normans, he had to contact his family discreetly. The vow which he had taken would be fulfilled when he once again rejoined his family and then he could reveal himself in his true identity. Isaac had accepted that. Vows were very much in vogue and many of them seemed peculiar. They served, more often than not, merely to lend an air of glamor to the knights who took them. If Isaac could be persuaded that something had happened to Lucas, perhaps he would begin his journey to York, taking Hooker and the armor with him and retracing the route that Lucas was to have taken. The merchant would not travel alone. He would hire porters and guards, thereby making the trip safer not only for himself but for Hooker as well. After seeing his own corpse, Hooker had no desire to remain alone and vulnerable.

Asking Isaac directly did not seem to be the best course to take. It would be better to work on the young Rebecca.

She came to see him when she brought his meals. It was a function that should have been delegated to a servant, but Rebecca had her own reasons for bringing him his food herself. She wanted to find out more about the mysterious white knight, the handsome stranger who had defeated all the Normans at the tournament and who acted like no knight she had ever seen, quoting the prophet Isaiah in Hebrew.

At first, Hooker thought that revealing his knowledge of Hebrew had been a mistake for Lucas. Time commandos routinely had to speak in many different languages, which was facilitated by the implant programming. It became quite automatic, so that a soldier could not only speak in virtually any language, but think in it as well. It was imperative to a soldier's survival. Lucas might not even have intended to speak in Hebrew. Given such linguistic versatility, it was easy to slip if caught off guard. The natural tendency, if reciting a quotation, would be to do so in the original language rather than to translate it. It was the sort of thing soldiers had to be on guard against. But Rebecca was more than enough to catch anyone off guard.

She was, quite simply, the most beautiful woman Hooker had ever laid eyes on. He was still young, not yet a true veteran of the time wars and his service had been such that he had not had anything in the way of significant contact with women on the Minus side. He was used to modern women. The demure Rebecca, whose mercurial temper he had caught a glimpse of when she had chased off the physicians who had wanted to bleed Lucas, was quite unlike anyone he had ever met. One moment, she displayed all the spirit and vitality of the modern woman, the next, she was reserved and shy, a woman all too aware of the place she had been relegated to not only by her sex, but by her faith. She was a woman, real, tangible and indisputably human, but at the same time, she was to Hooker an embodiment of a romantic memory, a product of a simpler and more ethereal time. To the impressionable young corporal, she represented the romance which he had sought when he enlisted in the Temporal Corps. And, reality not withstanding, he was falling in love with her.

"How did your master learn the Hebrew tongue?" she asked him. "It is not knowledge one gains quickly. On your oath, now, speak the truth! Can it be that the white knight is, indeed, a Jew?"

"A Jew!" said Hooker. "How would a Jew come to embrace knighthood?"

"I do not know," she said. "It is a mystery. Yet, even though it is forbidden, it is not unheard of for a Jew to enter into a union outside the faith. A powerful love could perhaps accomplish such a thing, although it would be wrong. If a child were born of a Jewish father and a mother who was not a Jewess, then, in the eyes of our faith, that child would not be a true Jew. Our people have been sorely used and . . . " she blushed, "it sometimes came to pass that a child would be born of . . . of force and the father would not be known."

"But my master's father *is* known," said Hooker. "And Cedric the Saxon is no Jew."

"Cedric the Saxon! So your master *is* a Saxon, then!"

"Rebecca, I have already said too much," said Hooker.

"Oh, Poignard, I beg you, tell me his name! The secret would be safe with me. I would carry it with me to my grave if such were your master's wishes, on my God, I swear it!"

Hooker took her hand. "Very well, then, Rebecca, I will tell you. And you need not swear, for I believe you are in earnest. My master has long been away on the Crusades, fighting with the king to free the Holy Land. In truth, he does not speak Hebrew, he has but some knowledge of the tongue. He consoled himself with studies, learning what he could upon his travels to keep his mind from brooding, because he had a broken heart. Cedric was ill pleased when his son chose to follow Richard, for Cedric is a prideful Saxon and he does not love the Normans. But my master saw that Richard was a fair and noble man and that he thought of English people as his subjects, to be treated equally, not as Normans superior to Saxons. A people can only be strong when they are unified. Richard went to free the Holy Land because he felt that it was just and right. Cedric thinks only of freeing Saxons from the Normans.''

"So he has displeased his father and his heart is broken," said Rebecca.

"His heart was broken because his love was doomed," said Hooker, hating himself for manipulating her. "My master was in love with Cedric's ward, Rowena, who is promised to another.''

"You say he *was* in love?" Rebecca said, unable to hide the note of hope in her voice.

"Perhaps it was merely lust, though it is truly not my place to say," said Hooker. "Forbidden fruit sometimes seems sweeter. My master has come home a tired, but wiser man. He now understands that there are more important things than lustful passions.''

"You still have not told me his name," Rebecca said. "Cedric the Saxon is unknown to me. I do not know by what name he calls his son.''

"Wilfred," Hooker said. "Wilfred of Ivanhoe. A noble knight to whom the king, in recognition of his service, has granted a barony. Yet, with Richard away, Prince John has seized the reins of power and has taken away the lands of many of Richard's faithful knights. Just as Prince John steals from Isaac, taking loans which are really tribute, so he has stolen from my master. Ivanhoe has come to aid the king in getting back his throne and, should his identity be known, John and his followers would try to stop him. Even now, Rebecca, I fear for his safety. He should have returned by now. He has gone to secure from Cedric his pardon and the monies to repay your father's loan. I fear something has happened to him. Perhaps he was attacked by outlaws, or thrown from his horse to lie senseless on the road somewhere. And here I sit, unable to go and search for him or help him!''

"Then you must depart at once," Rebecca said. "Find him, Poignard!''

"I cannot," said Hooker, averting his eyes. He couldn't look at her. She was so obviously infatuated with Lucas and he was using that against her. It wasn't fair. If she only felt that way for him, he'd desert the service, convert to Judaism and . . . but that was unthinkable. He had to control his emotions. He was a soldier and he had a job to do.

"But you *must* go seek him out!" Rebecca said.

"I am given in pledge to your father, along with my master's arms," said Hooker. "If I were to leave now, I would be an escaped bondsman and the penalty for that is severe."

"My father would not declare you outlaw," said Rebecca. "Who would listen to a Jew? And I would make him understand that—"

"It is no use, Rebecca," Hooker said. "I cannot go. My master has given his word that I will remain with Isaac and remain I must."

"Perhaps there is another way," Rebecca said. "We must go to York. We would have left already had not my father business with Sir Wilfred. We could leave at once and take the same road taken by your master. That way, if he is somewhere injured on the road, we would be sure to find him. And if not, we could leave word here for him to seek us out at York. Since you would remain with us, your master's pledge would not be broken and we could inquire about him on the way."

"But would Isaac do this?" Hooker said.

"I will convince him," said Rebecca. "Surely, he will see that he has more to gain by such an act and, if Wilfred is in trouble, it is only right that we should try to aid him. If King Richard is, indeed, as fair and noble as you say, perhaps he would treat us more kindly than does his brother, John."

"If you help Ivanhoe, then you help Richard," Hooker said. "And you will find that the king will not be ungrateful."

"I will go and speak to my father at once," Rebecca said.

When she had left, Hooker sighed and looked miserably at the food which she had brought him. Suddenly, he had no appetite.

Maurice De Bracy and Brian de Bois-Guilbert rode slowly with a small company of men on the road that led through the forest to Torquilstone. They were in a festive mood. The sun was high and so were their spirits. De Bracy planned yet another banquet, to celebrate his new status as lord of the manor at Torquilstone. They had been riding for several hours when they came upon an unusual scene.

It was Isaac of York and his party, or what had been his party. Lacking men at arms to insure the loyalty of the guards and porters he had hired, Isaac had been taken by his retainers. He had paid them half the sum in advance, the rest to be paid upon the safe delivery of himself and his goods, but these men felt that half the sum left them ahead of the game if they did not have to chance running across the outlaws of the forest. They had managed to make off with the horses and most of his belongings, but not without a price. Hooker had accounted for three of them before being wounded himself. What De Bracy and Bois-Guilbert beheld was a scene consisting of three corpses with daggers protruding from them, Hooker sitting on the ground and being tended to by Rebecca, and Isaac standing in the middle of the road and wailing.

"It is that Jew, Isaac of York," De Bracy said, "and the woman is his daughter, she to whom that white-garbed Saxon knight paid tribute at the tournament. The man who is with them I know not."

"Oh, gallant knights," wailed Isaac, running up to them and wringing his hands, "take pity on a poor Jew who has been robbed and abandoned on this lonely road! My hired porters have taken flight, fleeing with my worldly goods, leaving myself and my daughter at the mercy of the forest brigands! Surely, it is your Christian duty to stop and give aid to such as we, for—"

"Dog of an infidel!" said De Bracy. "You speak to us of Christian duty? You of that accursed race who killed Our Saviour? What care I if you've been robbed, you who have robbed so many with your usury?"

Isaac looked stricken. "No, no, valiant lords, I did not mean to give offence! Please do not desert poor stranded travelers such as we!" He clutched at De Bracy's stirrup. "We must make our way to York and if only—"

De Bracy kicked him away. "To hell with you and your whole tribe! Count yourself lucky that I do not run you down for daring to lay hands upon me!"

Bois-Guilbert reached over and touched De Bracy on the shoulder. "Hold your temper, Maurice. Let us not be too hasty, lest we waste an opportunity. This Jew is rich. It would only be our Christian duty to relieve him of his ill-gotten gains. Why not take him to Torquilstone and there make him pay ransom for his freedom?"

The color drained from Isaac's face and his mouth worked soundlessly.

"Why not, indeed?" De Bracy said. "And since we found this dog together, we can split the prize."

Bois-Guilbert smiled. "I will offer you a bargain, Maurice.

Take this offal and do with him what you will to pry his riches from him. For myself, I would lay sole claim to the pretty Jewess to warm my bed at Torquilstone.''

"Done," said De Bracy.

"No! No!" screamed Isaac. "I beg you, take me and do with me what you will, but spare my daughter! Do not dishonor a helpless maiden! I beseech you, do not bring her to ruin and humiliation! She is the very image of my deceased Rachael, the last of the six pledges of her love! Would you deprive a widowed father of his sole remaining comfort? Would you soil—"

"Be still, you whining baggage!" said De Bracy, leaning down and fetching Isaac a tremendous clout upon the head. Isaac fell to the ground, unconscious.

Sitting where he was, Hooker could not hear the exchange between Isaac and the two knights, but he recognized De Bracy and Bois-Guilbert at the head of their party and knew there could be trouble. When he heard Isaac start shouting and then saw him brought down, he knew trouble had arrived.

"Rebecca, run!" he said.

"No! I cannot leave my father!"

He struggled to his feet and pulled her, trying to get her to flee into the forest with him. Once they reached the protection of the woods, there was still a chance that, on foot, they might elude the more encumbered mounted men, but Rebecca resisted him with all her strength.

"No, I cannot abandon him, I tell you! You run, Poignard, and save yourself!"

"Hold!" cried Bois-Guilbert, riding up to them. They were quickly surrounded. "You," he said, pointing to Hooker, "what is your name?"

"I am called Poignard, my lord," said Hooker.

"You are a bondsman. How is it that you travel with this Jew?"

"He has been left with my father as a surety for the repayment of a loan," Rebecca said, "along with some possessions belonging to his master, a Norman fallen on hard times."

"What is your master's name, Poignard?" said Bois-Guilbert.

"Philip of Doncaster, my lord," said Hooker, improvising quickly.

"I do not know him. These three men," he pointed at the corpses, "you killed them?"

"He fought to protect his master's goods, my lord," Rebecca said. "He saved them and the mule which bears them and was wounded in his efforts."

"Your master is fortunate in having such a faithful bondsman," said the Templar. "Take his goods and go. Tell your master that Sir Brian de Bois-Guilbert has released him from his obligation."

"Wait, Brian!" called De Bracy. He came riding up to them with two young men beside him. He turned to his and the Templar's squires. "Are you certain this is the man?"

"There is no doubt, milord," said De Bracy's squire. "I recall that scar upon his face."

Bois-Guilbert's squire nodded. "It is the same man," he said. "The white knight's squire."

Bois-Guilbert leaned down, reaching out to the sole remaining mule and ripping away some of the rough cloth that was lashed over the load. The nysteel armor was revealed. He tore away the cloth and there was the shield with the uprooted oak upon it.

"A Norman fallen on hard times, you said?"

Rebecca looked away.

Hooker's heart sank. All he could think of was that vision of himself lying dead upon the ground, his head nearly severed from his shoulders.

9 ━━━━━━━━━━━━━━━━━━━━

Hunter poured Lucas a cup of tea and himself a glass of bourbon. "I'd offer you some of the good stuff," he said, "but you'd best take it easy for a while."

"This is amazing," Lucas said, slowly sipping the hot tea. "You've got Chinese tea and Kentucky bourbon, recordings of Bartok, Vivaldi, The Rolling Stones and P.J. Proby, Castello and Mastro De Paja pipes, Senior Service cigarettes, vintage Margeaux wine. . . ."

"I've always had a taste for the old-fashioned things," said Hunter with a note of pride, unable to conceal his pleasure at having a guest who could appreciate his acquisitions. "Would you care for a pipe?"

"Thank you, I would."

Hunter selected one for him, passing it to him along with a pouch of English blend tobacco, a mixture of the finest Oriental and Havana leaves. Lucas examined the pipe. It was a briar, a billiard shape, perfectly straight grained. He checked the stamping.

"This is a 1917 Dunhill," said Lucas. "It's almost brand new!"

"Picked it up in London not too long ago," said Hunter.

"How did it happen?" Lucas said. "What are you *doing* here?"

"Okay, I'll give you the abridged version," Hunter said. "I was floater-clocked into this time period with the 82nd Airborne."

Lucas nodded. He should have guessed as much when Hunter said he had a chronoplate. The 82nd Airborne had a long and extremely colorful history, dating back thousands of years. Once a crack division of paratroopers, the 82nd was now a floater division. They were para-time cartographers, pathfinders, without whom the time wars could not be fought.

In the early days of time travel, there had been disastrous accidents with people materializing inside walls, clocking back into the same location occupied by another person. Such accidents were still possible and they occurred from time to time, but to minimize their possibility, there were the floaters. These soldiers always preceded any fighting unit sent back into the past. They charted the geographical locations and the time periods in which the soldiers from the future would do battle, making extensive surveys of terrain and construction, population density, climatic conditions, in short, everything that would affect a soldier sent back into that time and place.

They were clocked out above ground, equipped with floater paks, so that they would appear in Minus Time at very high altitudes, which eliminated the possibility of their appearing in a space occupied by someone or something else. Using their floater paks, they would descend to isolated areas, where they would break up into teams, each team equipped with survey equipment and a chronoplate. These were crack troops, the cream of the Temporal Corps, the most disciplined of soldiers.

"I know what you're thinking," Hunter said. "It's not like a floater to desert."

"As a matter of fact," said Lucas, "that's exactly what I was thinking."

"Well, don't be too quick to pass judgment, pilgrim," Hunter said. "Put yourself in my place, first. We were sent to map out this area, preparatory to a mission in this sector and this time period. Come to think of it, I wouldn't be at all surprised if whatever hitch you're in on had something to do with it, although I can't be sure. I've been here for a while and I've clocked around some, so I kinda lost track of time, if you know what I mean. Anyway, to make a long story short, my team ran into trouble. Some of us came back dressed up like knights, nysteel armor and the works, others came done up like peasants, outlaws, serfs, whatever. My team were woodsmen. We had weapons that should have seen to our survival, but you oughtta know that it doesn't always work out that way.

"We came down in a deserted section of the forest, not too far from here. Plenty of game and the deer didn't run from you all the time, which meant that some of them had seen men and some of them hadn't. Anyway, I'm getting off the track. Point is, things were so damn quiet that we dropped our guard. We watched ourselves whenever we surveyed sectors that were populated or that had seen some traffic, but every time we came back here, we just felt real safe, you know? Of course, the moment we got to feeling that way, the shit hit the fan. We got to feeling too safe. We posted a guard every night, naturally, but this one night, one of the boys fell asleep. Maybe he fell off by accident one night and nothing happened, and after that he just took to nipping out on duty, I don't know. Whatever the case was, Jase was asleep the night we got hit.

"They were outlaws. Locksley's bunch. They shouldn't have even been in this neck of the woods; we had them charted miles away and we'd observed that they didn't like to wander too far from their stomping grounds, but this time they did. Maybe one of us got careless and was spotted. Either way, I woke up that night to find all hell had broken loose. There were about fifteen or twenty of them and only seven of us. We had no chance. They took us completely by surprise. None of us so much as got off a shot. Fortunately, we had our gear under a safety field and they couldn't get at it. They must've thought it was black magic or something.

"We had always figured they were pretty harmless. Bunch of crazy woodsmen who were drunk on their asses half the time. Just goes to show you, never underestimate the opposition. I was the only one who survived. Four of the boys had their throats cut in their sleep. The rest of us got taken out by arrows. I took two, one in the shoulder—" he pulled back his robe to display an ugly scar, "and one in the leg. Missed my femoral artery by about a fraction of an inch. On top of that, one of 'em practically caved in my skull with a quarterstaff.

"They must have figured I was done for, because when I

came to, double vision and the whole trip, they were gone and our camp was in a shambles. They wrecked everything they could get their hands on, looking for something worth stealing. They must have departed in a hurry once they came across the gear within the safety field. That probably made them think they'd just wasted a den of sorcerers. I helped them along in that direction later. Alexei was still alive. I found him with four arrows sticking out of him. No chance to save him, he died in my arms, laughing, *laughing* for God's sake, at how stupid it all was. And that left just yours truly."

Hunter took a healthy sip of bourbon. "I waited around for several days for S&R to show up. But there must have been some sort of slip-up. I don't know what the hell went down. They never showed. The implants of the dead men should have reported six KIAs, but no one ever showed. It finally occurred to me to test out my own implant. I stuck my finger in the hollow just behind my right ear, you know the drill, we all do it whenever we get to feeling paranoid, and nothing. No test tone. I just kept poking myself and poking myself, but no beeps went off inside my head. Only one conclusion. That rap on the head took out my implant. Still beats hell out of me why none of the others registered, but near as I can figure it, someone must've screwed up in S&R and our team never got logged. I assume the others all made it back all right, I never heard anything about them. But my team was the lost patrol. No one even knew we were back here. Typical army efficiency."

"But you still had your chronoplate," said Lucas. "You could have clocked back on your own."

Hunter nodded. "I had intended to. I doctored myself up as best I could and then I waited for the S&R pick-up. And I waited. And I waited. I finally decided to bury the dead. By that time, they had started stinking. I figured I'd put 'em in the ground and say a few words, then clock myself back. At least, that was the plan. Anyway . . . I buried them all. They're all out there, just beyond the front door of this cabin. But when I was covering up the last man . . . Jase, I think it was, it hit me. Why bother going back?"

Hunter started to pour himself another shot of bourbon, then changed his mind and drank from the bottle instead. He was chain-smoking cigarettes.

"Why bother going back? Nobody knew about me. Nobody cared. So . . . why bother?"

The thing that struck Lucas the most about Hunter, while he spoke, was the calm way in which he related this story. Hunter spoke without emotion. There was an animated quality about his speech, but that was not the same thing. There was a frightening coldness about the man, as if a part of him was dead. Or had never really lived. Lucas realized, with something of a shock, that he was listening to the perfect soldier, the ideal assassin. This was a man who would not panic under any circumstances. This was a man who would not know fear. It would be as alien an emotion to him as any other.

"It was raining," Hunter said, "and I was all covered with muck from burying six corpses. I sat down on the ground, right in the mud, right on top of Jase, and I considered my options. Only four branches of the service have steady access to chronoplates. Referee Corps, Observer Corps, Search and Retrieve and Airborne. The big boys keep real careful track of theirs, but us grunts can lose one once in a while. S&R might be able to home in on a lost chronoplate, like they home in on the coded implants, but suppose somebody picked the damn thing up and walked off with it? No big deal. They're fail safe. You don't know the sequence, the whole thing goes ka-boom. No problem. If there are any witnesses, it just becomes another crazy story. There are risks involved, but they're minimal compared to the risk of having a loose plate floating around.

"Okay, so I knew the sequence for my plate. I could program it. Sure, S&R could trace it, but then why didn't they trace the team through any of their implants?"

"Perhaps it was just a temporary mix-up," Lucas said. "Separations happen all the time."

"Yeah, maybe. It could happen," Hunter said. "So I decided to wait some more. I mean, what else was there to do? I could've clocked back, but all the time, I kept on thinking, what's in it for me if I return? They don't give a flying fuck about me, why should I give a damn? Well, after a while, I simply decided that I didn't. It took me about a week or two to figure out how to work a bypass on the tracer function. Then I was free and clear. My implant was out and they couldn't trace me through the plate. If they even knew a plate was missing, they'd figure it got into the wrong hands and self-destructed. I just mustered myself out. I built myself this cabin and then I set about making myself comfortable. It was easy. I had a full pathfinders program file to choose from. After a while, I started getting cocky. Started clocking into peacetime periods and locations. Just floated in, scouted around, blended in, did a little shopping and went home. I'll tell you, pilgrim, it's a fine life. I just pick myself a place and go. Paris in the 1920's, New York City in the 1890's, San Francisco in the 1980's, Greece, Singapore, Majorca, you name it. When I've had enough, I just clock back here. It's nice and quiet, no one bothers me and I go out there and tell the boys about the good times I've had."

"What about the outlaws?" Lucas said.

Hunter laughed. "They don't mess with me. We've got an understanding. They don't bother the wizard in the woods and I don't bother them. Fact is, we do each other little favors on occasion."

"What about your men?" said Lucas. "The outlaws killed them. Doesn't that mean anything to you?"

Hunter took a long pull from the bottle. "I don't forget things like that," he said. He got up and walked over to a shelf, from which he took down an ancient .45 caliber automatic pistol, a Colt Combat Commander. "I've got more sophisticated weapons," he said, "but I find this very effective, especially at night. All the noise and the muzzle flash, makes 'em think I'm throwing lightning bolts at 'em." He gestured at his robe. "This outfit sorta completes the image. Impresses the shit outta them. I just gave them a few convincing demonstrations and then I told them that I wanted the men who killed my boys or they were all dead meat. They delivered."

"What did you do with them?" said Lucas.

Hunter smiled. "I clocked 'em out."

"Where?"

"Oh, North America, back in the Upper Cretaceous. Figured they'd get a real bang out of that. I wonder how much good bows and arrows were against the likes of Tyrannosaurus Rex?"

Lucas swallowed heavily. The man was diabolical. Worse

than that, he was raving mad.

But he had a chronoplate.

Life was no longer simple for the merry men and, as a result, they were all somewhat less than merry. Marion was so impressed with Bobby's performance that with Finn Delaney's aid she mounted a G.I. inspection of the camp, destroying all the ale and wine that she could find. She laid down the law on drinking. From that moment on, it was to be strictly moderated.

The merry men were made to rise at dawn and given one hour in which to make themselves presentable for breakfast. Finn and Bobby had instituted the practice of bathing, which had been greeted with a great deal of alarm. Bathing was generally believed to be a health hazard and it took no small amount of cajoling and pummeling to get the outlaws to comply.

Many of the men were lice infested and this malady was cured by making all the outlaws shave all the hair from their bodies and scrub vigorously in wooden tubs while fire-heated water was poured over them. The complaints they made as a result of this were greatly multiplied when there followed the obligatory period of itching from the stubble as their hair grew back. Finn and Bobby did not exempt themselves from this; Finn shaved because he believed in setting a good example and not demanding anything of "his men" that he would not do himself. Bobby followed suit because he had discovered, to his great disgust, that Marion had gifted him with crabs.

It had taken both of them to wet her down and shave her, which task was accomplished only after her struggles had resulted in her taking some bad cuts from Finn. He finally smashed her in the jaw and told her that if she would not lie still, he would skin her alive. She suffered the treatment stoically from then on, but when it came time to scrub her down, she fought them, clawing like a wildcat. The merry men were more than eager to assist Finn and Bobby in the task.

When it was all done, they all looked like Army boots in training. And, not surprisingly, the process had taken a good deal of the resistance out of them. They were also pleasantly surprised to be free of their tiny livestock at long last.

Breakfast was followed by a general clean-up of the camp as

their existence became regimented. The clean-up was followed by inspection, which was followed by a period of drill and calisthenics. Finn was a ruthless taskmaster and he was ably assisted by Marion, who would not be outdone by any of the others. Finn and Bobby also saw to it that there was a variation in their diet and that cooked food was cooked properly. They worked hard and they ate well. Whatever recalcitrance remained vanished the moment they were able to put their new training into practice.

The soldiers had no desire to reform the merry men. They were outlaws and outlaws they would remain. Plying their trade helped them to put their training into practice. The first time, Finn and Bobby directed them in a foray against one of the sheriff's tax collecting parties.

The sheriff's tax collector was well protected by a party of knights and men at arms, a force that ordinarily the outlaws would have refrained from attacking. Finn had Bobby, with a group of about ten outlaws, block the party's progress by jumping out from under cover ahead of them with shouts of "Stand and deliver!" The sheriff's men reacted in the proper fashion to such a confrontation. The knights couched their lances and, closely followed by the men at arms, they charged —right into the line of fire of the twenty some odd archers Finn was commanding, who were under cover to the right of the trail. The result was that the sheriff's men were caught in a deadly crossfire, from the front and from their flank. At that distance, with the cloth-yard shafts and the incredibly powerful pull of the longbows, armor provided only the most superficial protection. The ambush was devastatingly effective and the outlaws made a tidy haul. Alan-a-dale was inspired to compose a song about the incident. In a short time, Finn and Bobby had instilled within the outlaws something which they had sorely lacked up to that point—*esprit de corps*.

But there was still one dark cloud on the horizon. There was no word from Lucas.

"He should have been here days ago," said Bobby. It was late and he and Finn were sitting by the embers of a fire. It would be dawn soon.

"How long has it been?" said Finn.

"I don't know," said Bobby. "A week? More? You think maybe Goldblum got him?"

"I don't know," said Finn. "I've had men making inquiries. No one seems to have seen either him or Hooker. Last word I had on Hooker was that he was staying with Isaac of York, but there's been no sign of him, either. He's vacated his rooms in the village of Ashby and he's not in York. I've sent men to Rotherwood, but Lucas isn't there. Nor is Cedric there, or Athelstane, or Rowena. It's like they've all just disappeared."

"They would have had to travel through Sherwood," Bobby said. "You don't think maybe—"

"No chance," said Finn. "If our guys had anything to do with it, I'd know about it."

Bobby smiled. "You really like them, don't you?"

"Like them? Yes, I suppose I do, at that. They're a good bunch. They work hard and they play hard. In a way, they sort of remind me of Eric's men."

"Eric?"

Finn chuckled. "Eric the Red. Nastiest son of a bitch it was ever my pleasure to serve under. You think this is a heavy gig? I'll tell you what a rough gig is. Try heading out to open sea in a longboat. Seventy-five feet from bow to stern, about ten feet in the beam, rigged with a Nordic square sail. God, those men were really something. Vikings. Greatest sailors ever lived, except maybe the Polynesians. I'll tell you something, we've got us a rough and ready bunch here, but they wouldn't last five minutes in a set-to with the Vikings."

"You know something, Finn? I think you were born too late."

"No way. I was born right smack on time. I wouldn't trade my life for anything. You and I, we're the ultimate soldiers. We can fight with anyone, anytime, anywhere. We've got all of human history to play with. I'll tell you one soldier who would've given his eyeteeth for living in our time and serving in the Temporal Corps. Fella by the name of Patton. Now there's a guy who was born too late, but not late enough."

"You're a romantic, Finn," said Bobby, softly.

"I guess I am, kid."

"I'm not." Bobby sighed. "I'm a realist. I can appreciate the way you feel, but what we're doing is dangerous, damned dangerous. Man never should have traveled back through time, Finn. It's wrong. It's crazy. Worse than that, it's stupid.

They're afraid to travel to the future because no one knows just what the future is. Is there *a* future? I mean, how many possibilities are there? Who knows what kind of bends and twists the timestream takes up ahead? Maybe someday some lunatic will actually try it, but they're scared of that right now and so long as they remain scared, I think there's still a chance that they'll come to their senses and stop the time wars. I don't know what it would take. Maybe something like this, maybe something worse, I just don't know, but I wish to hell they'd stop."

He stared at the embers silently as the sun came up.

"I want to go home," he said.

10

Andre was exhausted. She was grateful to drop Cedric off at Nottingham Castle. Blindfolding him had not been enough, it had finally been necessary to gag him, as well. She had had more than she could stand of his defiant epithets, Athelstane's ceaseless grumbling and Rowena's whining. She had finally ordered them all gagged, although she had to call one of the men over with a hand signal and whisper the command, since she could not imitate De Bracy's voice. The blindfolds served a dual purpose, protecting her masquerade as well as preventing the prisoners from seeing that they were being taken to Nottingham, rather than Torquilstone. Had the prisoners been able to see, they might have realized that she was not De Bracy; something might have given it away.

Taking them had been simple enough. The attack had been a complete surprise and every member of their party save for the three of them had been killed. It was a shame about the palmer who had been traveling with them. A simple pilgrim who had only desired safe passage through the wood, he was an innocent bystander. He had not even been armed. Still, she had her orders. She consoled herself that she had not hit him all that hard; perhaps there was a chance that the blow had not been fatal. It was a small consolation, but it was something.

Her stay at Nottingham had been extremely brief. She had remained there only long enough to see the prisoners turned over to the sheriff's men at arms and to pick up Marcel and change back into her own clothing and armor. Now, with Marcel riding at her side, she was once again the red knight, on her way to Torquilstone. De Bracy would welcome Andre de la Croix, never suspecting that he would be admitting his own murderer to his castle.

She was growing tired of playing ceaseless games of charade. Her breasts were hurting from the cloth that they were tightly swaddled in and she was badly in need of sleep. How long would it go on? How long *could* it go on? With all the constant intrigue, the pressure was increasing. Her greatest fear was not that she would die, but that she would somehow make a mistake and be caught, that her true sex would be discovered. All things considered, it was remarkable that she had been able to get away with it for so long.

What would they do, she wondered, if they were to find out? Kill her? It was certainly possible. Imprison her? More than likely. On the other hand, it was much more than a case of a peasant passing for a knight. She was a woman passing for a knight and she did not think that the men whom she had deceived would settle for any of the more traditional punishments. No, without doubt, for her they would devise something a bit more imaginative. Men such as Maurice De Bracy and Brian de Bois-Guilbert would never be able to accept that a woman had been able to hold her own with them, to prevail where they could not. There was no question of her ever being allowed to go free so that others might find out. Yes, they might very well kill her in some extremely unpleasant manner, but men had other ways of getting revenge. She thought that death would be preferable.

Most of all, she was concerned about Marcel. Without her, what would become of him? To minimize the risk of discovery, she and Marcel had never stayed very long in any one place, had never accepted service for an extended period of time. It was past time for them to move on, her every instinct told her so. However, there would be no moving on so long as the black knight knew her secret and could expose her at will. The smart thing to do would be to kill him. Only . . . how?

He claimed to be *Coeur de Lion*, but she no longer believed him. She did not know exactly *why* she did not believe him, but she was certain that he wasn't Richard any more than she was. Obviously, he was the very image of the departed king, since Sir Guy accepted him as such and the sheriff had known Richard well, and had at one time been among his men at arms. She had never seen Richard Plantagenet, so she had no way of knowing in what ways he had "changed" since returning from the Third Crusade. Whoever this was, he had thus far kept her secret. Certainly, Sir Guy did not suspect she was a woman. He treated her as an equal and they had spent many nights together, drinking and talking. She wasn't sure who repelled her more, Sir Guy or "Richard."

"He's returned a different man," the sheriff had said to her one night, while they sat before the fireplace drinking ale.

"Different in what ways?" she had said.

"In some ways, he seems more patient," said the sheriff. "And yet, the demons seem to drive him more than ever. I am the older man, and yet at times he seems to speak to me as if I were a child. Indeed, he acts like an older man now." He nodded slowly. "War can age a man like that. War can make men old before their time, or it can turn them into mewling infants. He does not speak of it, you know."

"The Crusade?"

Guy nodded. "I have asked him once or twice what it was like. Each time, he turned the talk to something else. He will not speak of Saladin, of Philip, or of his captivity. He speaks only of winning back his throne and of John's treachery."

"Why does he choose to array himself in black, I wonder?" Andre said.

The sheriff chuckled. "Perhaps to match his thoughts."

"He thinks black thoughts and is driven by demons," Andre said. "You make the king sound like a warlock."

Guy laughed. "A warlock he is, by God, in battle! He fights with the strength of ten!"

"Perhaps he has gained secret knowledge in his travels."

"Secret knowledge? Black arts, you mean? Absurd! The king has no need to learn the art of making lead into gold or of consorting with demons. The demons driving Richard are all of his own making. They exist within his mind and heart. Now if it's witches you want, I'll show you one, soon as I lay my hands upon the treacherous bitch!"

"You know a witch?"

"I *married* one, God spurn her!"

"I did not know you had a wife, Sir Guy."

"There's the malady, I do *not* have her. She ran off to join the forest brigands, damn her eyes."

"The *outlaws?* Surely, you jest! Why would a lady go—"

"Because she is no lady, that's why! It's why I married her, too. Perhaps, de la Croix, you can understand, being a knight errant. I serve my king, but being sheriff of Nottingham shire is a soft job for a soft man. I am a fighting man. I have always been a fighting man. I have fought for everything I've won in life and I fought for my women, too. There is pleasure in a hard won victory. I have little use for pampered willows who will bend before the slightest wind. By God, give me a woman who will fight and scratch and kick! I took Marion from her father and he was glad to be rid of a troublesome wench, but I liked her spirit! Oh, how she fought me on our wedding night! Damn near took my eyes out and wrecked my manhood! I beat her black and blue and still she would not submit. By God, there was a woman, I thought!"

"Indeed," said Andre, dryly.

"Within the first week of our marriage, three times she tried to kill me," the sheriff said. "Once, she tried to stab me in my sleep. I still bear the scar upon my shoulder. After that, I tied her up when I was through with her and gagged her, so that I might sleep undisturbed. The second time, she tried poisoning my food. It was my good fortune that I had no appetite that day and but drank and ate some fruit. Still her effort cost me my best hound. I stripped some skin from off her shoulders with my lash and thereafter made her taste my meals first. The third time she involved the outlaws. She had often heard me speak of cleaning out these vermin from the forest and, before the king's return, I often led patrols into the wood myself. Well, she managed to get word to the outlaws through one of the stableboys and they arranged an ambush for me. Fortunately, they are as inept as they are unprincipled and I escaped, killing a good number of them and capturing several. My good wife, doubtless fearing that her part in the plot would be discovered by myself, freed the prisoners from my dungeons and escaped with them in the dead of night, little suspecting that I already knew of it and made the escape possible, hoping to trail them back to their hidden camp."

"And did you?"

"No. I lost them in the woods, worse luck."

"And your wife?"

"She has been with them ever since."

"I should think that you would be glad to be rid of her," said Andre.

"It might seem so, but I miss the bloodthirsty bitch. She made life interesting in these placid times. But I'll get her back one day, mark my word. She's a peculiar woman, de la Croix. Truth be told, I don't think she ever forgave God for making her a woman. Perhaps such an overabundance of spirit is misplaced in one of her sex." Guy chuckled. "She should have been a man."

"Indeed," said Andre, "it is hard to imagine a woman who would not be satisfied with so passionate a husband as yourself."

"I thought you would understand," the sheriff said. "You're a man after my own heart, de la Croix. What say the two of us go wenching some night?"

"Perhaps we will," said Andre, "when our present duties have been done."

"Yes, one must always think of duty first. Still, a man must have time in which to be a man, eh?"

"True," said Andre. "Else women will forget their role in life."

"The sheriff laughed. "We can't have that, now, can we?"

"No, indeed. What kind of world would it be if women were to forget their place?"

"Perhaps they would even take to wearing spurs and entering the lists," said Guy, laughing. "That would be a sight, eh?"

"I think perhaps the ale has overstimulated your imagination."

"No doubt. God made woman to serve man and that is how it should be."

"Maybe someday you will find one who will serve you properly," said Andre, smiling.

"I'll drink to that," the sheriff said.

"So will I, Sir Guy."

"Why so quiet, Andre?" said Marcel.

"I was thinking of the sheriff, little brother."

Marcel frowned. "I don't like him. He frightens me."

"I don't like him either, Marcel. He's an animal, not a man. But then, the difference is a small one, is it not? We serve strange masters these days."

"Andre, why must we ride to Torquilstone? I'm afraid. I feel that no good will come of it."

Andre reined up her horse. "I have learned to trust your feelings, little brother. Have you a premonition?"

"The closer we get to Torquilstone, the stronger my fear becomes," Marcel said. "Let us not go there. Our horses are fresh, the day is young, we can put many miles between us and our troubles before the day is out."

Andre sat astride her horse silently for a moment, listening to the birds sing.

"Andre?"

"I am sorely tempted, Marcel. But I, too, am afraid. This black knight is some sort of sorcerer. One moment, there is nothing there, the next, he is standing at my shoulder. He is the devil's own, Marcel."

"Then we must fight him."

"I fear we lack the proper weapons. How does one fight a warlock?"

"I do not know."

"Nor do I. Perhaps we will find a way. Until then, we must bide our time and do his bidding."

"And what if we run out of time?"

"Yes, time always was our enemy, Marcel. But then, one cannot master time."

"So we ride on to Torquilstone?"

"Yes, little brother. We ride on."

His bonds were almost loose.

Hooker had tensed the muscles in his arms and wrists when they had tied him and now, as he walked ahead of his mule and behind the two Norman knights, he was making the best of the slight amount of slack by trying to work his hands free. The trail was narrow. If he could free his hands, he stood a good chance of being able to make a break for it. Perhaps he would be able to lose the men in the forest, but his progress would be drastically impeded with his hands tied behind his back. He had to get them free first. Fortunately, his position in the column made it possible for him to try. De Bracy and Bois-Guilbert rode their horses at a slow walk just ahead of him. Behind him was the mule with the nysteel armor lashed to it and behind the mule was Isaac, who was followed closely by the men at arms. Every time he had voiced a protest, one of them had cuffed him, so he was now reduced to mumbling incoherently under his breath. Hooker could not make out what he was saying, but he thought he caught a word or two of Hebrew. The old man was praying.

Hooker was flanked by two men at arms. The one on his right was left handed and he wore his sword on the right side of his body. The one on his left was right handed and wore his sword on his left side. That effectively put both swords out of his reach in the event that he could free himself and make a quick grab. It did, however, leave both their daggers within his reach. It was a weapon he was far more comfortable with.

His wrists were wet. He guessed that he had rubbed right through the skin so deeply that he didn't even feel the pain. The danger in that was that the blood would soak his bonds and make them more difficult to work loose. He struggled feverishly, keeping a careful watch with his peripheral vision on the men at arms to either side of him. They looked bored and tired, but if they noticed his efforts, they would quickly come alert.

Hooker was close to abject panic. He was sweating profusely. He didn't want to die. From time to time, in his brief career as a soldier, he had tried to imagine what it would be like to die. It was a morbid preoccupation, but he had not been able to resist it. He thought that getting shot would not be too bad, though there were ways one get could shot that would result in a slow and painful death. He had once made a list, mentally, in an idle moment, of ways in which he would prefer to go. He never told anyone about it for fear of being ridiculed. He had listed all possible ways of meeting his Maker in order of preference. At the top of the list were all the most immediate ways of dying—in a bomb blast; from a sonic weapon or a laser; a fatal bullet wound that would kill him before he knew what hit him. Following that, he considered more primitive methods such as decapitation, either by a guillotine or a headsman's axe; a sword thrust through the heart; an arrow wound, a slit throat. . . . He had also dwelled upon the more terrifying ways of dying. Drowning was said to be an easy death, but the prospect of it horrified him. There was death by slow torture; death by burning; death by irradiation or disease; death by chemical poisoning. . . . There was one method of execution that made Hooker's guts crawl. He was possessed of a lively imagination and, in this regard, he was his own worst enemy. He knew there was no rational logic to fear. What petrified one man would hardly give pause to another. Hooker was obsessed with his fear of death and one manner of demise horrified him more than any other. Hanging.

He had nightmares about being hanged. He had even researched it. There was a mythology concerning hanging that held that in most cases, strangulation did not truly occur. If placed upon a gallows, on an elevation, or if sat astride a horse preparatory to the dirty deed, it was said that the noose would often break the neck and death would be instantaneous, especially if a weight were used. Hooker knew that such was not the case. It was the exception rather than the rule. The image of men dancing at the end of a rope did not spring from nothing. Depending on the type of knot used, it could take a man as long as fifteen minutes to die.

When Hooker had seen his own corpse, he had been violently sick. Now he could not push the sight from his mind. He imagined the garotte slowly cutting into his throat, the blood running in rivulets down his neck, his tongue protruding from his mouth, his fingers madly scrabbling for the wire and failing to catch hold of it, fighting for breath with every fiber of his being and not succeeding. . . .

His head had been practically severed from his neck by the monofilament garotte. A weapon from the future. A weapon such as the one hidden in one of Lucas' gauntlets, just at the inside of the wrist. There was a small metal button there. One quick pull and the deadly wire could be brought into play. The nysteel gear was right behind him, lashed to the mule. It was all there, the mail, the armor, the shield, the *gauntlets*. . . . How long would it be before one of the Norman knights riding just ahead of him would discover the secrets of the armor? Hooker felt a moistness on his face that he first thought was sweat running down from his forehead, but he was astonished to discover that he was weeping silently. His wrists were growing numb. It felt very slippery back there. If only he could work his hands free! If only no one would notice—

There! He had worked one knot loose! He had hardly any feeling left in his fingers. They prickled as if stabbed with a thousand tiny needles. His fingers kept slipping off the knots, which were slick with blood. Please, God, he thought, abandoning his atheism, *help me!* He could now almost slip one hand free of the ropes. He gritted his teeth and pulled with all his might. He felt his left thumb being scraped raw, he felt his left wrist dislocate . . . and he was free!

He slammed his left fist into the face of the man to his left, crying out from the pain that shot up his arm as the dislocated wrist broke. With his right hand, he plucked the dagger from the man's sheath; moving with every ounce of speed that he could muster, he slashed it across the face of the man to his right, opening him up from his right eye to the bottom of his jaw. Then he made a headlong dive for the brush at the side of the trail.

"Catch that man!" he heard someone yell and then he rolled and was on his feet, running through the brambles, his one useless hand hanging limp at his side, the other clutching the dagger. He heard the pounding of horses' hooves behind him and the thrashing of men plunging into the brush. He ran as hard as he could, whimpering with fear. He tripped over a root and fell, striking his head.

"I have him!" someone cried.

Hooker looked up to see a man at arms bearing down upon him, sword drawn. He hurled the dagger. It stuck in the man's throat and he fell to the ground, gurgling horribly. De Bracy was upon him in an instant. He swung his sword, trying to strike Hooker with the flat of the blade, so as to take him alive. Hooker caught the blow on his right arm and he cried out as he felt his elbow break. Ignoring the pain, he snagged De Bracy's arm and pulled him from the saddle. The knight's horse shied away from him and he heard the others close behind. He ran. A crossbow bolt whizzed by him, then another. He ran, heedless of the branches lashing at his face, tripping, falling, getting up and running; he fled deeper into the forest, trying to outdistance his pursuers. He ran without looking back. He ran for his life, not knowing that he had escaped the frying pan only to fall into the fire.

There was a knock at the door of Irving's chambers.

"Yes?"

"We have taken a prisoner, Sire," said the sheriff, from the other side of the door. Irving got up and opened the door to admit Sir Guy.

"Well?"

"You did say to keep you informed, Sire."

"What of it?"

"One of my forest patrols has taken a prisoner. An escaped bondsman, it would seem. He stumbled out upon the trail before them and went wild."

"What do you mean?"

"He seems to be a raving madman, Sire. Possessed by demons or else mad with fear. He had a wrist broken on one arm and an elbow on the other and still he made a struggle. My men said that he spoke in tongues, screaming and babbling like a lunatic. He has been held captive, that much is certain. His hands are rubbed raw from where he slipped his bonds."

"A Saxon?"

"No, Sire. I do not know what he is, but I have seen him somewhere before, I think. He has a scar upon his face. I have seen that face recently, but I cannot remember where."

"In Nottingham? At York?"

"No, Sire. Perhaps at Ashby . . . Yes, at the tournament. I'm sure I saw him among the knights' pavilions, but I cannot remember whom he served."

"Where is he now?"

"Locked in the dungeons, below."

"Very well, I will see him presently. Await me there."

The sheriff left and Irving closed the door. A bondsman, but not a Saxon. Spoke in tongues. Was it possible? There was one way to make sure. Irving locked the door and pulled the case containing the chronoplate out from beneath his bed. He opened it and took out the border circuits which, when assembled, formed the chronoplate. Inside the case was the computer and the tracer apparatus. Irving turned it on, then selected close range implant scan. Yes! There it was! The implant proximity signal! He was right on top of it. It was an amazing stroke of luck. The sheriff's men had caught themselves a temporal trooper. That could only mean that it was one of the adjustment team! He quickly packed the gear away and hurried to join the sheriff in the dungeons.

The nether regions of the castle were dark and damp. There was a fetid odor of decay in the stagnant air and rats scurried away before him as he descended into the torchlit dungeons. The sheriff awaited him with the turnkey, a hideous old man who smelled as if he had been three weeks dead himself. The turnkey lived down in the depths of Nottingham Castle and he had not seen the light of day in years. He was half blind and his skin was the color of the underbelly of a fish. As they passed several of the cells, Irving could hear Cedric shouting behind one of the doors.

"Silence, you!" The turnkey pounded on the door with his gnarled fist. "Nothing but noise from that one," he said. He cackled. "He'll scream himself hoarse soon enough." He paused by another door. "This one's the lady," he said, smacking his lips. "Tender morsel, that. Will you be torturing her, Your Highness? I'm a good man with the bellows, that I am. I can heat the coals so that they glow red hot!"

"Shut him up," said Irving.

"Quiet!" said the sheriff, belting the turnkey alongside the head hard enough to stagger him.

"Thank you, milord."

The turnkey paused by the door of one of the cells and fumbled with his keys. It took him an eternity to fit the key into the hole—he kept missing it. Finally, he opened the door.

Irving gagged on the smell. He spun away, holding his hand over his nose and mouth.

"Bring him out," the sheriff said.

The turnkey entered the cell and, after a moment, he could be heard fumbling with the prisoner's manacles. Then there were the sounds of a scuffle and a blow falling and Hooker hurtled through the door. The sheriff felled him with one blow. Hooker collapsed to the floor, moaning. The sheriff stuck his head into the cell.

"You alive, you wretch?"

"Yes, thank you, milord."

The sheriff slammed the door on the cell, leaving the turnkey inside. He bent down and lifted Hooker bodily, throwing him over his shoulder. Together with Irving, he walked to the end of the hall, carrying Hooker. They descended another flight of steps to the torture chamber.

Once there, the sheriff threw Hooker up against a wall, holding the semi-conscious man with one hand on his chest while with the other he fastened on the manacles.

"Bring him around," said Irving.

Sir Guy picked up a bucket containing viscous, stagnant water and dashed it into Hooker's face. Then he grabbed the corporal by the hair and shook him.

"He's coming to his senses, Sire."

"Leave us."

"Sire?"

"Await me in the upper level," Irving said. "I would question this man myself."

"As you wish, Sire."

The sheriff left. Irving pulled a crude wooden stool over with his booted foot and sat down, waiting for Hooker to fully come to. When Hooker opened his eyes, the first thing he saw was Irving sitting on the stool a few feet away from him, smiling slightly.

"Oh, Christ," said Hooker.

"Hardly," Irving said, "but I do see that you know me, don't you?"

Hooker did not reply.

"Let us not waste time," said Irving. "I don't know who you are, but I do know *what* you are and that's more to the point. You are a member of a temporal adjustment team sent back to stop me. There's no use denying it, my equipment has registered your implant. I also know that there are at least three others; I've picked up their implants, as well. All of you were at the tournament. Unfortunately, I have not yet been able to take the time to pinpoint the location of the others, but I know they're somewhere in Sherwood."

"If you can locate them, what do you want from me?" said Hooker.

"Only a few simple answers to a few simple questions," Irving said.

"The name is Hooker, J.D., Corporal, serial number—"

Irving chuckled. "Look around you, Hooker. This is a medieval torture chamber. The equipment here is admittedly primitive, but nevertheless, quite effective. There really isn't any need to resort to such unpleasant means of persuasion, is there? You really can't win. I could have taken all of you earlier had I wished to, but I had other things to attend to. You had not yet become an inconvenience. You see, I can take you men out almost anytime I wish to."

"Then why don't you?"

"Expedience, Mr. Hooker. Your superior and I have been engaged in an elaborate game. He's a formidable player, but each time around, I learn the rules a little better. So does he, I expect. I daresay it's a learning experience for both of us. Well, be that as it may, one of the things I've learned is that the moment it becomes necessary for me to sanction the adjustment team, my rival immediately begins the game all over. Just once, I'd like to play it through to the end. Would you care for a cigarette?''

He removed a pack from a pouch on his belt and offered one to Hooker.

"Quite safe, I assure you. There's nothing in this more elaborate than tobacco. I do want you alive for now and given the condition you're in, I wouldn't chance dosing you with anything. Chances are you've been made drug resistant, anyway.''

Hooker opened his mouth and Irving placed the cigarette between his lips, then lighted it.

"Sometimes, the old-fashioned methods really are the best,'' said Irving. He walked over to an iron maiden and slowly forced it closed. It made a hideous scraping noise. "You know, there was a time when agents were equipped with all sorts of fascinating devices to enable them to avoid breaking under interrogation, cyanide capsules in the teeth and so on. Terrible waste of manpower. It's encouraging to know that we've progressed beyond such things.''

Hooker watched him silently, cigarette between clenched teeth.

"The assumption is that anyone can break, Mr. Hooker. It really doesn't matter. After all, there's no point to wasting manpower needlessly, isn't that so?''

"Get to the point,'' said Hooker.

"Certainly. The point is, I've had my fill of all this interference. It grows tiresome. This is like some strange game of chess, wherein the black king is beset by pawns. The pawns are very vulnerable, this is taken for granted, and they're really not all that important. The king can continue to take pawns almost at will, but there is always the chance that he will maneuver himself into a corner and a rather undignified checkmate. So the white king is prepared to sacrifice his pawns left and right, banking on those odds. All the black king can hope for is a stalemate, wherein no more pawns arrive. Only, in this game, the black king wins with a stalemate.

"You see, Mr. Hooker, in this strange game so long as there are pawns upon the board, my chances for a stalemate are increased. The rules are a bit peculiar. The white king is allowed an almost inexhaustible amount of pawns. They serve me better by remaining in the game. Unless you present a threat to me, you're quite safe. Really. I'd be a fool to kill any of you unless it was absolutely unavoidable. I just want you to make that easier for me, helping you to stay in the game, that is. Cooperate with me and you can sit the rest of the game out in comfort. You will be well provided for and you'll be out of it. Look at yourself. Broken bones, lacerations, you're on the edge of a total nervous collapse . . . and *why?* There's no reason for it. All you have to do is tell me what I want to know and that will be the end of it. I'll see to it that you're treated for your injuries and I'll see to it that you'll be comfortable. All you have to do is identify the other members of your team for me.''

"Is that all?"

Irving took the butt out of Hooker's mouth before it burned his lips.

"Well, there is one other thing. You see, I'm in a bit of a bind here. I have certain things I must accomplish and the other referee is determined to make matters very complicated for me. It is in both our interests, as I'm sure you'll understand, to keep the disruptions of the timestream to a minimum. So far, we've been able to do that, but it has not been easy. In order for you to appreciate my situation, you must understand the mechanics of the game. It involves a series of limited disruptions. Each one invites an increased possibility of creating a paradox.

"Each time, we progress a little farther, but I have yet to succeed in taking the throne. Once I've accomplished that, I will be in a stronger position, but still not invulnerable. I need to know two things from you in order to bring this charade to an end. I can't spend all my time scanning for the other members of your team and, unless I'm right on top of them and scanning, it becomes a little difficult for me to pinpoint them, especially if there's a crowd around. If push comes to shove, there will be fighting. I expect that to happen very soon and I don't want to kill any of your team unintentionally. If I can find out who they are, I can take steps to avoid them. I don't want to strike out at them except in self-defense, only if it's absolutely necessary. I just want you to make that easier for me. Help me to help you stay alive. And the other thing I need to know is where the other referee is."

"Can't you trace him?"

"Neither of us have implants, Mr. Hooker, and both of us

have bypassed the tracer functions on our chronoplates. He doesn't know where I am and I don't know where he is. However, you can remedy that situation, can't you?''

''If I do, then he's a dead man,'' Hooker said.

''Well, yes, I'm afraid that I have no choice but to kill him. It won't be a simple matter, I assume he's well protected, but that should not concern you. He doesn't care what happens to you. You're just a pawn to him. He sent you out to die.''

Hooker closed his eyes and remained silent.

''I respect your loyalty, Mr. Hooker, but it's sadly misplaced.''

Hooker stared at him. He became aware of the fact that he was in a cold sweat. His knees were starting to shake.

''Do you really think you can resist torture, Mr. Hooker?''

Hooker swallowed hard. ''Other men have.''

''Only because the interrogators were inept. You're already in a great deal of pain, aren't you? You're afraid. I can see it in your face. So far, this has all been relatively simple, even pleasant. Don't force me to have to hurt you.''

''Go to hell, Goldblum.''

Irving sighed. ''Very well, then. You leave me no choice. I'm really very sorry about this.''

He walked over to the racks and picked up a thumbscrew. It would do for a beginning.

11

"How are you feeling?" Hunter said.

Lucas sat up in bed. "I've been better, but I guess I'm okay."

"Glad to hear that," Hunter said. "Feel up to some traveling?"

Lucas took a deep breath. "Where am I going?"

"We."

"I don't understand."

"We're going, you and I. Or have you given up on Irving?"

"You mean you're going to *help* me?"

"Well, now what the hell did you expect me to do, pilgrim?" Hunter said.

Lucas made a wry face and started to get up. "Frankly, I felt sure that you were going to take advantage of my somewhat weakened condition to clock me out somewhere. I haven't got an implant anymore and you could've sent me just about anywhere with no hope of my ever being found."

Hunter stared at him. "Now why would I want to do a thing like that?"

"I may be digging my own grave," said Lucas, "but I didn't think that you could afford to let me go. What's to prevent me from reporting you?"

"Nothing," Hunter said. "So?"

"So?"

"Come on, now, they didn't hit you all *that* hard," said Hunter, chuckling. "So what if you reported me? What good would that do? They can't trace me and I've got my own plate. At worst, I'd have to give up this cozy little cabin, but that's no big deal. I could find another place. Hell, I can go anywhere I want to and there ain't an awful lot anyone can do about it, is there?"

Lucas smiled. "You've got a point. I suppose I simply wasn't thinking. But why should you want to get involved?"

"All sorts of reasons," Hunter said. "Things have been pretty quiet around here lately. I wouldn't mind a chance to raise some Cain and take on a rogue referee. Sounds interesting. There's also the fact that, without me, you just don't stand a chance unless you get damned lucky. And not the least of my reasons is the fact that I've got to protect my own interests. This guy Irving is vandalizing my playground. He's fooling around with the timestream and that could put me in a sticky situation if I decided to clock out ahead of where he's been mucking about. I'd have no idea of what I'd be getting into. See, I don't want any changes. I like things just the way they are. That way, I've got my edge."

"So what do you propose?"

"We may as well write off your nysteel gear," said Hunter. "It's not really a major loss now that you've got me and I am not without some equipment of my own. The way it stands right now, we're in pretty good shape, since the opposition is completely in the dark about yours truly. He's got no idea you now have access to a chronoplate and he won't know that I can supply you with special gear. I'm not as conservative as your mission commander in that respect. What's more, he can't trace you anymore without your implant."

Lucas glanced at him sharply. "What are you talking about?"

Hunter sighed. "Oh, boy. They really sent out a bunch of suckers on this one, didn't they?"

"I thought only S&R had tracer gear."

"Yeah, well, I guess I shouldn't be surprised that you weren't briefed," said Hunter. "You've never been cleared for duty that would have you assigned to a plate, that much is obvious. S&R does have some specialized equipment, but the fact is that any chronoplate can read an implant signal."

"Jesus Christ," said Lucas, sitting back and exhaling heavily. "That means Irving knew about us all along! He knows where we are at any given time!"

"Well, yes and no," said Hunter. "I mean, I can see why they didn't make a point of briefing you. Besides, chronoplates are restricted ordnance. The folks who get to play with them don't usually fraternize with the regular troops and they tend to be a bit closemouthed about them, anyway. Orders, you know. It's a safe bet Irving always had a fairly good idea where you were, but he'd be limited unless he had S&R gear, which I don't think he's got. If he did, this whole thing would have been over long ago. Maybe. There are variables involved."

"I don't get it."

"Okay, put yourself in his place. You've got access to a plate, but you don't have the Search and Retrieve Personnel Tracking System. You might have been able to get your hands on one, but a PTS probably wouldn't serve your purpose. It's designed for team use, so it's not as portable and it would be a hell of a lot more obvious. You'd want to be in a position where you could transport your equipment fairly inconspicuously. S&R wouldn't have your particular problems.

"So," he said, reaching for the bourbon bottle and taking a long pull, "you've got yourself a standard issue plate without the fancy PTS back-up system. Still gives you a lot to play with. For one thing, it gives you complete mobility. S&R generally works from a field base with scouting units. We'll assume some versatility, with a safety field and a PRU remote, we're still talking about an easily concealable kit. Now the standard gear allows you to scan for implant signals, but you only have a limited degree of accuracy without the PTS. You can't pin an implant down as well. That means Irving knows what I know. I read two implants west of us, smack dab in the middle of Locksley's territory. That will be your Johnson and Delaney. I can find their camp if I have to, but that's about as close as I can get. I could be standing in the middle of a group of ten or twenty people, say, and I wouldn't be able to tell which of them had implants unless I pulled my gear out there and then and took some time about it, which would hardly prove practical for Irving, right? So he can track you, but he can't nail you down absolutely without exposing himself to danger."

"I still don't see what kept him from moving in on us," said Lucas.

"A couple of things. First off, he wouldn't know *exactly* where you were or *who* you were. Not unless he was right on top of you and scanning. That still puts him in a good position to take you out, but what happens then? Remember, put yourself in his place. Suppose he takes you prisoner. The other ref still reads you. He can get a rough reading on you and figure a fairly close location with a little time. He might figure out that you were taken. If Irving wastes you, your implant sends a KIA signal. If your signal winks out, that means a probable KIA with implant damage. See, that's why they didn't bother to brief you. They knew Irving could read you, but *they* had to read you, too, because if the adjustment team fails, what happens then?"

"They try to get another team," said Lucas, dryly.

"Right. Insurgents are easier to neutralize if you can identify and isolate them. So long as you're not a direct threat to Irving and he's got some idea where you are, he leaves you alone and the scenario progresses in a roughly linear fashion. Irving's either got to try and effect a change that's radical enough to throw the mission out or he's got to get to your mission commander."

"So what happens now?" said Lucas.

"Now, he probably figures you got killed somehow. These are dangerous times, after all. What we do is rendezvous with Johnson and Delaney and put our heads together. The outlaws might prove useful, too."

"I've got to pick up Hooker," Lucas said.

"I'm afraid that's not going to happen," Hunter said. He passed Lucas the bottle. "I had him scanned in Nottingham Castle somewhere. While I was taking the reading, his implant sent a KIA signal."

He had made an unforgiveable error in judgment.

It had taken him a long time to break Hooker, much longer than he had anticipated. He had hated having to do the work himself, but he had not been able to delegate the responsibility. What he had to say to Hooker and what he had hoped the man would tell him were things he did not want anyone else to overhear.

Hooker had yielded up only one piece of useful information, but it had taken far more effort than Irving had expected. He had kept the work up steadily, had spoken in a soft and pleasant voice, repeating over and over again how it was all unnecessary, how all Hooker had to do was to cooperate and it would all be over for him. Yet, the man had resisted with an astonishing force of will.

He had been wild with fear; he had blubbered pathetically; he had screamed with pain, but he had held on. There was a moment when he finally broke, when Irving thought that he was ready to go all the way, but something within him had galvanized and he screamed with rage and passed out. He had escaped, temporarily, in the only way left open to him.

Irving had freed him then. He had called the sheriff, who had entered the torture chamber and unfastened the manacles holding the unconscious Hooker to the wall. The look on Sir Guy's face had been difficult to read. Irving tried to imagine what the man was thinking, what had gone through his mind while he stood in the upper level of the dungeons, listening to the screams coming from below.

That's my king down there, torturing some escaped bondsman.

The sheriff had picked Hooker up and carried him to Irving's chambers. Irving told him to place Hooker on the bed and leave. Sir Guy complied without a word. Let the man rest, Irving had thought. Let him wake up in more pleasant surroundings. Allow him to accept that there was an alternative to the stinking dungeons. Irving left him alone, first taking the precaution of activating the safety field on his chronoplate and removing all the weapons from the room. But he had committed a serious error. He had underestimated Hooker's resolve and he had forgotten to take away the gauntlets that lay on a chair, unnoticed.

Irving stood looking at Hooker's corpse, cursing himself.

The man had taken one of the gauntlets and pulled out the garotte, looping the wire around the torch sconce set into the wall and then around his own neck. It was a grisly sight. The man must have gone mad. No rational human being would ever have committed such a horrifying act. Fighting his nausea, Irving took him down.

Perhaps there was still a way to turn this to his advantage. Hooker had revealed to him the identity of one of the adjustment team. So Ivanhoe wasn't really Ivanhoe in this scenario.

He was a temporal agent named Lucas Priest. He should have guessed when he had seen the man's performance in the melee, but the real Ivanhoe was a deadly fighter and Irving had expected that the adjustment team would have been infiltrated into the Norman camp, where they would at least have some protection. He had suspected De Bracy and Bois-Guilbert, for which reason he had recruited Andre de la Croix to stay close to them. At least he was certain of her.

Who could the other two men be? There were only two implant signals remaining, which meant that one of them was probably dead, but which one? Chances were that it was Priest, since he had been teamed with Hooker and Hooker had obviously run into trouble before falling into his hands. Hooker hadn't known about the missing signal, Irving was sure of that. Two signals left, both somewhere in Sherwood, in outlaw territory.

An outlaw archer had split a Norman arrow during the tournament at Ashby. A guided arrow? It was certainly possible for such a shot to occur naturally, but the odds against it were incredible. Still . . . hadn't there been a story in the legend of Robin Hood about . . . of course! What better way to use the outlaws against him than to infiltrate into their midst men who would be in a position of leadership? He wished he could have seen that archer from a closer distance. It could have been Locksley. On the other hand, it could easily have been one of the others and the act later attributed to Locksley. For that matter, it could have been a woman. Marion? Why not? He would proceed on the assumption that anyone in a position of leadership among the outlaws could be a temporal agent. He could clock back and observe the contest once again. For that matter, he could clock back and observe Priest and see whom he came in contact with.

They would be proceeding with extreme caution, knowing full well how inferior their position was. Irving smiled. What if he was to shake them up a bit?

Hooker was already dead. Very well, then let him know in Minus Time that he would die. Throw them for a loop. If he could avoid splitting the timestream, at that point he could reinforce his present position. He would clock back and observe the contest and his own part in it. Then he would ascertain which of the pavilions belonged to Priest, clock forward to his present position, pick up Hooker's body and drop it off with them. He would have to watch himself, but the effect on them would be devastating. They would know that he had penetrated at least two of their identities and most likely the others, as well. Hooker would be forced to face the prospect of his eventual demise. The alternative would be a paradox. Considering that, he understood why he had not been able to break Hooker easily. Perhaps he had already done as he was planning and the only way to preserve the timeline was to go ahead and do it now.

He was getting a headache. The migraines were coming more and more frequently now. He *had* to stop the game. It was wearing him out. He rubbed his head, trying to make the pain go away. What if he killed Prince John? Would the other referee be able to split the timeline, creating an alternate scenario in which his action would be canceled out somehow? He didn't know. He had to seize the throne. He knew that he was most vulnerable until he accomplished that goal. The other referee would not want to resort to setting up a parallel timeline. That would prove dangerous. Once he was firmly entrenched as Richard, King of England, nothing short of a major historical disruption would stop him, since Richard died at Chaluz, near Limoges, and Irving had no intention of setting foot anywhere near the place. Still, the game was making him more and more uncertain. If only they hadn't discovered his departure before he had been able to act. . . .

"God, when will it end?" he moaned, holding his head. He looked down at Hooker's corpse. "How many more of you will they send against me? How many more must die?"

He had to keep going. He had to keep struggling, forever hoping that some action he would take would result in a future scenario in which they did not send a team back after him. Meanwhile, he had to play it carefully. Sooner or later, he would prevail. The demands upon him were enormous, but he accepted that. Great men had to overcome great obstacles.

All right, he thought, time to bring things to a boil. Andre de la Croix was, by now, already at Torquilstone, in a position to move against De Bracy and Bois-Guilbert. That would deprive John of his two strongest allies. The Saxon leaders were in his hands, he could now clock them directly into De Bracy's dungeons. He reached under his bed, first deactivating the safety field on the chronoplate with his remote unit. He opened the case and began to assemble the border circuits. He wasn't quite through with Hooker yet.

Hooker would, indeed, be in a unique position. After all, how many men would ever know the exact manner of their death?

Lucas and Hunter materialized in the exact center of the camp, so near to Alan-a-dale that he jumped a foot and promptly passed out.

"Ooops," said Hunter. "That was a little close, wasn't it?"

Lucas was too busy upchucking to reply. He was still a little weak and his stomach had reacted badly to the chronoplate.

"Sorry about that," said Hunter. "I would've floater-clocked us in, but I don't want to pull out any technology that might alert our friend. Someone might've spotted us coming in that way."

"Suppose I had clocked in right in his space," said Lucas, wiping his mouth and looking at the unconscious minstrel.

"Hey, you gotta bring some to get some, pilgrim. I'll try to be more careful from now on."

"I would appreciate that."

Within seconds of their dramatic appearance, they were surrounded by the merry men, who gazed at Hunter with a mixture of awe and fear. Delaney and Johnson, accompanied by Marion, pushed their way through. At the sight of Hunter, Finn's jaw dropped.

"What the—"

"Silence!" Hunter took out his .45 and fired into the ground at Delaney's feet. Finn jumped back, eyes wide. "Any insolence will be severely dealt with," said Hunter.

"Holy shit," said Bobby.

Hunter pointed the weapon at him and Bobby quickly raised his hands.

"What do you demand of us?" said Marion.

Finn and Bobby exchanged quick glances. They were profoundly relieved to see Lucas alive, but who in God's name was the guy with the automatic?

"Some of you know this man," said Hunter, scowling at the outlaws. They were clearly terrified of him. "He is the white knight, Sir Wilfred of Ivanhoe. You are to give him shelter. You are to obey him as you would obey me. You are to say nothing of his presence here to anyone. You know the consequences."

They were all deathly silent.

"You. And you," said Hunter, pointing out Finn and Bobby. "Come with me." To Marion, he said, "See to it that we are not disturbed. The rest of you go on about your business."

"A deserter with a chronoplate," said Finn. "Man, you must be living the life of Riley."

Hunter grinned. "It suits me."

"These men obviously know you," said Bobby. "If I was really Robin Hood, I suppose I would have known about you, too, but how is it that we've never even heard anyone mention you?"

"Fear," said Hunter. "It makes for an effective deterrent. It's not hard to preserve your anonymity in an age where there isn't much mobility, but I couldn't hope to hide from everyone. I put the fear of God into these people, or fear of the devil, if you prefer. I value my privacy, so I told them that there was a spell protecting me. Anyone who speaks of me aloud will be struck down, unless they're addressing me personally. And just to keep them in line, to remind them of the consequences of giving in to temptation, every so often I waste a couple of them. Something showy like laser beam decapitation or a pyrogel grenade."

"I guess that would do it," Finn said softly.

"You mean you just . . . kill a number of them . . . *at random*?" said Bobby, shocked.

"I told you, they killed my boys," said Hunter. "Why should I care about their lives? Besides, I've got a strong streak of self-preservation."

"Seems to me I've heard that phrase before," said Finn, glancing at Bobby.

"It works," said Hunter. "I always make sure the hit is witnessed, so the horrible story gets back to the others, ten times exaggerated. It reminds them that I have magical powers and I always take care that I'm not seen, so they simply assume that the poor deceased must have spoken about me."

"That's crazy," Bobby said.

"No, it is, perhaps, a bit draconian, but that's not out of line in these times. I'm just taking advantage of Clarke's Axiom. Any sufficiently advanced technology is going to seem like magic to those who don't understand it. If that offends your moral sensibilities, tough shit. Besides, considering your line of work, that would be splitting hairs, wouldn't it?"

"You sure you want this guy on our side?" Bobby said to Lucas.

Hunter laughed. "Listen, pilgrim, without me, you're dead meat and you know it. Besides, you haven't got any choice. Our friend Irving is threatening me as well as you, by his very intervention in this period. If you're going to stop him, you'll need all the help you can get."

"Look, arguing amongst ourselves isn't going to help us any," Finn said. "He's right. Irving presents a threat and we've got to neutralize it."

"What about the threat *he's* presenting?" Bobby said.

"I'm not stupid," Hunter said. "I've taken steps to keep my presence here from affecting history. So I bring some artifacts from the future. So what? You think any of these people know what the hell an automatic pistol is? Obviously, there's no guarantee that my presence here will remain a secret. Again, so what? These are superstitious times. What's another story about a sorcerer with deadly powers?"

"Suppose something you brought back falls into the wrong hands?" said Bobby. "Have you thought of that?"

"I seriously doubt that would change the course of history," said Hunter. "Besides, odds are it would be destroyed. Sorcerous paraphernalia, you know. You got any other questions, or can we get down to business?"

"I think that's a sensible suggestion," Lucas said. "First off, Finn, how are the outlaws shaping up?"

"Well, a crack military unit they're not, but they'll do in a pinch. The only problem right now is a question of priorities."

"How's that?"

"They're impossible to control right now," said Finn. "Evidently, De Bracy's attack on Cedric's party was seen by someone. Word's gotten around that the prisoners are being kept at Torquilstone. What's more, rumor has it that the outlaws were paid off to help De Bracy. That kind of talk isn't doing these people any good. Many of them have families in the local villages and not a few of them are Saxon patriots."

"Is there any chance the rumor's true?" said Lucas.

"It's possible," said Finn, "although I doubt it. We've got ourselves a small army here and there are a lot of other bands spread out throughout the forest. I don't think any of

Locksley's people were involved, but the point is, whether it's true or not, Cedric's very well regarded in these parts. If times are tough, you can always get a meal at Rotherwood. And Cedric doesn't mind if you hunt on his land. These are his people. They might be outlaws, but they're Saxon outlaws and they've got a lot of pride. De Bracy went and put the arm on the last of the house of Alfred. If he wanted to start a revolution, he couldn't have gone about it in a better way."

"Word's gone out to all the outlaw bands," said Bobby. "They've already started arriving. They want to lay siege to Torquilstone."

"Can they pull it off?" said Lucas.

Finn shrugged. "They've got the numbers. And their blood is up. If they march on Torquilstone, nothing short of a major military action will stop them."

"A Saxon uprising did occur in this period," said Bobby. "I don't think there's anything that we can do to stop it. Irving knows that, too. It will provide him with an ideal opportunity to make his move."

Hunter nodded. "That makes sense. There will be the knights who've returned from the Crusades; they'll be loyal to Richard. My guess is he's probably contacted many of them and they'll be awaiting his orders to move. When the outlaws attack Torquilstone, they'll pin down John's strongest knights. If Irving shows up to help them, he'll have a Saxon army to follow him against Prince John. I wouldn't be at all surprised to learn that he even engineered Cedric's capture somehow."

"But he'll have to know that we'll be there," said Bobby. "How can he hope to join the action, knowing that temporal agents are waiting to take him out right then and there?"

"Well, obviously it will be taking a risk," said Hunter, "but if it was me, I'll tell you how I'd do it. I'd announce myself as King Richard, returned to end tyranny and oppression and all that sort of thing. Then I'd declare a blanket pardon for all the outlaws in exchange for their help. When it hits the fan, you might be able to draw a bead on him in the middle of it all, but he won't be alone. And he'll have all the outlaws watching out for him."

"That won't necessarily stop us from killing him," said Bobby.

"It'll make it hard as hell," said Hunter. "But just for a

minute, suppose you do get a clear shot at him. If one of the outlaws doesn't stop you, how are you going to survive killing the king? Worse than that, you'll have an army of witnesses to testify to the fact that Richard died at Torquilstone. Be a little awkward if another Richard showed up after that, wouldn't it?''

"You think he'd gamble on that?" said Lucas.

"Why not? We're the only ones interested in preserving history. Irving's the guy who wants to change it.''

12

De Bracy was losing his patience. "I am not here to bargain with you, Jew," he said to Isaac. He reached out and grabbed the man by his beard, giving it a vicious yank. Isaac cried out in pain. "I know you're a rich man, the banker of your accursed tribe. It is not as if I'm asking for the moon."

"I would sooner be able to give you the moon, Sir Knight," said Isaac, "than gather together the ransom you demand!"

"A thousand pounds in silver," said De Bracy. "Those are my terms. I will not bargain. I am a reasonable man. If silver be scarce, I will not refuse gold. Is your life not worth such a sum?"

"And what of my daughter's life?" said Isaac.

"You need not fear for Rebecca's life," said De Bracy, chuckling. "Brian de Bois-Guilbert's desire is for love, not death. She will be safe enough from violence so long as she pleases him. When he grows tired of her, I'm certain you will have her back."

"No," said Isaac, "I beg you, save her from such shame. I will do anything you ask; her dishonor would be more than I could bear!"

"You will bear much more before I am through with you," De Bracy said. "Look around you. You are in my dungeons now, not your house in York, where you are free to dictate terms to those from whose disadvantages you prosper. Prisoners ten thousand times more distinguished than yourself have died within these walls. But their deaths would be luxuries compared to yours. A man can be made to suffer untold pain and still be kept alive to suffer more. Do you see that range of iron bars above the glowing charcoal? You'll be stripped of all your clothes and placed on that warm couch. You will be basted like a roast, so that you do not cook too quickly. Is not a thousand pounds of silver a paltry sum compared to such a fate? Choose and choose now, for I am running out of patience! A slow death upon the coals, or a thousand pounds of silver, those are my terms!''

"I will pay your ransom," Isaac said, "only preserve my daughter's honor and let her go free."

"I told you, Jew, I will not bargain with you! Besides, I have already given my word that Bois-Guilbert shall have her. I would not go back on my word as a knight, not for the sake of a pathetic Jew."

"Then you will get nothing," Isaac said, staring at him with hatred. "Not an ounce of silver will I give you, unless I were to pour it molten down your avaricious throat! Do your worst. Take my life if you will and let it be said that the Jew, in spite of all his tortures, knew how to disappoint the Christian!''

"Very well, then," said De Bracy. "I will put your resolve to the test. You'll be whimpering for mercy within moments. Strip him!''

At that moment, a trumpet call was sounded and there was a commotion up above, the sounds of men yelling to each other. Andre de la Croix ran into the dungeon.

"Maurice, come quickly! The Saxons are attacking!"

"*What?* Are you mad?"

"It's true, I tell you! Listen. It is the outlaws. They have gathered in force and are even at this moment attempting to storm the castle!"

"What absurdity is this?" De Bracy said. "Why would the outlaws attack Torquilstone?"

"They cry for Cedric's freedom."

"The Saxon? I have but two Jews, I have no Saxon!"

"So Bois-Guilbert says. He commands the castle in your

absence. They will not listen. Brian says that only force is good for dealing with them.''

''How many of them are there?''

''A thousand, at the least.''

''Brian is a fool. With such a number, they might well take the castle if they are determined enough. I will show them that Cedric is not here.''

Isaac momentarily forgotten, De Bracy started out of the dungeons, on his way to the castle above. Andre followed him.

''I don't know what insanity has overtaken them,'' De Bracy said, ''but these cells are all empty! See for yourself. I—''

At that moment, the sound of Cedric's voice was heard shouting from within one of the cells.

''What the devil?'' said De Bracy. He flung open the tiny window of the door and peered inside. ''*Cedric!*''

''Release me, villain!'' Cedric shouted, launching himself against the door.

De Bracy slammed the window shut, stunned. He opened the window in the door of the next cell and saw Athelstane. In the adjoining cell, he found Rowena.

''Is this your doing, de la Croix?''

''I rode into the castle with just my squire,'' Andre said. ''You know that. You, yourself, admitted me.''

''*But how in God's name did they get here?*''

''There is no need to attempt to deceive *me*, Maurice,'' said Andre, smiling. ''I am on *your* side.''

''Don't you jest with *me*, de la Croix!'' said De Bracy, grabbing her by the cloth of her doublet and slamming her into the wall. He felt the swaddling cloth beneath. ''What's this?''

He ripped open her doublet with a quick motion, revealing the cloth. ''You're wounded! No, you're . . .'' He saw the bulges beneath the cloth and his eyes grew wide. In that moment, Andre stuck her dagger into his stomach up to its hilt. As De Bracy jerked, she leaned into him, placing both hands on the dagger. She twisted the blade and used her weight to drive into him, jerking the dagger up several times in a ripping motion.

De Bracy sagged to the floor and she pulled the dagger out of him, wiping its blade on his clothing. Clutching his stomach, he stared up at her in disbelief, making choking noises.

She glanced at him only briefly, to make certain that the wound was fatal, then she left him to die in his own dungeons.

The word spread through the outlaws' ranks like wildfire. Richard had returned. No one knew who had been the original bearer of the news, but Lucas was convinced that Irving had infiltrated runners into the attacking force. The news was passed rapidly. Richard, it seemed, had returned to England to take back his throne and to restore justice to the land. No one was exactly sure what "justice" was, but it was generally supposed that the Saxons were going to get a fair shake at last. Evidently, the king had met up with one of the outlaw bands and was even now on his way with a party of knights to join in the attack on Torquiistone. It was, of course, the sensible thing for him to do. Even the outlaws understood that De Bracy and Bois-Guilbert were allied with John and, as such, posed a threat to Richard. The news that was greeted with the greatest jubilation was that the king had decreed a blanket pardon for all the outlaws who would help him in his cause. Irving had done precisely as Hunter had surmised.

"You can bet that he won't make an appearance until he's certain that everyone has heard the news," said Bobby, sourly. "Well, that might make our job a little more difficult, but it still won't make it impossible. Before the day is out, we'll know which way this thing is going to go."

So far, it was going pretty much of its own accord. It was next to impossible to control such a large and undisciplined band of men. Outlaws from all over the countryside had arrived to take part in the revolt and they were out for blood. Finn, trying to do the best he could under the circumstances, was trying to direct the assault upon the barbican. It wasn't the ideal way to take a castle, but they were forced to follow the momentum of the attack and control its flow to whatever degree they could. Besides, the outcome of the battle was of no consequence to them. In that respect, there was a familiarity about the situation. It was like a standard temporal action. The soldiers from the future were fighting a war within a war. Irving was their objective. So long as they were able to take him out, what happened to Torquilstone didn't really matter.

The air above the castle was a hailstorm of arrows. Most of the cloth-yard shafts failed to find a mark, but given such a profusion of arrows, the archers took their inevitable toll. Anyone who risked showing themselves upon the battlements stood to become a pincushion in short order. Each lattice and aperture became a target for the bowmen and the Norman men at arms returned the fire with their crossbows at their peril. Finn's men were moving forward under the protection of mantelets and pavisses, which provided at least some protection from the arbalests being used to defend the barbican. Once that was taken, then the other outlaws could move forward for a mass assault upon the outer walls and postern with rams and scaling ladders. It would be a bloody conflict with heavy losses.

Above the din of battle, a trumpet call was heard and, from across the meadow, a formation of knights approached at full gallop. In their vanguard, a knight wearing the three lions of Richard Plantagenet rode beside his banner.

"He must have completely lost his mind," said Bobby. He removed one of his warhead arrows from his quiver and fitted it to the bow. "This is going to be like shooting fish in a barrel. The moment he gets in range, I'm going to let him have it."

"I don't know if that's wise," said Lucas. "Maybe we should wait until he gets into the thick of it. If he falls in the middle of the battle, it might not be as noticeable."

"I really don't give a damn," said Bobby.

"Don't be hasty," Lucas said. "There are outlaws all around us who are very pleased to see this man. Remember, he just pardoned all of them. They're not going to take it too kindly if they see you drawing a bead on him. The idea *is* for us to get the job done and get back alive."

"Maybe. But it might be best just to take our chances. Finn's right. Our job is to take him out and then let the refs worry about fixing things up."

"All right. So we'll take him out. But let's not rush it and blow the deal. Has it occurred to you that he knows we're here? Do you think he'd be so stupid as to make such an obvious target of himself?"

"What are you getting at?"

"What I'm getting at is that there's no guarantee that the

guy wearing Richard's armor is really Irving. He might be one of the others and the man in Richard's armor just a decoy to enable him to get past us."

"The man's got a point," said Hunter. He had come up right behind them and now he beckoned them back under the cover of the trees. They went a short distance away from the drawn lines of the outlaws and found that Hunter had brought his chronoplate with him, along with some other equipment. "Okay, I'm going to make it fast, so listen up. I just hope to hell you guys have been cleared on these weapons at some time, because I haven't got the time or the inclination to start giving lessons right now. I brought back a couple of Swedish "K" grease guns. Lucas, you hang on to my Colt, I've brought back another. Bobby, here's a .45 for you, too. If things get really hairy, I brought back a few pyrogel grenades, Mark Fours. Here's a bunch of magazines—"

"Are you kidding?" Bobby said. "This stuff's prehistoric!"

"Not in the 12th century it ain't, pilgrim. Listen, I had a hell of a time just getting those grenades. What do you want, a GE/Krupp four-barrel pulser? I almost got myself fried getting my hands on these. TC ordnance isn't exactly just lying around for the taking, you know. I'm not putting my ass on the line for anybody. If you can't do the job with this stuff, you just can't do the job, so hang it up."

"Okay, okay," said Bobby. "So what's the plan?"

"The plan is to move fast as hell," said Hunter. "Lucas is right. You don't know which of those jokers is Irving, so Bobby, old friend, you just take one of these pretty little Swedes and you open up on *all* of 'em."

"If Irving's wearing nysteel, a submachine gun isn't going to do the trick. It might beat his armor all to hell, but it's going to be pretty iffy."

"Right. But you can bet your ass it's going to knock him down," said Hunter. "It'll kill anybody who isn't wearing nysteel. The guy who gets back up is your man. *Then* you can use one of your fancy arrows on him. Right?"

"Great," said Bobby. "Give me that thing." He took the grease gun and quickly checked it.

"You all still got the PRU's I gave you?" Hunter said. "Where's Delaney?"

"He's up with the assault force," Lucas said. "Yeah, we've all got 'em."

"Good. They're all slaved to this unit." He indicated the chronoplate. "I'll stay back here and try to keep my eye on you. Like I said, I'm not going to lay my ass on the line if I can help it. If I see you're in trouble, I'll yank you right back here. Likewise, if you're in a jam, the PRU will bring you right back to this spot, so we've got a double safety, your control and mine. Any questions?"

"No," said Bobby. "Let's do it."

"Get a move on. Those knights are coming on fast."

They moved back forward, Bobby using his body to shield the "K." As the knights rode up to the scene of battle, the barbican fell to the outlaws and the Norman men at arms began to sally forth from the castle to defend the postern. Hunter bent over his chronoplate and, seconds later, Finn Delaney stood in front of him.

"What the hell?" Finn said.

"I used the PRU to snatch you back here," Hunter said. He tossed Finn the other grease gun, then handed him a Browning nine-millimeter and a satchel of grenades. "Now listen up. We could be in deep shit unless we find Irving's chronoplate. You can bet your ass he hasn't got it with him."

"How the hell are we going to do that?" said Finn. "We haven't got enough manpower to institute a radius search—"

"We don't have to. It's a gamble, but I think his plate is in Nottingham Castle. I scanned Hooker over there just before he died. I could still be wrong, but it's the best guess I can make right now. I'm going to clock you over there. Now there will be people in your way, but you've got them at a disadvantage now. You go through that castle and you *find* that damn plate. There's some plastique in that satchel. You find it and you blow it, got it? And then our friend won't be able to get away."

"That's assuming that you're right and the plate is there," said Finn.

Hunter shrugged. "You got a better idea?"

"No. Okay. Clock me out."

"Good luck."

Finn disappeared.

• • •

Irving rode at the rear of the formation, his nysteel armor relacquered from its original black shade to one of green. Up ahead of him, the sheriff rode at the front of the formation, wearing the three lions of Richard Plantagenet. Some of the other knights had unlacquered armor, others, who held lands, wore the colors they were known by. Irving had no doubt that if the temporal agents were to strike, they would move first against Sir Guy. He would have to remain on his guard, watching out for them. Once he had them spotted, he could move to neutralize them. He kept his hand on his PRU. As they approached the battle, suddenly there erupted from the outlaw ranks a staccato clattering and Sir Guy and the two knights immediately to either side went down. Irving looked wildly about the scene. The formation was broken up when the first three knights were hit. Three more died before Irving had the man spotted.

It wasn't hard to spot him. He stood all alone, firing a sub-machine gun. A submachine gun! Incredible! They must have reached total desperation. All around the man, the outlaws were drawing back in panic, fleeing from the noise and the destruction that they could never understand. Even as he watched, more men went down in front of him as the man kept firing in short, steady bursts, and then bullets were ripping into him. It had all happened so fast, he barely had time to think. He hit the ground hard, caught his breath and struggled to his feet, thankful that he had kept his grip on the PRU.

"Bingo!" said Bobby, tossing the grease gun to Lucas, who came running up beside him. "The green knight! Cover me!"

He nocked his warhead arrow and drew back his bow.

"Game's over!" Bobby said.

As Irving got up, he hit the PRU and clocked himself back to Nottingham. He reappeared inside his chambers in the castle. The temporal agents were desperate men and they had resorted to desperate tactics. Well, the game wasn't over yet. He still had his chronoplate and that was where he had them, superior firepower notwithstanding. He could still outflank them. He quickly made the necessary adjustments on the plate, then clocked himself back onto the scene of the battle, in a different location, seconds before he had clocked back to Nottingham.

Bobby had drawn his bow and was aiming at the green knight, but even as he let the arrow fly, Irving disappeared. At that same instant, Irving appeared behind him. Even as the Irving Bobby was shooting at was clocking out, the Irving who had clocked in behind him plunged a dagger into him.

"*Bobby!*" Lucas shouted. He swung the grease gun around and fired, but Irving was no longer there. Instantly realizing his error, Lucas spun around and only had enough time to hurl himself sideways as Irving brought his sword down in a vicious arc. The sword missed him, but just barely.

Suddenly, Lucas was on the ground at Hunter's feet. Hunter had used the PRU to yank him away.

"Son of a bitch is playing fugue games," Hunter said.

"I've still got the gun, give me some grenades," said Lucas.

"Forget it, man. You don't want to go filling the air with slugs when you might be clocking right into 'em. We're just going to have to play that game ourselves. No other way."

"I've got no armor!" Lucas said.

"I've got some mail and half-plate. It ain't nysteel, but it's the best I can do. Throw it on and get back out there."

"This is crazy!"

"Tell me about it. Only two ways it can end like this. One of you dies or Finn finds that plate. Better cross your fingers, pilgrim."

He clocked Lucas back into the action, at a point just before he left.

Even as Irving was bringing his sword down on Lucas, Lucas appeared behind him. Before Lucas could strike Irving, another Irving appeared behind *him* and Lucas felt a momentary shock as Irving's sword glanced off him even as he was clocking once again. Irving had the advantage in that his armor was effectively impregnable. Lucas made up for his disadvantage in that he did not have to worry about clocking himself out or in. Hunter was at the controls. The only thing he had to worry about was that Hunter would stay on the ball. The action began to accelerate with amazing speed. There was no chance to use the weapons Hunter had brought back. He was right. In a fugue situation, the last thing you wanted to do was to fill the air with bullets, cutting through space into which you might be clocking. Given the speed with which the combat took place, it was only possible to fight with the weapons at hand.

To the outlaws and men at arms observing the action, the world seemed to have gone mad. One moment, there was one knight fighting another. The next, two knights fighting two. Three knights fighting three. Four knights fighting four.

Each of the antagonists used their PRU units to return to their respective chronoplates again and again, where quick calculations and recalibrations would be made as they fought to catch their breath. Then they would clock back into the battle, materializing on the scene in their own immediate past, seconds or minutes before they had departed. The pressures of the temporal fugue were immense. One error in calculation, one slip in concentration and it would all be over. As the cycle progressed, those not involved in the fugue were confronted with a dizzying reality. Events happened at a much faster pace for them than for the combatants. In an instant, there were suddenly dozens of green knights and dozens of Ivanhoes hacking away at each other, more appearing as others winked out as though they had never been there to begin with.

Many of those who observed the phenomenon came to a gaping halt, mesmerized by the impossibility of what they were confronting. Not a few were killed as they stood staring in shock. It was an eerie scene: the fugue combatants going at each other for all they were worth, those around them either fighting, oblivious to what was happening around them, or simply standing with their weapons in their hands, staring uncomprehendingly. Many simply dropped their arms and ran.

Finn materialized in the courtyard of Nottingham Castle. It took perhaps a moment before anybody noticed him. By the time they did, he had quickly taken stock of his surroundings and was already on the move, firing as he ran. He wasn't taking any chances. His weapons gave him a devastating superiority, but all it took was one archer who would not panic and he would become just another statistic. Fortunately, most of them did panic. They had no reference for gunpower or lead projectiles fired too fast to be seen. Some of the guards stood frozen on the battlements, watching in disbelief as the bodies of their comrades literally came apart before their eyes. Those who survived the initial burst of firing fled, screaming with terror. By that time, Finn had already aimed and thrown one of the pyrogel grenades. The courtyard became a place of havoc, filled with the sounds of submachine gun fire and men screaming in agony as they fled from a horror they did not understand. Those who had survived the blast of the pyrogel grenade, but were still near enough to catch the fury of the explosion, became wreathed in flame and were consumed in seconds. Walking corpses in a halo of fire, charred crisp as a cinder, vocal chords seared away so that screaming was no longer possible, they made several halting steps and fell into a pile of ashes on the ground.

Finn didn't waste time with the door. He hurled a grenade and dived through, rolling and firing as he came up. Those who died didn't even have enough time to draw their swords. There was a brutal simplicity to Finn's tactics. He simply had to slaughter everyone in sight before he could take time to search for the plate. He only hoped that Hunter had guessed right and that it was here. As he ran down the corridor, slipping in a fresh magazine, a group of men came running to meet him, responding to the alarm. He cut them down to the last man, then reached for another clip. He jerked as a crossbow bolt hit him from behind, entering his shoulder from the back and coming almost completely through the other side. He dropped his grease gun. Throwing himself to the side, he came up with the 9mm Browning. Three quick shots dropped the archer even as he was drawing back his crossbow to fire a second quarrel.

For a moment, all was silent, save for the sounds of running footsteps somewhere close by, echoing all around him. Finn glanced quickly at his wound. He left the quarrel where it was. Removing it meant risking a flow of blood, since it could be the only thing holding a blood vessel together. The wound didn't look fatal unless, possibly, it became infected. There was no point to worrying about that now. He didn't even feel any pain. He retrieved his SMG and loaded another clip, then took off at a run down the corridor, staying close to the wall and keeping an eye on what was behind him. He couldn't risk being surprised again. He had to clean the castle out and find the chronoplate.

It could be anywhere. He had to search the entire castle for something the size of a briefcase.

Andre ran directly to her quarters, oblivious of all the commotion around her. The castle was under attack and its commander lay dead or dying beneath her in the dungeons. She had only three things on her mind. She had to get her armor, she had to take steps to protect Marcel, and she had to find a way to dispose of Bois-Guilbert. She was what the black knight had called his "inside man," and her duty was to defeat the defenders of the castle from within by depriving them of their leaders.

She had resented his remark at the time he made it and she had said so, protesting that she was not at all a man on the inside and that she had no desire to be a man; then he had told her that the term was used to describe someone who attacked a force from within their own ranks, a spy, one who pretended loyalty until the time to act was ripe.

"You mean a traitor," she had said.

"Treason is defined purely subjectively," he had told her. "I could have called you an 'inside woman,' but seeing as how you are a man on the outside, within the walls of Torquilstone you will . . . oh, never mind. You can't see the humor in it, can you?"

"I see no humor in being asked to play the part of a traitor," she replied.

"You will be treasonous to John if you do as I command. If you do not, then you will be treasonous to me. I ask you to consider which of the two you would prefer. It seems contrary to your profession to speak of treason. You are a mass of ambiguities, de la Croix."

"Of what?"

"Never mind. I'll make the matter of your honor simple for you. As a mercenary, your loyalty rests with your paymaster. Since I have outbid the competition, your course would seem to be quite clear. Does that satisfy you?"

"I suppose that it will have to."

"Good, I'm so glad. Take this." He handed her a PRU.

"What is it?"

"Where you will be going, you will encounter danger. This is a charm of sorts. Keep it with you at all times. It will protect you."

She started to examine it.

"Do not play with it," he said, sternly. "It has powers you would not understand. Merely keep it on your person. Take it as a token of my concern for you."

She stared at him steadily. "Who are you?"

He raised his eyebrows. "I am your king."

"Or the devil," she said.

"If you like."

As she reached her quarters, she took out the charm that he had given her and, for a moment, she considered throwing it away. She wanted nothing to do with black arts, but it was too late for that. She had allied herself with a sorcerer and, king or not, he was her master. She hated him. She would kill him if she could, but could the sorcerer be killed? She had tried before and failed. Perhaps he had such a charm himself. She stared at it. If it could give her some measure of protection, she would do well to keep it. She knew that she would need all the protection she could get before the day was out.

Marcel assisted her in arming for battle.

"I will go with you, Andre. You'll need my help."

"No, little brother. You remain here, where it will be safe until I come for you. I would not want to lose you now."

"Nor I you," Marcel said. "Sir Brian is a strong knight. He will make a dangerous opponent."

"And I will fight better knowing you are safe," said Andre, "than I would if you were by my side and I had to constantly watch out for you."

Marcel drew back indignantly. "I can take care of myself," he said in a wounded tone.

She pulled him to her. "Of course you can. But I would worry anyway. Indulge me and set my mind at rest. There will be other battles for you when you're older. Now I must go. Remember, stay here and do not be tempted to look outside upon the battle. The Saxon archers shoot straight and true."

With sword and shield in hand, she left him and walked quickly down the corridor. Her heart was racing, as it always did in the excitement of a battle. She would have to find a way to kill Bois-Guilbert in such a manner as to not leave herself vulnerable to the men whom he commanded in defense of the castle. She stopped by an aperture and, holding her shield ready to protect her face, risked a quick glance outside. The barbican had fallen. Any moment now, they would begin to attack the outer walls with scaling ladders and they would start ramming at the gates. Given their number, it was inevitable that they would soon gain entry to the castle. Given a firm hand and strong leadership, the defenders of Torquilstone might still repulse them, but not if they were deprived of their commanders. De Bracy was already accounted for. Only one remained.

She stopped a man at arms who went rushing by her in the corridor. He looked terrified.

"You!" She approached him. "Where are you going?"

"I . . . I was . . ."

He was running away to find a place to hide, no doubt. "Where is Sir Brian?"

The man was near hysteria. "You ask for Sir Brian," he said. "Sir Brian bellows for Sir Maurice! The Saxons bellow for our blood! They are on us like flies upon a carcass and where is De Bracy?"

"De Bracy's dead!"

They both turned toward the sound of the voice and saw De Bracy's torturer. Andre cursed her luck. She had bolted the door to the dungeons, but the man must have broken through. He held a mace in his hand. The beefy torturer had murder in his eyes as he pointed at her with his mace.

"There stands the culprit! Sir Maurice breathed his name before he died!"

Andre ran the man at arms beside her through with her sword and pushed his body aside. Holding the mace with both hands, the torturer advanced upon her. Suddenly, he stiffened and dropped his mace, a look of surprise upon his face. He pitched forward. As he fell, Marcel stood revealed, a bloody dagger in his hand.

"Marcel! I told you to remain behind! I could have dealt with—"

Marcel's eyes widened. "*Andre! Beware, behind you!*"

Instinctively, she threw herself to one side, thereby avoiding the killing stroke. The nysteel armor might have saved her, but her reflexes were too quick for her to think of that. As it was, she caught a glancing blow on her brassard and, stunned, she dropped her shield and staggered. Marcel leapt forward with his dagger.

Andre heard him cry out and raised her head in time to see

Bois-Guilbert withdrawing his sword from her little brother's stomach.

"*God! Marcel!*"

"So," said Bois-Guilbert, "De Bracy's dead and we have a traitor in our midst. As God is my judge, I will show you the price of treason, de la Croix!"

"I have already paid that price," said Andre, glancing at Marcel. "And in a moment, God *will* be judging you."

What opposition there was was either dead, in flight, or hiding. Finn had to find the chronoplate. It would not be where anyone could readily see it. If Irving had been using Nottingham Castle as his base of operations, then it stood to reason that he'd keep the chronoplate secure within his chambers. But which of the rooms were his?

Finn ransacked them all systematically, tearing everything apart to find the object of his search. In several of the rooms, he found men and women cowering in fright. There was a chance that they would not have attempted to interfere with him, but he could not afford to take it. He shot them all. If they succeeded in their mission, the refs would have a lot of cleaning up to do. If not, the point was moot. There were a lot of lives at stake. Somehow, that thought did very little to comfort him.

The crossbow bolt in his shoulder was beginning to cause him a great deal of pain now. He could not afford to dwell on it. Hunter had to be right, he *had* to be. The thought of so much killing to no purpose . . .

Where was it?

There remained two more places where he had not searched. Please, God, Finn thought, let it be in one of them, please. He tried the door. It was bolted from within, like several of the others had been, where people had attempted to hide from him. He took a small amount of the plastique and blew it open. A man rushed at him with a sword. Finn shot him. There was no one else inside. He looked down at his attacker.

He wasn't even old enough to shave.

Irving clocked back into his chambers. Safe, for the moment, behind a bolted door. He was breathing hard. He was almost completely spent. Each time, he tried to rest a little, to catch his breath, but the strain of the temporal fugue was beginning to wear him out.

He had almost bought it when the fugue began. They were using a chronoplate as well! He had been certain that the other referee would not have risked it, would not have had a plate issued to his team. This changed everything. Obviously, there was no chance of tracing the plate. He hadn't been aware of it before and that meant that the tracer function had been bypassed, just as he had done on his unit. Those fools! Didn't they realize what they were forcing him to do? He had gone to a great deal of trouble to become Richard and he hated to abandon his role, but he had to recognize the possibility that he would have to clock out to another period, start a new scenario. They might never find him then. They had forced his hand. He hated to leave now when he had come so close, but it appeared that he would have little choice.

But before he did anything else, he had to bring the fugue to a conclusion. He could not risk being outmaneuvered. He had to stop that man; he was the only one left. . . . And perhaps that would even end it. He had killed the other agent. Perhaps when he killed this one the scenario would take a turn in his favor. Maybe this time the other ref would be too late. He still had a hole card.

Andre de la Croix.

She was carrying a PRU slaved to his chronoplate. He could clock her back into his chambers and bring her back into the fugue with him. He could not hope to explain the mechanics of a temporal fugue to her, but she already believed him to be a wizard, he could pass it all off as sorcery and tell her that the only thing she needed to concern herself with was the death of his opponent. Together, they would outnumber him and he would stand no chance. He had given her the unit in expectation of trouble, but he had not suspected just how badly he would need her. He would end it now.

Reaching for the control console of the chronoplate, he punched out the sequence that would clock her back to Nottingham. Then, when her usefulness was ended, he could kill her at his leisure.

Bois-Guilbert was putting up a valiant struggle, but he was being hammered into the ground. He couldn't understand how de la Croix's armor was standing up so well under his repeated assaults. Both knights were exhausted, but where Bois-Guilbert's armor bore the marks of Andre's assaults, de la Croix's armor was undamaged. She had already drawn blood.

Andre was fighting with a fury unlike anything that she had known before. For the first time, she felt the fire of blood lust coursing through her. She was tired and Bois-Guilbert was strong, but her ensorcelled armor and her charm gave her protection he did not enjoy. He had killed Marcel and he would pay.

With a savage stroke, she smashed at him. He caught the blow on his shield, which was badly battered, and the force of it was too great for him to hold on. She struck again and he lost his shield. Holding his sword with both hands, he attempted to strike back, but de la Croix was on him with a vengeance, pounding away at him, breaking through his armor, getting past his defenses . . . .

He was growing weak from loss of blood. He could not accept that he was losing. It could not be happening, it was impossible. Her sword came down in a vicious chopping stroke and he felt it bite into his armor, penetrate through into his arm. He cried out and felt his sword slip from his hand, felt the floor come up beneath him . . . .

For a moment, there was an incandescent respite. He looked up and saw de la Croix poised with sword held overhead.

"Damn," he whispered softly.

The sword—

—came down.

Irving never knew what killed him.

Andre froze. She did not know what had happened. One moment, Bois-Guilbert was at her mercy, prepared to meet his maker. The next, she was . . . elsewhere. And her sword had split the sorcerer's head right down the middle. He was at her feet, kneeling before some strange and mystifying apparatus. His helmet was on the floor, inches away, as though he had only just removed it. Dazed, she backed away and watched the corpse topple.

The door exploded inward and Finn Delaney barged into the room. He fired a quick burst into her chest, knocking her off her feet, and then he saw the chronoplate and Irving's corpse. Andre lay on her back, not moving. She was in shock. Not giving her a second glance, Finn set the charge on the chronoplate and hit his PRU. When Andre looked up, he was gone.

13 ————————————————

It was over before Lucas realized that it had ended. The fugue had run its course and, as time caught up to them, all the Irvings and all his other selves began to disappear until only he was left, standing all alone and spinning madly, swinging his sword in all directions. As the battle raged around him, he stood alone in a cleared space as some of the outlaws looked on, jaws hanging agape, the attack on Torquilstone forgotten.

In the fury of the battle, only a few of those involved were aware of the strange scene being played out in their midst. The Saxons had broken through and were even at that moment pouring into the castle and slaughtering the Normans. Cedric and his family were being released, along with a sorrowful Isaac of York. As Lucas stopped hacking at the air and stood alone, those who had been watching began to back away, questioning their own sanity. No one approached him. No one attempted to speak to him.

What they had seen—or had thought that they had seen—had taken place in what was little more than an instant, a few moments, a brief span of unreality. Two knights had come together in deadly battle and suddenly, they seemed to have multiplied. Two became two armies and, just as suddenly, only one remained. It couldn't have been real, could it? One knight stood alone. In a brief span, surely too brief, his armor had been battered and dented, he was bloodied, he was exhausted, he was chopping at the air. They wandered away in a daze. More sophisticated men might have believed that they had succumbed to some sort of mass psychosis, but these men did not know the meaning of the word. The word would not exist in the vocabulary of men for many, many years to come. It was sorcery. They knew of only one sorcerer. They knew better than to speak of him.

Lucas let his sword drop to the ground.

"My God," he said. "I think I've won. What happened?"

Finn Delaney walked up beside him.

"It's over," he said, putting his arm around Lucas. "Irving's dead. His chronoplate's destroyed."

Lucas stared at him, his eyes slightly unfocused.

"Did I kill him?"

"No, but it doesn't matter. He's dead just the same."

Lucas looked back at Torquilstone. The sounds of battle were still coming from within its walls. The Saxons were still invading the castle.

"Forget it," Finn said. "That doesn't concern us anymore. We've done our job, Lucas. Let's go home."

"Hunter?"

Finn smiled. "He's gone. Like the man said, he's not putting his ass on the line for anybody. He popped in out of nowhere, saved our bacon, and now he's disappeared again and taken his toys with him. Back into retirement."

"Is there any way that we can keep him out of it?" said Lucas.

Finn shrugged. "What difference does it make? We'll be debriefed. We can tell them everything we know. Hunter's smart. He won't stay around here. He'll pick himself another time, another place . . . they'll never find him." He took Lucas' PRU. "I gave mine back to him. I've still got some explosive left. He can probably change the code, but what do you say we blow these anyway?"

"These?"

Finn sighed. "Yeah. Bobby's too. Hunter wasn't fast enough to save him. For what it's worth, he said he was sorry."

They stood over Bobby's body.

"It's worth something," Lucas said.

For a moment, there was an incandescent respite. He looked up and saw de la Croix poised with sword held overhead.

"Damn," he whispered softly.

The sword—

—never came down. At the last moment, he had shut his eyes, resigned to his fate. He waited for the blow that never came. He waited . . . and he waited, then it occurred to him that de la Croix was waiting for him to open his eyes, waiting before giving him the *coup de grace* so that he would open his eyes, so that the last thing he would ever see was—

He sighed. Very well, then. Let it be. He would die looking his executioner in the eye. After all, it was only fitting. He opened his eyes.

And de la Croix was gone.

He blinked. He turned around. He remained on the floor, puzzled. *Why?* It made no sense. How . . . where . . .

His wounds were hurting him. The most serious was the one in his arm. Yet it was not a fatal wound. He would live.

He would live!

He got to his feet and retrieved his sword. He looked outside. The Saxons were swarming over the walls. His men—De Bracy's men—were being defeated. Perhaps de la Croix was saving him for a more ignoble fate, leaving him to the devices of the Saxon outlaws. Well, it would not be. He would escape. He looked down at his shield, which had been hammered into uselessness. No matter. He could quickly get another. And he had yet another shield in mind. Not even Saxon outlaws would draw a bow back on a woman.

He ran quickly to his chambers.

Rebecca, bruised and disheveled, lay on the bed. She stared up at the ceiling. Her eyes were vacant and unfocused and tears slid down her cheeks. She was utterly silent.

"Rebecca, come quickly!" said Bois-Guilbert. "The outlaws are storming the castle. All is lost."

She did not respond.

"Damn you," swore Sir Brian. "You're far more trouble than you're worth." He picked her up and ran for the stables.

He was right. The Saxon outlaws would not shoot at a woman. They were already swarming into the courtyard by the time he mounted. With Rebecca held in front of him, he spurred hard and rode through the press, scattering those who tried to stop him. With De Bracy dead and Richard back in England, things suddenly looked grim. It would be a bad time for him to be alone. With one arm clutching Rebecca, he turned his horse toward the Preceptory of Templestowe.

Andre blinked hard.

One moment, Bois-Guilbert was at her feet, awaiting her killing stroke, the next, she was in the wizard's chambers and her sword was embedded in his skull. No sooner had the realization sunk in than another sorcerer—for what else could he have been?—burst into the room, throwing lightning at her and striking her down. Yet, he had not killed her. For a moment, she had not been certain, but now she knew she was alive. Perhaps the man was merely an apprentice and his power not yet strong enough to slay her. When she raised her head, he was gone, but now, scant seconds later, another stood in his place, appearing out of nowhere.

This one was dressed in a satanic robe, with dragons on both sides. His long brown hair was streaked with gray, as was his beard, and he looked at her only briefly before bending down over the black knight's evil apparatus.

"This place is going to be the scene of a small cataclysm in a moment," Hunter said, removing the explosive from the chronoplate and tossing it beneath the bed. "It would be wise if we vacated the premises and quickly. Come with me."

He held out a hand and helped her up, then picked up the chronoplate. "These things are a bit difficult to get a hold of," he said. "And I could use a spare. Don't be frightened. We're going to take a little trip, you and I."

"Am I to be killed?" said Andre.

"I don't think you have to worry about that," said Hunter. "You might get a little sick, but it won't be serious. Come on now, that thing's going to blow."

"Blow?"

"I'll explain later," Hunter said. "We need an explosion in this room to keep things in order. Now, just stand over here. If you like, you can close your eyes. It will only take a moment."

Resigning herself to whatever fate awaited her, Andre closed her eyes. When she opened them again, she was no longer in Nottingham Castle.

She became violently ill.

Albert Beaumanoir, Grand Master of the Order of the Knights Templars, was considerably less than happy with his charges. Recently returned from a conference with Philip of France, the Grand Master had come to England and had established himself in residency at the Preceptory of Temple-stowe. He was an old man with gray hair, a long gray beard and deep-sunken eyes in which glittered the light of fanaticism. Conrad Mont-Fitchet, the preceptor who attended him, walked slightly behind him in the garden of Templestowe, listening to his superior and nodding at his words.

Beaumanoir was extremely displeased at what he perceived as being a fall from grace among many of the Templars. He took his office and his vows seriously, with a zealot's pride. To Beaumanoir, the white burrel mantle of a Knight Templar, with the red octagonal cross on the left shoulder, was a simple statement that identified its wearer as a warrior of God. Yet he had come to England to find that the Templars there had abandoned the severity of their vows, granting themselves many dispensations.

"Since I have come to England," said the Grand Master, "I have seen little of the practices of our brethren here upon which I can look with favor. It distresses me."

"It's true," said Conrad. "The irregularities of our knights in England are even more gross than of those in France."

"It is because they are more wealthy," said Beaumanoir. "Wealth can be the lifeblood of the Church, but wealth can also corrupt. See how it has affected those here. Our vows proclaim that we should wear no vain or worldly ornaments, no crests upon our helmets, no gold upon our bridle or our stirrups, yet look how our brothers of the sword array themselves in England! They have embraced all crass material pursuits, from falconry to debauchery. They are forbidden to read save what their Superior permits, yet they are engrossed in the study of the cabalistical secrets of the Jews and the magic of the Saracens. Simplicity of diet was prescribed to them and look how their tables groan under the weight of princely fare! Their drink was to be water, but now to drink like a Templar is the boast of each jolly boon companion! The souls of our pure founders, the spirits of Hugh de Payen and Godfrey de Saint Omer, and of the blessed Seven who first joined in dedicating their lives to the service of the Temple, are disturbed even in paradise itself! I have seen them in the visions of the night. They say to me, Beaumanoir, awake! There is a stain in the fabric of the Temple, as deep and foul as that left by the streaks of leprosy on the walls of the infected houses of old! The soldiers of the Cross, who should shun the glance of a woman as the eye of a basilisk, live in open sin, not only with females of their own race, but with the daughters of the accursed heathen and the more accursed Jew. I *will* purify the fabric of the Temple, Conrad, and the unclean stones in which the plague is, I will remove and cast out of the building!''

At that moment, a squire approached them.

"Grand Master," he said, "a Jew stands without the gate, begging admission to speak with our brother, Brian de Bois-Guilbert."

"You were right to give me knowledge of this," said Beaumanoir. "It imports us especially to know of this Bois-Guilbert's proceedings."

"Report speaks him brave and valiant," Conrad said.

"And truly he is so spoken of," said the Grand Master. "But brother Brian came into our Order a moody and a disappointed man, stirred, perhaps, to take our vows and to renounce the world not in the sincerity of the soul, but as one whom some light touch of discontent has driven into penitence. Since then, he has become an earnest agitator, a leader among those who impugn our authority. I am curious to know what this Jew would want with him. Bring him into our presence, Damian."

The terrified Isaac of York was brought into the hall to meet with the Grand Master. He approached, but when he was three paces distant, Beaumanoir motioned him to halt and Isaac dropped to his knees in supplication.

"Speak, Jew, and be brief," said the Grand Master. "What is the purpose of your dealings with Bois-Guilbert? And beware, Jew, should you speak falsely. If your tongue deceives me, I'll see that it's torn out."

"I am the bearer of a letter," Isaac stammered. "A letter to Sir Brian de Bois-Guilbert, from Prior Aymer of the Abbey of Jorvaulx."

"Did I not say that these were evil times, Conrad?" said Beaumanoir. "A Cistercian prior sends a letter to a soldier of the Temple and can find no more fitting messenger than an unbelieving Jew. Give me the letter."

Isaac stretched forth the letter, but Beaumanoir recoiled from him, waiting until Conrad took it and broke the seal.

"Read it," said Beaumanoir.
Conrad read the letter.

Aymer, by divine grace, Prior of the Cistercian house of Saint Mary's of Jorvaulx, to Sir Brian de Bois-Guilbert, a knight of the Holy Order of the Temple, wishing health, with the bounties of King Bacchus and my Lady Venus. Touching our present condition, dear Brother, we are a captive in the hands of certain lawless and godless men, who have not feared to detain our person and put it to ransom; whereby we have also learned of De Bracy's misfortune and of your escape with that fair Jewish sorceress whose black eyes have bewitched you. We rejoice in your safety. Nevertheless, we pray you to be on your guard against this second Witch of Endor. Your Grand Master, who cares not a bean for black eyes and cherry cheeks, is said to be en route from Normandy to diminish your mirth and amend your misdoings. Wherefore we pray you heartily to beware, and to be found watching. The wealthy Jew, Isaac of York, has pleaded with me to give him letters in his behalf. The woman is his daughter. I entreat you to hold the damsel to ransom. He will pay you as much as may find fifty damsels upon safer terms, whereof I trust to have my part when we make merry together, as true brothers. Until that merry meeting, we wish you farewell. Given from this den of thieves, about the hour of matins,

Aymer, Pr. S.M. Jorvolciensis

"What say you to this, Conrad?" said Beaumanoir. "Small wonder the hand of God is upon us, when we have such churchmen as this Aymer. A den of thieves is a fit residence for the likes of him! Yet, what does he mean by this second Witch of Endor?"

"I think I know, but I will endeavor to find out for certain," Conrad said. "Jew, is your daughter a prisoner of Bois-Guilbert?"

"Rebecca was taken from me, reverend sir, by that same knight," said Isaac, taking great pains to maintain a subservient tone. "Whatsoever ransom a poor man may pay for her deliverance—"

"Your daughter, Rebecca, practiced the art of healing, did she not?" said Conrad.

"Indeed, gracious sir, my daughter is the very soul of goodness. Many a knight and yeoman, squire and vassal, may bless the gift which Heaven has assigned to her. She has helped many when every other human aid had failed. The blessing of the God of Jacob is upon her."

"Behold the deceptions of the devouring Enemy," said Conrad Mont-Fitchet. "I doubt not your words, Jew. Your daughter cures by words and sigils and other cabalistical mysteries not known to good Christian souls."

"No, no, reverend knight," said Isaac. "She cures in chief measure by balsams of marvelous virtue, not by any mystical art!"

"Where had she that secret?" said the Grand Master.

"It was delivered to her by Miriam, a sage matron of our tribe," said Isaac, reluctantly.

"And was this not the same witch, Miriam of Endor, the abomination of whose enchantments caused her to be burnt at the stake, her ashes scattered to the four winds?" said Mont-Fitchet. Turning to Beaumanoir, he said, "The matter seems quite clear now, reverend father. This Rebecca of York was a pupil of this Witch of Endor and she has enchanted Bois-Guilbert so that he has forsaken his sacred vows."

"*No!* My daughter is no witch, I swear by—"

"False Jew!" said Beaumanoir. "I will teach this witch daughter of yours to throw spells and incantations over the soldiers of the blessed Temple! Damian, spurn this Jew from the gate and shoot him dead if he oppose or turn again! We will deal with his daughter as the Christian law and our own high office warrant!"

Bois-Guilbert stood before Rebecca. She sat silently by a small window, looking out across the surrounding countryside. She did not turn when he entered.

"Rebecca," he said. "Rebecca, please look at me."

She turned an empty gaze upon him.

"Rebecca, I have brought you more grief than I had intended. I would it had been otherwise."

"You should have thought of that before you took me against my will," she said softly.

"A passionate man takes what he wants," Sir Brian said,

"and I wanted you from the first day I set eyes on you at Ashby. Had we more time, you would have grown to love me, Rebecca."

"You flatter yourself, Sir Brian. I did not think that it was my love you wanted."

"What's done is done," he said. "Still, I would that it were otherwise. I could have given you a life such as you had never known. What future is there for a daughter of a lowly Jewish merchant? You could be the woman of a Knight Templar, a lady to be treated with respect."

"The way you treated me?"

"You are bitter."

"I am dishonored."

"Yet you are still alive. When I brought you here to Templestowe, it was not my intention to place your life in danger, yet that is what I have done. Albert Beaumanoir has returned to Templestowe. I have just come from him. The Grand Master is not a man of vision. He clings stubbornly to the old ways. In time, his influence would become inconsequential, but as yet, he is still Grand Master of our Order. I had sought to keep your presence here a secret from him, but he has found out."

"Then he will set me free?"

"He means to set your spirit free," Sir Brian said. "There is to be a trial and you are the accused."

She looked up at him, startled. "Accused of what? I have done nothing."

"The charge is sorcery," said Bois-Guilbert.

"Then I will trust to God to see me delivered," said Rebecca, "for I am innocent."

"You are innocent, indeed," said Bois-Guilbert. "Innocent of the ways of the world. You are closer to your God than you know. The trial has not been held yet, but rest assured that the outcome has already been decided. You have but one chance to avoid the stake. Demand a champion."

"I do not understand."

"If you demand a champion, then according to our ways, and the ways of chivalry, your fate will be decided in a trial by combat. Choose me as your champion and I will fight for you with my last breath."

"And if you lose?"

"Then I lose my life and you will be burnt at the stake,"

said Bois-Guilbert. "But I will not lose. No man will take from me that which I have gone to so many pains to obtain. You are mine, Rebecca. You must choose me. It is your only hope."

"Then I have no hope," she said.

"Think well on this," said Bois-Guilbert. "There would be no purpose served if you threw your life away. If you do not choose me, who else would fight for you? Who cares what happens to a Jew?"

"God will care for me," she said.

"Your death would be a tragic waste," said Bois-Guilbert. "Think on the agonies of death by fire, Rebecca. I pray that you will change your mind."

The men did not have long to wait. They were not sure exactly how the pick-up would be arranged, but when the contact came, it proved to be a surprise. And it stood to reason. There must have been someone keeping an eye on them, someone who had taken the tremendous risk of undertaking his mission with implant removed, so that he could not be scanned. He was a captain in the Observer Corps. They knew him as Alan-a-dale.

"So it's almost over," Alan-a-dale said to them when they returned to camp.

"Almost?" said Finn.

"Well, the hard part's over," said the minstrel, winking at them. "Irving's dead."

"Son-of-a-bitch," said Finn. "You're a ringer."

"Only for a little while longer," said the bogus minstrel. "The name's Bannerman. Captain Richard Bannerman, Observer Corps. And I must say I'm very much relieved to see you men have pulled it off. I was just about resigned to spending the rest of my days back here. Who knows, if Irving had succeeded, I might have been better off."

"So what happens now?" said Lucas.

"I've already contacted the mission commander," Bannerman said. "Since we have no idea what really happened to King Richard, we're going to have to proceed on the assumption that he's dead. I doubt Irving would have let him live; it would have been too risky."

"Suppose he turns up after all?" said Lucas.

"Well, he might," said Bannerman, "although it's one hell

of a long shot. He won't, I'm sure of that. But if he does, well, there's already going to be one King Richard on the throne of England and he'll be a member of the Referee Corps. If anyone else shows up claiming that title, it will be our job to dispose of him."

"So the ref's going to have to die at Chaluz," said Finn.

Bannerman was silent for a moment. "I'm afraid so. Perhaps we'll be able to fake it. But, if not, well, what's one life to preserve the course of history?"

"It's been more than one life already," Lucas said.

"I know," said Bannerman. "If we can pull it off without him getting killed, believe me, we'll try. But he knew what the mission entailed when he took the job. There's a lot more to being a ref than just deciding point spreads."

"I think I'm better off just being a simple dog soldier," Finn said. "What's the drill for us now?"

"You and Priest will simply disappear," said Bannerman. He smiled. "Little John is going to be grieving for Robin Hood. He's going to take off on a bender somewhere. When he returns, he'll be the real McCoy, suitably conditioned to recall events in which he did not take part. And Ivanhoe will turn up again, at the appropriate time. There are still some details to work out."

"So the legend of Robin Hood ends right here," said Lucas. "I'll be curious to learn how history explains it."

"That's where you're wrong," said Bannerman. "Both Poignard and Robin Hood will return. Poignard is, so far as we know, of no great significance to history. As for Robin Hood, well, the legend about him has always been a legend. We don't know exactly how he died. The real Locksley will return and those who thought they saw him die will help the legend grow. Just between you and me, I wouldn't be surprised if Marion turns out to be the end of him at last."

"That wraps up the adjustment then," said Lucas.

"Well, not quite. There are still a few loose ends, not the least of which are Andre de la Croix and your friend, Hunter."

"He's long gone," said Finn. "You guys will never get him."

Bannerman smiled. "Perhaps. If we don't, I won't really mind. After all, without him, we could not have done it. We really need people like Hunter."

"Come again?" said Lucas.

"Surely, you don't think he's the only one," said Bannerman. "We've had quite a few deserters from the Temporal Corps. It's not exactly common knowledge, as I'm sure you'll appreciate. We can't broadcast the fact that there are temporal renegades spread throughout all of time. Deserting isn't easy and those who try are punished quite severely, which fact I hope you men will keep in mind. Still, quite a number have succeeded, as has Hunter. We didn't even know about him until he surfaced during this operation."

"What do you plan to do?" said Finn.

"Apprehend him, if we can. I don't think we can, though. Still, people like your friend Hunter are very useful to us. In order for their existence to remain relatively safe, they must constantly strive to preserve the timeline. The underground—"

"The *underground?*" said Finn.

"Oh, yes. They have an organization of sorts. Quite fascinating, actually. We have established that there are points in time which they have pinpointed for rendezvous purposes. It's quite a sophisticated network. In order to protect themselves, they police themselves and the timeline, as well. It's ironic, really. They think that they've beaten the system and are out of it, yet effectively, they still work for us. We find them very useful."

"I wonder what Hunter would make of that," said Lucas.

"I doubt he really cares," said Finn.

"Well, *Lieutenant* Delaney, and *Lieutenant* Priest," said Bannerman, smiling, "if you're quite ready?"

"You mean we're leaving now?" said Lucas.

"If you like. I've got a plate hidden not too far from here. No tracer function, naturally, but I warn you, should you get any ideas, I'll have both of you covered every inch of the way."

"I'll bet you will," said Finn.

"God, this is really it," said Lucas. "After this, we're just going to be plain old citizens."

"Not me," said Finn. "I never got used to being an officer, but who knows? I've been busted down before. I think I'll just stay a soldier. It's all I know. And, when it gets right down to it, it's all I really want. The straight life would bore the hell out of me after this."

"He may have a point, Mr. Priest," Bannerman said. "You can, of course, retire now, with the the full pension of a first lieutenant in the Temporal Corps. But ask yourself, what will you do back in the straight life? I suppose you'll be able to get by on your pension, but won't life seem just a little . . . well, ordinary?"

"I'll settle for ordinary," Lucas said.

"Then I won't try to talk you out of it," said Bannerman. "But the Corps could use men like you, who have proven themselves in the field. With each mission served in the past, with each successful adjustment completed, more anomalies arise that must be corrected. I'd be very surprised if something up ahead was not affected by what you men have done right here. After an assignment such as this, should you elect to remain in the service, we couldn't possibly return you to the regular Corps."

"Oh?" said Finn.

"Since you intend to re-up, *Captain*, your commission is in the Time Commandos now. From now on, it's just adjustment missions for you. More pay, more perks, more risk. It's a highly irregular unit, but from what I know of you, I believe you'll find it to your liking. In the Commandos, there's room for mavericks like you."

"We'll see," said Finn.

"Well, if you want to spend the rest of your life laying your ass on the line, as Hunter would say, it's okay with me," said Lucas. "Count me out. It's back to 2613 and the easy life for me."

"And you're more than entitled," said Bannerman. "But if you should ever change your mind—"

"I won't."

"—there'll still be a place for you. You can re-enlist in the Commandos with the rank of captain anytime."

"Don't hold your breath," said Lucas.

Bannerman smiled. "I won't. At any rate, you men have some R&R coming, courtesy of the Temporal Corps. Six months paid vacation, anytime, anyplace."

"No strings?" said Lucas.

"None, Mr. Priest. You have *carte blanche*."

"It'll cost you, then."

Bannerman grinned. "We can afford it."

14 _____

Andre woke up to the sound of music, but it was music unlike anything that she had ever heard. The recorder did not sound strange to her, but the instruments of the symphony orchestra that supported it in the concerto by Bartok both mesmerized and frightened her. Her fear and lack of understanding were compounded by the fact that the sound came from all around her, yet she saw no musicians. Had she been transported to some faery land? Had she died?

She sat up slowly, then stood upon the floor, looking all around her. Where was the music coming from? What strange instruments produced such sounds?

She was in a woodsman's cabin, but this was the abode of no ordinary woodsman. This cabin had a floor and shutters. . . . She opened one of the shutters and saw that it was night outside. Night! And yet it was bright as daylight in the cabin. It was warm, although she could see no fire. In the center of the room, there stood some strange black apparatus with an appendage that stretched out of its top and through the ceiling. It squatted on four legs like some evil gnome. It was from this black thing that the warmth emanated. She reached out and touched it, then jerked her hand back quickly. It had burned her. It was like touching fire. She backed away, moving toward the bed once more. She sat down, mystified.

Suddenly, she moved quickly toward the door and flung it

open, thinking to escape the evil place. The sorcerer stood before her.

"Going somewhere?" Hunter said.

She backed into the room. "I am damned, then," she said softly.

Hunter raised his eyebrows. "What makes you say that?"

"I have escaped from the clutches of one wizard only to fall into the hands of another," she said. "This is what comes of serving the devil's own. There will be no escape for me. My soul is forfeit. What do you want of me? Am I to suffer your revenge for killing the other wizard? I do not even know how that happened. I cannot think. It is all too much to reason out. Do with me what you will and make an end of it."

"Are you finished?"

"I have nothing more to say."

"Well, that's good. Sit down. Please."

She sat.

"First of all," said Hunter, "your soul is not in peril, at least, not from me. I serve neither God nor the devil, I serve myself. If you prefer to think of me as a sorcerer, go right ahead, I won't stop you. It so happens that I'm not a sorcerer, or a wizard, or a warlock, or anything else except a man. I realize that may be hard for you to accept right now, but try."

"But the magic—"

"Is not magic. At least, not in the sense that you understand it. To some savage who has never seen a suit of armor, a knight would seem to be a devilish apparition. Imagine, if you can, that you have never seen an armored knight. That you know nothing of the craft involved in making armor, that you know nothing of its properties. Having lived in a world in which a knight has never been seen, might you not assume, upon seeing one, that it was not even a human being you were seeing, but some terrifying creature whose flesh was metal animated by black magic? Well, as uncomplimentary as it may seem, in this case, I am that knight and you are that savage. What I do seems like magic to you because you do not understand it and you know nothing of the craft involved. I merely have more knowledge than you have."

He reached for a bottle of bourbon.

"Would you like some?"

"What is it?" said Andre, cautiously.

"A beverage. No mystical potion, I promise you. It's made

from a mash of corn and malt and rye. It's called whiskey. The effects of drinking it are much like drinking ale, only this is a far more potent brew.''

He held out the bottle and Andre took it carefully.

Her eyes bulged after the first swallow and she coughed. ''By God! You *drink* this swill?''

''It takes some getting used to,'' Hunter said, ''because of its strength. Once you grow accustomed to the taste, you actually enjoy it.''

''It does give a pleasant warmth,'' said Andre.

''Just drink a little,'' Hunter said. ''To one who's never had a taste before, the effects can be overpowering, like giving ale to an infant.''

''This knowledge of which you spoke,'' she said, ''you called it a craft. Yet, there is a craft to magic, is there not? It is one thing to craft a suit of armor, and yet it is another to bring forth music from the empty air and to appear and disappear at will. How can this not be magic? And this black apparatus which gives forth heat—''

''Is called a stove,'' said Hunter. ''Look.'' He kicked open the door, showing the flames inside. ''Nothing but a fancy fireplace, only a more efficient one. All it is is metal to contain a fire of wood and coal.''

''But will the metal not grow red and soft from the fire's heat?'' said Andre.

''Not if it's made properly,'' said Hunter. ''The metal is thick and the fire is never hot enough to soften it. Simple, isn't it?''

''And this metal tube?''

''Is just a chimney to carry the smoke away.''

''And the music?''

''That's a little harder to explain,'' said Hunter.

''I will attempt to understand.''

''Well . . . let me put it this way. There are musical instruments with which you are familiar, such as the wood flute and the lute, for instance. There are other musical instruments which you have never heard of. They produce very different sounds. Look here,'' he said, showing her the sound system. ''All this is is a device that records the sound of music made by musicians. Just as a monk records holy works on paper, through the art of writing, so this device records *sounds*. It reproduces them.''

"How?"

"How. Good question. How do you explain electronic recording to a woman of the Middle Ages? Well, for now, you'll just have to be satisfied with this: there is a method of preserving sounds made by a musician. The method of preserving spoken words is called writing. One speaks, another writes those words down and later, still another who knows how to read can reproduce those words by reading what was written. In a way, this is similar, but the knowledge involved is far greater. This is a . . . tool . . . which preserves sounds, just as writing preserves words. Only with this tool, there is no need of reading. The tool records the sounds and then plays them back to you. It can even reproduce the sound of your own voice. Perhaps I'll show you, later."

"This is not magic?"

"No, it is a simple craft, but men will not know how to make such tools for many, many years to come."

"Then how have you learned this?"

Hunter sighed. "I was afraid you were going to ask that."

"The knowledge is secret, then."

"No, it's not a secret, it's just . . . very difficult to explain."

"I would like to learn, if this is possible."

"Oh, it's possible, all right, but you're going to have to be very patient. And forbearing."

"It will not endanger my soul to learn of this?"

"It will not."

"Do you dare swear this before God?" said Andre.

"I swear this before God."

Andre frowned. "I do not think a sorcerer can so swear. Very well, then, I will risk to listen."

Hunter sighed. "Where do I begin?"

"At the beginning, if this is not asking too much," said Andre.

Hunter shrugged. "What the hell? All right. I was a soldier."

"A man at arms?"

"A man at arms, if you will. Now shut up and listen. And don't interrupt. I was a soldier. I served in an army mightier than anything you have ever seen or heard of. An army that will not exist for centuries."

Andre started to speak, but held back.

"Thank you. I said you would have to be patient. Try to imagine what it must have been like for the first men to walk the earth. And the first women, too. They were simple savages, little more than animals. They had not yet discovered fire or clothing. They did not know how to build shelters, so they slept in the open or in caves. They knew only how to eat and kill and little else. For their weapons, they used simple clubs of wood or axes made of stone. Now, take such a man or woman and imagine what it would be like for them today, if they were to suddenly be transported to this time and place. They would see castles and not know what they were, since they did not know how to build with stone and wood. They would see a crossbow or an arbalest and think it was the work of the devil, for they would know nothing of the craft involved in making such weapons. They would see armored knights and take them for horrifying monsters or even gods."

Andre nodded slowly.

"Now, what if we were able, you and I, to have some mastery over time?" said Hunter. "What if we had a mode of travel that would take us not from one place to another, but from one *time* to another? What if I were to take you far into the future, to this very place, only a thousand years from now? You would be like that savage from the dawn of time, failing to comprehend everything you saw around you, for with time, man's knowledge grows ever greater. What would you see a thousand years from now?"

"I do not know."

"I'll tell you. You would see cities a thousand times greater than the towns you know. You would see many more people. You would see a world in which simple wagons and carts had been replaced by conveyances that would enable you to make a journey that would now take you months in just a matter of minutes. Just as men have learned to craft a crossbow or a suit of armor, so will they have learned to build devices that enable them to fly."

"*To fly!*"

"A thousand years from now," said Hunter, "flying will be as commonplace as riding a horse is today. You would look at those men and women of the future and think that they were gods, or sorcerers, since you would not understand how they can do the things they do. They will live much longer than people do today, for they will have learned to overcome disease. They will wear different clothing. They will have machines—artifacts they made—perform work for them that men must do for themselves today, only these machines will do the work far more efficiently and much faster. They will have even traveled to the stars."

Andre sighed, shaking her head.

"You think I'm mad," Hunter said. "Listen to me. When the first crossbow was made, it was said that the world was coming to an end. How could the society of man survive such a devastating weapon? Yet, a thousand years from now, there will be weapons so devastating that they will make the crossbow seem like the wooden club of the simple savage."

Hunter took out his .45 and held it up so she could see it.

"This is one such weapon. And there are others, far more powerful than you could imagine in your wildest nightmares."

Andre stared at the gun. "It does not look very formidable," she said. "What use would it be against a crossbow or a sword?"

Hunter smiled. "Watch," he said. He cocked the weapon and aimed it at a bottle on the shelf. He fired and the bottle shattered in an explosion of glass and whiskey.

Andre turned pale. "Sorcery," she whispered.

"No," said Hunter. "In a way, it is something like a crossbow, in that it shoots a projectile. The crossbow shoots a bolt or quarrel. This gun," he showed it to her and, in spite of herself, she leaned forward to look at it more closely, "shoots a tiny piece of lead. It has functioning parts, just like a crossbow, only there are more of them and they take a great deal of skill to make."

He removed the clip and he began to disassemble the gun.

"You see, there are many parts to this weapon. I will explain in the simplest way, just so you understand the principle. When I pull back on the slide here, it brings the bullet into position. The gun is now prepared to function. When I gently squeeze the trigger, it acts on these other parts here, so, and this hammer falls on the end of the bullet. This little metal piece here, the firing pin, strikes the primer, which causes the powder in the case to ignite. This creates a tremendous force which pushes the lead out of the case and down this barrel here with very great speed, causing it to fly out of the gun here, like an arrow leaves a bow, only far faster than the eye can follow. The sound you hear is caused by the force created when the powder ignites, and this same force causes the slide to be moved back again, bringing the next bullet into position. You can feel this force when you shoot the weapon. Would you like to try?''

"You would trust me with this magic weapon?''

"I'll be right next to you,'' said Hunter, smiling. "If you attempt to use it against me, I have enough skill to take it away from you before you can employ it.''

"How do I use it?'' she said.

He cocked the gun, having reassembled it, then stood at her side, carefully placing it into her hand and showing her how to take the proper position. She aimed, long and carefully, then gently squeezed the trigger. The .45 bucked in her hand and the bottle shattered. She almost dropped the gun.

"You see?''

"It will shoot again now?'' she said, her voice unsteady.

He took the gun. "Yes. But first I will remove the cartridges so you can hold the weapon safely and examine it.'' He did so and handed it back to her.

"Look at it. Feel it. It is only a tool, and nothing more. A dangerous tool, to be sure, but made by men, skilled artisans, not sorcerers. Can any artisans you know make such a weapon?''

She gazed at the gun with awe. "No. No artisans I have ever seen possess such skill or knowledge.''

"Now perhaps you can accept the other things I've told you,'' Hunter said. "I know it all sounds unbelievable, but nevertheless, it's all true. I am a soldier from that future time. The man you killed was also from that time. He was an evil and misguided man, insane. All of this will be very hard for you to understand and the story will take a long time to tell. I have much to tell you, about myself and the life I lead, about the mastery of time. You have much to learn.''

"Why?'' She had a confused expression on her face. "I try to understand all this, yet it eludes me. I only know that the things I've seen, the things of which you told me, seem like the fragments of some dream. How can they be real? And yet, how can I doubt my own senses, unless I have gone mad?''

"You will understand, in time,'' said Hunter.

She shook her head.

"Look,'' said Hunter, "sit down. I know this must be hard for you to deal with. You're doing very well, under the circumstances. You're quite a woman. That, in itself, was a surprise." He grinned. "Imagine how I felt when you fainted and I put you to bed and started to undress you. I first thought you were wounded and I meant to treat you. There was no hair on your chest, but young boys are often hairless and you appeared to be a pretty young man, not yet old enough to grow a beard. But then I discovered otherwise."

"I see," said Andre, tensing.

Hunter chuckled. "No, I did not take license with your body. My word of honor."

"Why do you offer to teach me, then? You think to make me your concubine? I will not—"

"Peace," said Hunter, holding up his hand. "My intentions toward you are strictly honorable. I hope to make you my friend. But first, I intend to save your life."

"And is my life endangered?"

"I'm afraid so," Hunter said. "You see, I am not alone here. In this time, there are others who came from the future to defeat Irving—the 'wizard' whom you killed. They must now take steps to erase all traces of their presence here. The fact that they were here, that they can master time, that *is* secret knowledge. Irving meant to take the place of *Coeur de Lion* and to set into motion events that would affect the time from which we came. That had to be prevented."

"Did I not kill him?"

"Yes, you certainly did. And later, I'll explain to you just how it must have happened. Yet now, another Richard must arrive. A Richard who will act as we know the real Richard will have acted, because we know all the events of his life. It is our history. And we must make certain that our history remains unchanged."

She sighed and shook her head again. "Once more, you mystify me. How can I ever hope to understand all this?"

"You will," said Hunter. "Only now, you must understand that you know things you were never meant to know. You have seen things you were never meant to see. You are not alone in this, but many of the others who have been affected by our presence here are either dead or ways can be found to keep their knowledge from being a threat. You, on the other hand, have seen far more than anyone else. You have seen one Richard die and now you will see another Richard return. You possess a suit of armor such as no armorer of this day can make. Perhaps all this is insignificant in the grand scheme of things, but the soldiers from my time can't be sure of that."

"They will try to kill me?"

"Perhaps. That would be the simplest way. Or they may capture you and take away your memory."

"They can do this?"

"Easily."

"And I would forget everything? I would forget my part in this, I would forget the things that you have shown me, even though I hardly understand them all? I would forget Marcel—"

She shut her eyes.

"No. No, it must not be."

"It doesn't have to be," said Hunter.

"Why do you take my part in this? Are you not one of them?"

"I *was* one of them," said Hunter. "Now, I live life on my own terms. As for why I want to help you, well, there are many reasons and none. You interest me. I like you. I admire your spirit and determination. In a way, we are alike. You could not live by the rules of your society, so you made your own rules. You were born before your time and I was born too late for mine. We're kindred spirits, you and I. Thanks to you, a threat to my existence has been removed and I now have Irving's chronoplate—his apparatus for traveling from one time or place to another. I propose to take you with me."

"As your woman."

"As your own woman. The time from which I come does not hold women to be inferior to men. And you are the superior of most. In exchange for your companionship, on your own terms, I can offer you the world and almost all of time. I can show you these things I've spoken of. I can teach you how to understand them. I can offer you experiences that would defy your wildest dreams."

"I would like to see these things you spoke of," Andre said. "And I would like to see a world in which I did not have to act the part of a man to live life on my terms. You may be a devil tempting me into damnation for all I know, but this world in which I now reside has lost its sweetness. Yet, I cannot go. Not while Bois-Guilbert lives. If it costs me my life, I will bring him to justice before God for the murder of my brother."

"That's easily enough accomplished," Hunter said. "Take my gun and shoot the bastard."

"No. With such an awesome weapon, his death would be too swift and I could take no pleasure in it. He dies by my sword, gazing at my face."

"Well, I won't try to talk you out of it," said Hunter. "Revenge is something I can understand. However, do you see that your being abroad now constitutes a risk, and that if you remain here after you have avenged your brother, they will surely find you? I assure you, you would be defenseless against them."

"Once I have avenged Marcel, if you are still willling, I will seek you out and gratefully accept your offer of escape, since I wish to survive and I am most curious to learn of these strange and wonderful things you speak of. Perhaps it will prove the end of me, but I have never been one to turn back from a challenge. I will go with you, but we go as comrades in arms and nothing more, else I do not go."

"Understood."

"Then I must leave you now to seek out Bois-Guilbert."

"If you will allow me—"

"This is a thing which I must do myself," she said.

"And so you shall. But there is no reason not to take precautions. There is still time in which we can be safe here. Let *me* seek out Bois-Guilbert. I have greater mobility than you and can do so quickly. Then, once I've found him, I'll take you to him. Past that, I promise not to interfere. Is it agreed?"

"Agreed."

15 ————————————

"I've found him," Hunter said.

"What, so quickly?" Andre shook her head in wonder. "And this is not sorcery, you say. You vanish before my very eyes and then appear again as if by magic, and yet it is not magic. I wish that I could accept this."

"You will," said Hunter. "It won't take a bargain with the devil, either. There's a way to gain a lot of knowledge very quickly. There are others like me, in other times and other places. We speak in many different languages, yet we understand each other. We are a strong society." He grinned. "There's such a thing as an implant that can't be traced. You don't know what that is yet, but it will enable you to learn and understand. Meanwhile, there still remains the matter of your revenge."

"Where is Bois-Guilbert? Take me to him!"

"It's not as simple as that," said Hunter. "I found him for you. But he won't be easy to get at. He's very well protected. He fled to Templestowe with Rebecca of York as a hostage."

"The Jewess?"

Hunter nodded. "No doubt, he wanted to set up light housekeeping at the Templars' residence. The only problem is, there's a shake up in the works."

"A . . . shake up?"

"I beg your pardon. A series of radical reforms. Albert

Beaumanoir, Grand Master of the Order of the Knights
Templars, has arrived at Templestowe with the intent of showing his warrior priests the error of their ways. Consequently, it
would look bad for Bois-Guilbert to co-habit with a woman at
this time, and a Jew no less."

"So he is in disfavor with his superiors," said Andre. "How
can this work against me?"

"Well, he would have been in trouble with the Grand
Master if it wasn't for the fact that friends interceded for him.
They convinced Beaumanoir that Sir Brian's been ensorcelled
by Rebecca and the poor woman was made to stand trial for
witchcraft. Naturally, they convicted her."

"The countryside teems with sorcerers these days," said
Andre wryly.

"That poor girl has been made a victim, by Bois-Guilbert
and now by Beaumanoir. She's to be burned at the stake. But
she has appealed for trial by combat. Bois-Guilbert's advice,
no doubt. She'd never have thought of it on her own."

"It is good advice," said Andre. "If Bois-Guilbert appears
in the lists as her champion, the matter will be decided by the
will of God. Should Bois-Guilbert win, and there are few who
could defeat him, then he could not have been ensorcelled,
since God would have granted him the victory. Rebecca will be
cleared of the charge of witchcraft and Sir Brian will be free to
find another way to keep her. A sound plan."

"Only the plan has a hitch," said Hunter. "It seems that the
Grand Master has selected Bois-Guilbert to champion the
Temple. I guess they don't mind if an ensorcelled knight
represents them."

Andre smiled. "Sir Brian has been neatly outflanked. If he
loses, he forfeits his life and the charge is proven true. If he
wins, as he must strive to do, since he will not want to give up
life and breath for a lowly Jewess, then God will have over-
powered the enchantment. Rebecca will die and Bois-Guilbert
will have to go into retreat for purification. If he chooses not
to enter the lists, then he is disgraced. He will lose his rank and
armor and his dreams of leading the Knights Templars will
come to nought. And if no champion appears to defend
Rebecca, she dies at the stake."

"Isaac of York is desperately trying to find a champion to
represent his daughter," Hunter said.

"There are few who would undertake such a cause, even for

money," Andre said. "Brian's prowess is well known. Yet she will have a champion. I will appear for her."

"I was expecting you to say that," Hunter said. "But I just want you to be aware of the risk involved."

"There is no risk," said Andre. "With this armor made by those master artisans you spoke of, Brian will stand no chance against me. It will all go as before, when he should have died beneath my blade."

"Yes, well, that's precisely why it's risky," Hunter said. "The nysteel will protect you, but it won't make you completely invulnerable. You'll have to get it over with quickly. If you and Bois-Guilbert spend any time slamming away at each other, they're bound to notice that the combat is affecting his armor and not yours. Remember, they'll be primed for a witch burning. If you are seen to take his strongest blows with barely any visible damage to your armor, they just might decide that one witch has summoned another to defend her. And you *can* be brought down if they attack you in sufficient numbers."

"It is a risk that I will have to take," said Andre.

"I figured that you'd say that, too. So here, take this, then."

He handed her a PRU.

"The wizard's charm?"

"Call it a charm, if you like," said Hunter. "I control it now. Keep it as my favor when you fight with Bois-Guilbert."

"I will keep it."

"Just don't lose it."

"I do not accept a favor lightly," Andre said stiffly. "I will not lose it and I will try to do it honor."

Hunter smiled. "That's all I ask."

A great crowd had gathered at Templestowe to witness the witchburning and, with any luck, a lethal passage at arms, as well. A little sport before the roasting would be a welcome diversion, but no one truly expected it. All they had to do was look at Isaac to see that the man held out no hope at all for the deliverance of his daughter.

Isaac had offered up everything he owned in an effort to recruit a champion to represent his daughter, but there had been no takers. A fortune would be of little use if one did not live to spend it, and Bois-Guilbert was held in high esteem by those who had tilted at him in the lists and lived to tell the tale.

Only two knights were known to have bested him, Ivanhoe and *Coeur de Lion*, himself. Perhaps it was a lot of money, but to die fighting for a Jewess? Surely, it would be best to offer up one's life in a more fitting cause and one whose outcome was in some greater doubt.

Isaac wandered among the rapidly filling galleries, shredding his clothes and wailing. He called on God to visit whatever sins he had committed upon himself, rather than on his innocent daughter. There was absolutely nothing he could do except pray and he did not honestly expect his prayers to be answered.

A fanfare sounded and the gates of the preceptory were thrown open to the procession, which came forth beneath *Le Beau-seant*, the black and white standard of the Knights Templars. Bois-Guilbert rode just behind the standard bearers, looking proud and defiant in his brightly polished armor. Behind him, two squires carried his helmet and weapons, along with his shield.

His old shield had been rendered useless in his fight with de la Croix and there had not been time to obtain another from an armorer, made to his specification. In his flight from Torquilstone, he had grabbed the first shield that came to hand. It seemed unusually light, but he had tested it somewhat and was satisfied that it was well made and very strong. The only modification he had made was to have his skull-bearing raven painted over the uprooted oak.

Rebecca was brought out on foot. She wore a simple white dress, a stark contrast to the attire and livery of the Templars. Placed in the center of the procession, she was paraded past the galleries and the place of honor occupied by Beaumanoir, then brought to a black chair placed near the stake which would be her funeral pyre.

She watched silently as the members of the court took their places. The words of the heralds and the ceremonial accepting of the glove by the Grand Master, the charging of Bois-Guilbert with his pledge and vows, all were lost on her as her attention became focused inward. She was aware of the breeze upon her skin and she was acutely sensitive to the firmness of the chair upon which she sat. She felt the sun warming her face and wondered how much warmer the fire would feel when it began to eat away her flesh. She registered, to those who watched her, a calm, stoic acceptance of her fate. Yet, in fact, she had not accepted it, *could not* accept it. Intellectually, she realized that she was going to die an agonizing death. Emotionally, she was unable to deal with it. She knew only that she did not deserve to die and she could not understand why the court had thought she should. They had brought witnesses against her, people she did not even know, had never seen before. They had lied, perjuring themselves before God, ascribing to her all sorts of powers and evil deeds. Why? What purpose would her death serve?

She entertained, briefly, the thought that it was all the will of God, that the Lord was testing her and making her a martyr, but she could not accept that, either. She did not want to be a martyr, and martyrs were made of sterner stuff than she. To think that God intended a purging flame for her in order for her to become a martyr was an incredible conceit and, whatever other sins she might have committed, she would not go to her death having been guilty of the sin of pride. So she was left with nothing. She could see no rhyme or reason to their actions, she could take no comfort in knowing they were wrong. Silently, she began to weep.

They called for her champion.

There was total silence.

They waited. No champion appeared.

They summoned her champion once more.

Again, the silence, longer this time. Broken by the voice of Bois-Guilbert, who had ridden up beside her.

"Rebecca," he said softly, "know that I did not intend this. I would have fought as your champion, had not Beaumanoir appointed me to defend the Temple. I have no wish to see you die. To perish by the flame is not a pleasant death. Before your last breath leaves you, you will suffer the agonies of the damned. And your death would serve no purpose. I desired you more than I ever wanted any woman. I still desire you. I have no wish to be a party to your death."

"I do not see how you can absolve yourself of it," Rebecca said. "I take no comfort in knowing the strength of your desire. It was that which brought me to my ruin."

"Rebecca—"

"A champion!" someone cried, and the cry was taken up by others. "A champion appears!"

Bois-Guilbert glanced up and saw a mounted knight approaching at the gallop. He frowned. "I can't see . . . de la Croix!"

The assembled crowd began to cheer. There would be combat, after all! Isaac sank to his knees and offered up a prayer of thanks to God.

"Rebecca," Bois-Guilbert said quickly, "listen to me. There is still a way for you to avoid the grisly fate awaiting you. If I fail to appear in the lists, I forfeit my rank and honor. I will be disgraced and all that I have worked for will have come to nought. All this would I bear for you if you were to say to me, 'Bois-Guilbert, I accept you as my lover.' Climb up behind me and we will quit this place. My horse will easily outdistance all pursuit. We can go to Palestine, where my friend, the Marquis of Montserrat, will give us shelter. I could ally myself with Saladin and form new paths to greatness. Let Beaumanoir speak the doom which I despise, let them erase the name of Bois-Guilbert from their list of monastic slaves! I will wash out with blood whatever blot they may dare cast upon my scutcheon!"

"Foul tempter!" said Rebecca. "I would rather die than betray my faith and become the concubine of a bloody warlord! I will look to God for my salvation."

"Then look your last upon the sun and burn," said Bois-Guilbert. "I will not lay down my life and all that I hold dear for an ungrateful wench!"

He spurred his horse and rode away from her.

Andre de la Croix rode up to the Grand Master and, to the herald who had summoned her, she replied, "My name is Andre de la Croix, and I am a knight errant come to sustain with lance and sword the just and lawful quarrel of this damsel, Rebecca, daughter of Isaac of York; to uphold the doom pronounced against her to be false and truthless, and to defy Sir Brian de Bois-Guilbert as a traitor, a murderer, and liar, as I will prove in the field with my body against his by the aid of God."

"The words traitor and murderer coming from your lips are, indeed, an irony," said Bois-Guilbert. "You, who have slain Maurice De Bracy in a manner most foul and reprehensible, dare to impute my honor!"

"Does the Grand Master allow me the combat?" said de la Croix.

"I may not deny the challenge, provided the maiden accepts you as her champion, Sir Knight," said Beaumanoir. "If she does, then let whatever quarrel be between you and Bois-Guilbert be settled on this day, as well."

Andre rode up to Rebecca. "Do you accept me as your champion, Rebecca of York?"

"I do, Sir Knight," she said, "but you do not even know me. Why would you risk your life for mine?"

"Bois-Guilbert murdered my brother," Andre said. "His name was Marcel, and he was just a child. That, in itself, is reason enough that I should meet him with my sword, but there is yet another. A man who takes a woman against her will is a repugnant creature and deserves nothing less than death."

"Then my prayers go with you."

Both knights assumed their places at opposite ends of the lists. The herald announced that none, on pain of instant death, should dare to interfere with the combatants. The Grand Master, after a long moment of anticipatory silence, threw down Rebecca's glove and cried out the words, "*Laissez aller!*"

Hunter watched with a scope from a distance.

Bois-Guilbert and Andre spurred their horses and galloped at each other, lances couched. They came together hard, each taking the other's lance upon their shields. Both were unhorsed. Hunter could hear the crowd cheering the spectacle from where he stood, in the shelter of the trees. There was a moment during which both lay stunned upon the ground, then Bois-Guilbert got up, followed almost immediately by Andre. They drew their swords, advancing on each other on foot.

They struck at each other furiously, exchanging blow after blow, and Hunter wondered how long they would be able to keep up such a pace. Andre's nysteel armor should have given her a marked advantage, but Bois-Guilbert was taking the best she had to give and coming back. There was a limit to how much punishment a shield could take. If it was an ordinary shield. That was when Hunter remembered that Bois-Guilbert had seized Priest's nysteel armor.

He didn't think that Bois-Guilbert could fit into a suit of armor made for Lucas and still fight comfortably. It would be too large for him. But he could use the shield with no difficulty. As he watched the fight, he saw both of them slow down a little and then more as the effort took its toll. Andre and Bois-Guilbert had both managed to penetrate the other's guard and his armor showed some of the effects of her assault, even if his shield did not. They were now moving almost ponderously, as if in slow motion, both exhausted from the prodigious amount of energy they had expended during the first moments of their fight. The shields would sustain them; now it would only be a matter of who tired first. Andre raised her sword and, using her whole body to throw her weight into the stroke, brought it down on Bois-Guilbert's shield. Slowly, he raised his own blade and smashed it down on her shield. The recovery time of each was getting longer. They looked like two blacksmiths pounding at each other, like some grotesque wind-up toy that was running down.

The sound of distant hoofbeats distracted Hunter from the scene. He looked up and saw an armed party of men riding hard toward the tiltyard of Templestowe. He raised his scope. They rode under the banner of *Coeur de Lion*. Another imposter, but history would never know the difference.

It was going to be close. Hunter put down his scope and bent over the chronoplate on the ground before him, checking its programming. Then he picked up his laser and attached the scope to it. He raised it and sighted. Then he fired, aiming at Bois-Guilbert's visor.

Those who saw it weren't certain afterward that they had not imagined it. The flash of light had been astonishingly brief. Others insisted that it was the hand of God. An impossibly bright shaft of light, straight as an arrow, had struck Bois-Guilbert and he had grabbed at his helmet, dropping his shield and giving de la Croix the necessary opening to thrust into his throat.

As Bois-Guilbert fell to the ground, the knights rode into the tiltyard and there was no one who did not recognize the three lions on the chest of the one who led them. As they raised a welcoming cry for Richard of England, Andre raised her visor and slowly backed away from the corpse of Bois-Guilbert.

What happened? Why hadn't he defended himself? Had he been blinded by the sun?

Rebecca started to run across the field toward de la Croix.

At the same moment, "Richard" saw Andre and motioned to several of the knights behind him, but they were somewhat hampered in their progress toward the red knight by the crowd which pressed around them. When they had broken through, they could no longer see de la Croix. The red knight had disappeared.

Rebecca stood stock still in the middle of the tiltyard. Isaac came running up to her with tears in his eyes and he threw his arms around her, burying his head in her shoulder and sobbing, giving thanks to God.

Rebecca hardly even heard him. She stood staring, eyes glazed, at the spot where Andre de la Croix had stood. The knight had vanished before her very eyes.

EPILOGUE

It was recruiting day at Westerly Antiagathics. The army was back with its dog and pony show. The master of ceremonies, dressed casually and attractively in a clingsuit of muted terra cotta, was just finishing up his opening remarks and now the Parade of Uniforms was starting. They came from the wings of the stage, two from either side, a man and a woman dressed in period. They walked onto the stage in pairs and, as the army spokesman made some brief remarks about the periods which they were representing, they moved down the apron and onto the long runway, walking with the gait of experienced models.

Rick Cooper, a clerk in the administrative department, sat in the thirty-second row. He watched a Greek woman as she moved languidly past him on the long runway and he exhaled heavily.

"Boy, that's the life, eh? What I wouldn't give to get my hands on someone like her!"

The man beside him chuckled. "*That* lady ain't no trooper, son. The closest she ever came to ancient Greece was when she studied it in school."

"Well, maybe so," said Rick, "but you've got to admit that they don't make 'em like they used to."

"That's for sure," said Lucas. "As a temporal trooper, you'd be able to appreciate that. If you were lucky enough to find some time in which to enjoy a woman, she'd probably be some stinking prostitute with no teeth and a crotchful of lice. Let's hear it for the old days.''

"Oh, come on now," Rick said, "you're just focusing on the bad parts.''

"If the teeth and crotch are bad, I wouldn't give you much for the rest of her.''

"You know what I mean. Things were simpler back then. Men were men, not just cogs in some conglomerate machine. There's no adventure anymore, no glamor.''

"Sure. It's a lot more glamorous to be cannon fodder than to be a cog.''

"Oh, what would *you* know about it?''

"I was in the Corps," said Lucas. "Name's Lucas Priest, First Lieutenant, United States Army Temporal Corps, retired.''

"You were an officer? Really?''

"Well, my promotion and my honorable discharge came together.''

"So you know what it's all about, then. You know the score.''

Lucas nodded. "Don't let 'em scam you, kid. It's a hell of a rough gig. The roughest. They only tell you about how glamorous it is, a simpler time, the quest for adventure and glory and all that bullshit. It's a snow job. You join the service, chances are you'll never get out alive. Oh, you'll get to see all those wonderful places they tell you about, plus some they don't tell you about, like Stalingrad, Bataan, Carthage, Thermopylae. It's a real picnic—and you get a front row seat, too. Join the Temporal Corps, travel through time to wonderful, far off exotic places. Meet glamorous, exotic people. And kill them. Or get your own nuts shot off.''

"Maybe you've got a point," Rick said. "Maybe it *is* all just a snow job. Maybe it is a lot rougher and a lot more dangerous than they let on. Maybe I won't get back alive. Maybe I'll get shot or knifed or catch an arrow in my back or God only knows what else, come down with some disease and not get cured in time, but you went through it and you made it, didn't you?''

"Only because I was very lucky," Lucas said.

"Then you can't be the only one," said Rick. "I know they lay it on pretty thick, I'm not a fool. But look at me. I'm eighteen years old and I've done nothing but go to school all my damn life. I worked my ass off so I could get a decent job and now I've got one and what do I have to look forward to? Spending the next hundred years working for the corporation, filling out forms, programming computers, sitting on my duff all day and coming home to watch the holo at night. Anyplace where you can go for some excitement, I can't afford. So that's it, right? Okay, so maybe you're a little jaded, but you've *had* your shot. You took the gamble and you time traveled and you made it back and now that you're older, you can settle back and enjoy a boring job and have those memories to keep you going. Me? I never even had a chance to get any memories. I say the hell with it, I'm joining up. Maybe I'm throwing my life away. Maybe I'll go through all kinds of hell and feel sick and scared and hurt, but it beats being bored to death. This job might be all right for you, Mr. Priest, because you had a chance for some adventure while you were still young. Me, I'm not going to blow that chance.''

He got up and walked to the back of the hall, where the recruiting tables were set up.

Lucas sat still in his seat. "While I *was* still young?" he said to himself. He shook his head. "Damn kids. Think they know it all. Stupid fool's throwing his life away.''

He looked up to see an armored knight walking past him on the runway, nysteel gleaming, sword held at the ready.

Maybe he's the one who's got a point, thought Lucas. It does beat hell out of being bored.

He licked his lips, sighed, then got up and followed Rick toward the recruiting tables.

"Shit,'' he said. "I'm really going to hate myself tomorrow morning.''

BEST-SELLING
Science Fiction
and
Fantasy

COLLECTIONS OF FANTASY AND SCIENCE FICTION